To my brothers & sisters still on
the battlefield of retail.

"It's ironic that retailers and restaurants live or die on customer service, yet their employees have some of the lowest pay and worst benefits of any industry."

Howard Schultz
Chairman and CEO, Starbucks

CHAPTER 1

The world is full of stupid people.

The world is also full of stores, and stores are full of customers. None of this is coincidence.

I worked for years in one of the big box electronic stores. The kind of store that has a demonstration model of every single product they sell for hordes of customers to paw at and cover with their grime and germs.

I had always thought of myself a salesman, but since every job title has to be dressed up with some extravagant, useless label, I was not a mere salesman. I was a Customer Service Sales Specialist.

What started as a part-time position, while attending college, turned into a full-time sentence. I served six years.

I blame college. I couldn't find a course that held my interest for more than a couple of weeks and quickly developed a bullshit theory that real-world experience was worth more than education. At least, that's what I started telling people. Truth was, drinking beer and playing video games was way more fun than going to class.

I dropped out of school and started looking for a real job that would allow me to make a difference in the world. That lasted for about a week.

Once the store heard I wasn't in school, they offered me full-time hours. I reluctantly accepted since it would allow me to make a little more money until I found that real job I dreamed of.

Working full-time meant I was job-hunting part-time. Each week I put in a little less effort. Two months later I retired from job hunting and tried to convince myself that working retail was just as real a job as anything else.

The more I worked at the store, the more I found that I liked the job, at least in the beginning. The store managers referred to me as an example employee, which I realized later was like someone saying I could have won the Special Olympics.

I worked my way up the chain of command and rose to the respectable rank of Department Supervisor. Doesn't sound like much, but there were a lot of pointless positions I had to go through to get there, and had only a few more until Store Manager.

That's when I started to think the job could turn into a career. At the time it was a job easily tolerated and I was making decent money with benefits. More promotions were ahead and store managers made an unnecessarily high salary.

Then I found a big problem. Most human beings can't have a job in retail and maintain sanity. Retail shows a dark side of people and, to a smaller extent, society that is both shocking and disheartening. Staying too long makes cynical employees with all faith in the human race destroyed.

Just like me.

* * *

Chantelle always thought she was better than me because I worked in retail and she was a secretary, or as she would say, an executive assistant.

"I just don't understand you, Wade Williams! We've been together for, like, two years. We should be living together. It just makes sense." Every word sounded like she was whining.

She was twenty-four years old and still acted like a high school girl.

"What are you scared of?" she asked.

She was ruining my day off.

"I'm not scared of anything. I just don't want to live with you."

"Oh, that's great. You don't want to live with me. Maybe we should just break up then!"

All right, I thought. *I'll call your bluff.*

"That sounds good. Let's do that."

Tears welled in her eyes instantly. She cried for just about any reason.

I think it was the way she was brought up. As a kid, when she wanted to get her way, she must have thrown temper tantrums. If that didn't work her face would leak saltwater and, based on our relationship and her behavior as an adult, it must have worked every time.

It even worked on me countless times before. I had tried to break up with her on three prior occasions and each time she cried and laid down thick layers of guilt until I submitted. That night was different.

"If you're going to cry, would you mind doing it out in the hallway?"

"We were supposed to be together forever!" She stamped her foot, tight fists at her sides.

"Trust me. We were never supposed to be together forever."

"So, that's it? You're just giving up?" This was the first phase of her guilt trip. Six more to go.

"Truthfully, I gave up a long time ago," I said. "Now, I have the rest of the night off to relax and I don't want you ruining that. We've talked through everything there is to talk through, so the only thing left is for you to fuck off."

She stood there speechless, trying to find something else to say to evoke guilt or sympathy. In these moments, it always seemed to take her a long time to say something. Some might say she was arranging her thoughts and considering how to word her next reply. I think she was dumb.

"Don't you remember how many times you told me you loved me?"

Part two commenced.

I didn't keep track of the amount of times I told her I loved her, but I would wager it was the same amount of times we had sex.

With two cars of the guilt train down I realized I didn't have the energy to battle through another five.

"Listen..." I looked at her the way a mother looks at her child to make sure the kid is listening. "It's not you, it's me. You've changed, I've changed, people change. We've grown apart. I'm holding you back. You're holding me back. You're just not that same person I fell in love with. I don't feel the same way about you anymore. We need to spend some time apart. A lot of time apart. I think we should be just friends."

Anyone can refute one reason for a break-up, but who can come back from all the excuses? She continued to stand there goggling, a three-point shot that sat on the rim wobbling between in and out.

"And you're getting fat."

CHAPTER 2

Friday.

Friday shifts were an oddity. Without any particular reason a Friday could be extremely busy or completely dead. Either way no one would be able to explain why the traffic was what it was.

I had the closing shift, which had things to like and things to hate. Sleeping in was always nice and most cleaning was done throughout the day, but there were more customers to deal with and the shelves needed stocking after closing.

I was hiding in the lunchroom, pretending to work on my department's schedule, when Rory, a fellow department supervisor, walked in. His department was called Audio and consisted of stereos, MP3 players, boom boxes, etc.

"What up, Dub-dub?" Rory bellowed at me. Dub-dub was his nickname for me. It evolved from Wade Williams to WW to DoubleW to Double Dubs and finally to Dub-dub. He thought it was extremely clever. I thought it was fucking stupid.

"Hey, Rory. Nice to see you." The only good thing about Rory is that you could be as sarcastic as you wanted and he never picked it up. Ever.

"You stuck closing this bitch with me?" Rory asked.

"Yeah. It's you, me and Mikey." Mike Colburn was the department supervisor for the Tech Repair department, and one of my closest friends.

"Sweet. Have you heard the new Bose sub I got in my department? It packs, like, 1,500 watts in this really compact case. I'm telling you, it's incanny."

He meant uncanny.

"Yeah, I'll have to check that out." I had no intention of checking it out.

"Awesome. When you see Mike, tell him I want to get this fucker closed on time tonight. I'm gonna be hitting the bar, looking for some ladies and getting me some action, if you know what I'm saying."

"I'll be sure to tell him," I said, just as Mike walked in.

"Tell who what now?" Mike asked.

"Oh, yeah. Mike," I said. "Rory wanted me to tell you that he wants to get the store closed on time tonight, 'cause he's going to hit the bar, look for some ladies and get some action."

"Oh, well if you see Rory tell him I'll do my best," Mike replied.

"Yeah. I got the message. I'm standing right here," Rory said.

"Oh, hi, Rory!" said Mike, putting on a ridiculous smile.

"Oh, Rory," I said. "Mike wanted me to tell you he's going to do his best tonight."

"You guys suck," Rory said as he left the room.

"What are you doing in here?" Mike asked me.

"Hiding and pretending to work on the schedule. Got a half hour out of it so far."

"I bet you can get another hour, easy."

Most of the supervisors in the store had tricks for avoiding work. Counting and recounting inventory, employee assessments, and sales numbers analysis were all common, but working on the schedule was a classic that we all shared.

Secret of Retail #2: The higher rank you achieve in the store, the less actual work you had to do.

"I haven't seen you around lately. Where've you been?" I said.

"I had a few days off. Took my lady to the falls. It was fun."

"Did you have all kinds of crazy sex in seedy hotel rooms? Did you do the ultraviolet light thing to see all the other dudes' loads?"

"So, this is where all the supervisors are hiding." Laura was standing in the doorway looking at us. She worked at the customer service desk at the front of the store.

"That's right. And now we must kill you," Mike said.

"Funny guy," Laura said. "I need one of you to come to Customer Service. There's a woman demanding to speak to a manager."

Customers always demanded to speak to a manager any time they ran into the smallest bit of resistance. If a customer wanted to get something that wasn't on that sale that week, but had been on sale the week before, they'd demand to speak to a manager. If something was sold out, they'd demand to speak to a manager. If they couldn't seem to lose that five pounds they said they would back in January, they'd demand to speak to a manager.

Of course, the staff had been trained that customers who wanted to speak to a manager should speak to a supervisor first, and the supervisors had been trained to do everything possible to prevent having to involve an actual manager.

See Secret of Retail #2.

"Rock, paper, scissors?" I asked Mike.

He thrust a fist forward, and on the count of three his scissors beat my paper.

"Two out of three?" I asked.

"Fuck that. You lost. Go service customers."

"Damn."

The lunchroom was situated at the very back of the store. This was done on purpose so employees had to walk all the way through the store when they got to work, and then again when they were leaving work. This provided customers extra opportunities to bother an employee who just wanted to take a lunch or a smoke break. Most employees resorted to wearing a coat or sweater when making the long walk, which usually worked, but when it was really busy even covering the store uniform didn't seem to stop customers from asking for help.

The break room exited onto what we called 'the track'. The track runs around the store connecting every department. It's made up of a giant circle, encompassing most of the store, with an additional walkway going through the middle. This effectively cuts the store into six smaller pieces. Four of them reside outside of the large circular path, one in each direction, and the other two inside the circle.

At the back, near the break room, is the computer department. My department. I can't complain about its placement. It makes for easy access to duck in and out of the break room.

Tucked in the back corner of my department, right next to the warehouse doors, was Mike's Tech Repair desk where the technicians worked on faulty product.

On the east side of the path is the home theatre department. Home theatre quality surround sound systems, DVD players and more big screen TVs than you'll see in any other store.

Across from the home theatre department, on the inside of the track, is an area shared by the digital camera department and the cellular department. Digital cameras also included video cameras and few film cameras that were more relics than products. Mobile sold cell phones and all the little gadgets that go with them.

West of the outer path is Rory's audio department.

The area across from that, dubbed Media, consisted of video games, music and movies.

At the very front of the store were several cash registers.

Tucked right in between the audio department and the cashiers' area was the Customer Service desk and the Employees Only zone, which was a small back room where staff signed in for their shifts. There was also a door that led to an even smaller office which everyone called the managers' room. Mainly because the managers always seemed to be in there. They didn't have to come up with tricks for avoiding work. They just had to walk into that room and close the door.

As I walked from the lunchroom to the customer service desk I thought about the cyclical nature of customer service.

Businesses constantly competed in order to win customers and, more importantly, the money of those customers. Stores trained their employees to go out of their way to thrill the customer with great service. Customer tells all of his or her friends. Before long that level of customer service that was considered exceptional becomes standard.

Businesses and employees are now required to raise the level of service again, and go even further out of their way to win customers. Again, customers are thrilled, and again that level of service becomes the new standard.

The road to hell is paved with customer service.

A large woman was standing at the customer service counter with her arms crossed and a pissed off look on her face. I wished that I had picked rock.

CHAPTER 3

"Ma'am, this is Wade, he's going to help you out," said Laura who then backed away from the counter and the large lady.

"What can I do for you today?" I said trying to smile, but doing a terrible job.

"Are you the manager?"

I could have explained that even though I was only a supervisor I would do everything possible to find a solution. However, most of the time it's just easier to say, "Yes, I am. How can I help?"

"I want to return this." She dropped an iPod on the counter. "This piece of shit!"

"Is there a problem with it?" I asked, acting concerned.

"Yeah. It's a piece of shit."

"I'm going to do everything I can to help you, but there's no need for that kind of language." I had no problem with cursing, but asking customers like her to stop always pissed them off and made me feel a little better. "Is it broken?" I rephrased.

The woman sighed loudly. "Yes. It's broken."

I began taking the MP3 player out of its box when the woman interrupted. "What are you doing?"

"I'm going to test it."

"Why? You think I'm lying? Like I got time to go around trying to return shit for no reason?"

Some people did, and they loved to hang out at our store.

"I need to test it to see if I can find a problem more specific than 'it's broken.'"

Some statisticians in Sweden completed a study on North American retail. The results of the study said that half of electronics returned under the reason of 'malfunction' had no problem at all. The average consumer spent only 15 minutes trying to figure something out before giving up. And since people will never admit to failure, they bring it back to the store and say stupid things like 'this is a broken piece of shit'.

"I can tell you exactly what's wrong with it," said the lady. "It won't play."

She thought that was helpful advice.

Within 90 seconds I knew there was nothing wrong with the iPod. It turned on without an issue and I rolled my eyes when I saw her playlist was mostly Backstreet Boys and ABBA.

I brought the iPod over to the lady, had her put on the earphones and hit the play button. I heard the music start playing and tried not to grin.

At this point, most customers would ask a few more questions about operating their product, thank me for the advice, and be on their way. But, there were some customers that would persist on saying something like...

"Well, I still want to return it."

18

She was embarrassed. Customers like her hate that she couldn't figure out how to use an iPod and that I proved it worked in less than two minutes.

"I just don't like this one. It doesn't sound very good. I don't really like the color, and the earphones are uncomfortable in my ears."

"OK. So we'll do the return," I said.

"That's what I want, but this one over here says I can't."

'This one' referred to Laura, who was still standing behind me. I hate when people are that disrespectful.

"I'm sorry. This one?"

"Yeah."

"I don't understand."

"The girl standing behind you."

"Oh, you mean Laura. I'm sorry, I misunderstood, 'this one.'" There was a certain level of sarcasm I could use with customers before they would call me on it. I was pushing the boundaries. "Why did Laura say you can't return it?"

"She said I need a receipt."

"Laura's absolutely right. You do need a receipt."

"Well, I don't have one."

"We need to see one."

"Why? I bought it here."

"There's no way for me to know that."

"How many other stores sell this? Can't be that many."

"Last I checked, over a dozen. Not to mention all the websites that sell it."

"You made that up." She was right. I had made it up, but it was probably pretty close.

"Here's the deal. Our policy says I can't let you return this MP3 player without a receipt, but we care about our customers and appreciate your business." It took a lot of control not to laugh while saying things like that. "So, here's what I'm going to do. I'm going to let you return the iPod for store credit."

That was how most of these confrontations ended, but with that type of customer I had to make her think she was in for a fight to get anything. Then, when store credit is offered, it would seem like she won.

"Fine. Thank you." Her words were anything but appreciative.

"Have a nice day." At that point in my life those words no longer had any meaning.

I left Laura to process the return and headed toward the warehouse to continue hiding.

CHAPTER 4

There was usually only one of two people in the warehouse, which was good because I didn't have to work as hard at looking like I was working hard.

The warehouse was nearly the size of a football field with large, steel shelves `15 feet high. When the warehouse was full of product it could fill the store's shelves three times over.

Some commotion in the back corner led me to find Mike, who was arranging the stock of big screen televisions.

"Look at you," I said. "Doing real work!"

"We got a surplus of big screens, so Jameson sent me back here and told me to figure out a way to fit them all back here. He gave me the 'by any means necessary' line."

"Asshole."

We actually had two managers in our store; a sales manager and a store manager. Kevin Jameson was the store manager, he outranked the sales manager, and he really was an asshole.

"Yeah. I got two left and the only space left in the whole warehouse is on the top shelf."

"I'll get Big Bertha."

Big Bertha was a hydraulic lift used to put heavy items on high shelves, and it was the most fun to be had in the store while actually working.

When using Bertha, the employee got to ride up with the cargo. It was even fun to be the guy on the ground since the emergency stop button would leave someone up in the air, stranded and helpless.

Mike was on the top shelf, strapping the televisions in place when Jameson burst into the warehouse. "Colburn!"

Kevin Jameson was a short man, but made up for his lack of height with a rabid pugnacity. Along with being an asshole, Jameson enjoyed picking on Mike whenever he had the chance.

"What are you doing back here?" Jameson asked. "You've got a line up at the repair desk!"

"I'm putting these TVs away. Like you asked me to."

"Williams. What are you doing back here?"

"Just giving Mike a hand."

"Shouldn't you be on the floor selling something?"

From time to time, Jameson attempted to pick on me, probably because I was friends with Mike.

"That is a good place for me to be, Kevin," I said. "But, Mike is using Bertha to put those televisions on the top shelf. According to company policy, he has to have a spotter. Otherwise, it creates an unsafe work environment."

He turned his attention back onto Mike. "Get down from there, so both of you can get back to work."

"Sure," Mike agreed. "I just have to finish strapping this TV down."

"Nope. I need you two out there now."

"What about the TV?" Mike asked.

"I'll get that taken care of. Get out there."

The look on Mike's face said that he had a dozen things he wanted to say to Jameson, but he kept his mouth shut.

As Mike and I left the warehouse together, shaking our heads. "Hey, we'll take lunch in an hour, head across the street and I'll buy you a beer."

"I may not come back," Mike said with a smirk.

*   *   *

I spent the next hour trying to explain to an extremely elderly couple that if they wanted to buy a computer to play *the solitaire game* they should save themselves a thousand bucks and buy a deck of cards.

Afterwards, Mike and I walked across the street to The Draft, a pub-style bar and restaurant. It was a laid back place that provided free peanuts and encourages patrons to drop the shells on the floor.

We sat ourselves at our usual table and waved at one of the girls behind the bar. She brought two draft beers to the table before even saying 'hello'.

"Jameson is such a dick," Mike said.

"You don't have to tell me. I'm pretty sure that's in his job description."

"I just hate that he always picks on me."

"You're an easy target."

"How so?"

"You don't fight back."

"I fight back," Mike said, getting defensive.

"Let me rephrase. When you fight back, you make it

personal. You get upset. He feeds off that. He likes to make people insubordinate and then give them shit for it."

"He likes to suck cock. That's what he likes to do."

"I've heard stories," I said, laughing. "Next time he tries to pick on you, just keep it professional. He's so dumb that he still has no clue about policies and guidelines. You do. Use it against him."

Most store managers worked their way up through the chain of command. Not Kevin Jameson. He came from an outside company and was hired as a store manager. I heard a rumor once that he used to sell furniture and gave a good deal to one of the regional managers from our head office in order to get the job. Either that or he slept with someone to get it. I don't know which is worse.

Even after being the store manager for over a year he would still regularly run into policies or procedures that he didn't know. Each time, he would claim that he was still new to certain aspects of the job, even after a year. Most people knew all the aspects of a job after a few weeks.

"I can't think about policies when he starts in on me," Mike said. "I get so angry that I just want to scream obscenities about his mother."

"Well, Mikey, if worse comes to worst we'll get a couple of masks, drag Jameson out of his own house and beat his ass on the front lawn."

We heard a female voice from behind me. "Sounds like something I'd be interested in."

It was Becky, our fellow co-worker and supervisor of the store's mobile department.

"Beck, you hang out here on your day off?" I asked.

She shrugged. "It's cheap to play pool here."

"You here on a date?" Mike asked.

"No. Just here with some girlfriends."

"Too bad I have to go back to work," I said, using my most arrogant tone. "I'd love to play pool with you and your girlfriends. Make sure you're all using the right stroke."

"Charming," Becky said, rolling her eyes. "Maybe another time. See you guys later."

She walked away, smirking.

"I love that girl," I said.

I really did. Becky was fun to hang out with. If someone at the table made a comment about a girl, she had one to follow up with. She wasn't a lesbian, but she seemed to see the beauty in the female form. She was like one of the guys, but with a great rack.

We spent the rest of our lunch laughing at Jameson's expense. The only bad part about a great lunch break was that you still had to go back to work afterwards.

CHAPTER 5

The second Mike and I walked into the store, Laura, from customer service, waved me down. Thinking she had another bitchy customer for me to deal with I looked around for any potential escape.

Mike abandoned me, grinning as he went. I looked around for customers. There was one looking at a big screen TV, but that was at least a half hour commitment. I needed a customer with a quick question who would go away directly after. Then I her browsing the DVD section. She wasn't just beautiful, she was dream girl material, if I had believed in that sort of thing.

I was about to approach her, to see if she needed help finding a movie, or maybe finding a guy to watch the movie with, but I had stood staring too long. Laura was directly in front of me. "The managers said for you to go and see them as soon as you get back," she said.

"So?" I asked.

"So. You're back." She whirled and walked away, calling over her shoulder. "They're in the managers' room."

Big surprise. Managers were always in the managers' room. Its official name was actually something like the Sales Development Office, but it went from being an office to a room and instead of developing sales, managers sat on their asses.

The room wasn't very big. It held a long table, with room for four chairs on each side, and along one wall was a short bookcase filled with binders of company policies and procedures. Any who cared to look closely at the binders would find a thick layer of dust forming.

The walls were adorned with motivational propaganda provided by head office. Sales charts that had very little meaning, graphs that predicted the company's future success, and a poster of that stupid little cat holding onto a tree branch for dear life.

What they did in there was anyone's guess. My guess was hiding from customers. In that, our goal was the same, but I had to work much harder to hide. They had a designated spot. That seemed like an unfair advantage.

When I entered the manager's room Jameson was talking with Lewis Bailer, the store's Sales Manager. They were talking about the U.S. Open. Despite the laziness he was displaying now, Lewis was a good guy and good manager. He was fair to the employees and handled customers well, when it couldn't be avoided.

Since he was half of the management team, Jameson liked to allow him to sit in the manager's room so they could talk about meaningless shit. I can't blame Lewis for taking advantage of it. I probably would have too, even if it meant talking with an asshole like Jameson.

"Lewis. Kevin," I said. "Laura said you wanted to see me?" I had my suspicions as to why.

"Here. I need you to take this," Jameson said, thrusting a clipboard into my hands. My suspicions were right. "And be sales lead for me."

The sales lead was supposed to be aware of the current sales totals and compare them to head office's projected sales. When the store was lower than the projected, the sales lead was supposed to go around the store and motivate the staff to pull sales out of the store's collective ass. The staff was always really good at pretending to care.

Most of the employees were part-timers who just took the job to help with the cost of school, so most of them didn't know what the sales goal was and didn't care. They also weren't stressed when a customer wasn't getting the help they wanted. Which lead into another sales lead duty, coaxing sales people out of their various hiding places to shove them in the direction of customers.

Company policy said there always had to be someone filling the role of sales lead. Policy also said that it was supposed to be done by managers and should only ever have been handed off to a supervisor as a last resort.

I guess discussing the PGA warranted extreme need. Tiger must have been winning.

I took the clipboard, keeping a sarcastic comment unvoiced, and headed out to the sales floor. The numbers said we were behind in sales. I tried to care. There was a time when I cared.

I walked down an aisle of boom boxes and was ambushed at the end of it when Rory popped out from behind a stack of boxes.

"Dub-dub! You here to check out that Sony I was telling you about?" he asked.

"I wish I could, but I was just handed sales lead. So, I have to get out there and," I searched my brain for a good excuse. Any excuse. "Whatever. Show me."

Rory led me down another aisle. "Hey, have you talked to Christine lately?" he said, sounding nervous.

"No. Haven't you?"

"Well, I'm not exactly the most lavacious guy in the world."

He meant loquacious.

Christine was a part-timer and had been recently spending a lot of time with Rory.

"Aren't you her boyfriend? Or at least one of them?"

"Yeah, we were going out. But we're totally just friends now." He transformed his manner from nervous to cocky. "I mean, we still have sex and everything, but we're totally just friends."

"Sounds awesome." Again my sarcasm went undetected.

"Anyway, so this is the one," he said, stopping in front of one of the boom boxes. "You like Coldplay?"

"Not really."

"Yeah, but, through this..."

Before Rory could finish his sentence, a page boomed out over the intercom.

"Wade, can you come to the computer service desk? Wade, to the computer service desk, please."

"Sorry, Rory." I grinned and turned away.

Mike was waiting for me at the computer service desk.

"You owe me," he said.

"At least one. Thanks."

"Don't thank me too much. I let you squirm a little before making the page."

"Dick."

"Hey, you rocking sales lead?"

"Yeah. I'm here to motivate you so that we can strive to beat our target numbers."

"Oh yeah. How are you going to do that?"

"I have a motivational speech prepared."

"Do you? Lay it on me."

"Do better."

We stood in silence for a few seconds.

"That was great," he said. "I'm inspired."

"I'm bored. How long until we can kick everyone out?"

"Two and a half long hours."

There weren't many people in the store that night. On a normal Friday, there would have been a small rush of customers after dinner. Beyond that, most people were busy having a social life.

A lot of computer nerds spent their Friday nights with us, but they'd just hang out in the computer department talking amongst themselves about over clocked processors and refresh rates.

After two and a half hours of pretending to care about customers and their needs we said goodbye to the last one and locked the doors.

Jameson's voice boomed over the intercom. "Wade, I need to see you in the manager's room."

Jameson and Lewis were in the exact same spot they had been in before.

"Did you update those numbers?" Jameson asked.

"Yeah. 10 minutes ago."

"Good. Let me take a look." I slid the clipboard across the table. He studied the numbers quickly, nodding as he took them all in. "Not bad. Could have been better, but we'll take it." He stood up and smiled at me, not knowing how much of an asshole I thought he was. "Right?"

"I guess."

He clapped me on the shoulder and continued to smile like a jackass. "Listen, you're opening tomorrow, right?"

"Yeah."

"Good. I like having my dependable guys in Saturday mornings." He was about to ask me for something. "Could you do me a favor?"

"Sure. Why not?"

"I think Lewis and I need to have an off-site meeting. We have a few sensitive issues to discuss. So, I'm going to give you my keys to close up the store tonight. I'll just get them from you sometime tomorrow." It was Friday, so they were probably going to eat chicken wings and drink beer at Hooters.

"Yeah. No problem." We always closed the store faster when Jameson wasn't around.

"Thanks, Wade. Lewis, I'll meet you out front. I just have to grab my coat from the lunch room." Jameson left the room whistling.

Lewis stood up and stretched the kind of stretch a man does when he's been sitting for a long, long time.

"How's it going, Wade?" he asked.

"All right. Just looking forward to getting the store closed so I can have my own off-site meeting."

Lewis smiled. He knew that I knew they weren't having any kind of meeting. He also knew that I didn't really blame him for taking advantage of Jameson's favor.

"Hey, I'm in tomorrow morning too. So, don't worry about opening duties. Sleep in another half hour."

Like I said before, Lewis was a good guy. If only Jameson was a little more like him.

I unlocked the front doors for Lewis and Jameson and went to make sure people were stocking shelves instead of standing around talking.

Thirty seconds later I walked past a group of three part-timers standing in a circle talking.

"Hey, come on," I said. "At least pretend like you're working."

Back when I was a part-timer I had all kinds of tricks to make it seem like I was working. I would take a piece of paper and write down a few items that I needed to get from the back. Then I could just slack off until someone asked what I was doing, then I would show them the list and say I was on my way to the warehouse.

My favorite was just to walk around holding onto a product. It always looked like I was taking it somewhere. It either looked like I was stocking a shelf somewhere, or a shelf was overstocked and I was taking something back to the warehouse.

I made my way back to the computer service desk where Mike was tidying up the work bench, which was littered with tools, small screws and little bits of wire.

"Well, the managers are gone," I said.

"Bastards."

"At least no one will be looking over our shoulders tonight."

"You're in tomorrow, right?"

"Yeah. Open shift. You?"

"Nope."

"How the hell did you get a Saturday off?"

"Traded a shift with Becky."

"Lucky dog," I said. Although Saturdays off weren't any better than any other day off. If you wanted to go anywhere, you were sharing the time with most of the working world. Stores were packed, restaurants booked, all the good DVDs were already rented.

Everything was much more available during the week, but it meant dodging senior citizens. That's a whole other topic on its own.

"I think we're good to get out of here. The store's about as clean and stocked as it's going to get tonight," I said.

"Good. You want to grab a couple more beers?" Mike asked.

"As good as a beer sounds right now, I'd better not. I have to stop by the grocery store on my way home."

"Groceries at this time of night?"

"Yeah. Lendo's is open twenty-four seven." I chuckled. "How'd you like to work there?"

CHAPTER 6

There's a strange sense of camaraderie naturally inherent between employees of all retail and customer service environments. Walking through Lendo's grocery store that night I couldn't help but give a nod of respect to a stock boy. Since I was still wearing my store uniform he returned the gesture, like two soldiers who've never met but salute each other as equals.

My grocery list consisted of Doritos and Pizza Pops. Truthfully, my daily diet consisted of Doritos and Pizza Pops. As I stood in the frozen food section contemplating if I wanted pepperoni or deluxe, a pair of squeaky running shoes announced themselves at the end of the aisle, carrying their owner toward me. The squeaking grew louder until a man stood beside me with a stupid look on his face.

"Excuse me, but can you tell me where I can find barbecue sauce?" the man asked.

Secret of Retail #7: Never wear your uniform into other stores.

For some reason, customers could never tell the difference between one store uniform and another.

I pointed to the store logo embroidered on the breast of my shirt. "Sorry. I don't work here."

The man continued to stand there and traded his stupid look for a shocked one. He opened his mouth to spew more stupidity at me. "I don't think you should be wearing your uniform in another store. It might confuse people."

It obviously confused him.

"I came here straight from work. I don't normally dress in my uniform to go grocery shopping." He was defeated, but as truly stupid people often do, he kept fighting.

"A police officer doesn't wear his uniform when he's not on duty. What makes you any different?" the stupid man continued.

I didn't want to get into an argument, especially one that stupid. I just wanted to buy some junk food and go home. I didn't want to have to verbally slap this man, but it was about it happen.

"I don't fight fires and I don't catch criminals. I sell fucking electronics. And it's not my fault that you got confused. I'm wearing khakis and a black golf shirt. All the employees here wear black pants and red smocks. That's not the same type or color of clothing."

Again, that should have been enough for him to realize he was defeated.

"I don't think..." I cut him off. It was time to end this.

"Need more? I'm standing here with a basket full of groceries in my hand and you're looking for barbecue sauce in the frozen fucking foods section!"

The man's face turned a bright shade of red. He opened

his mouth to say something, but instead glanced around at the freezers on both sides of the aisle. He gave me another stare then turned and continued his search for barbecue sauce, shoes squeaking in his retreat. I bet he tried the produce section next.

Moments later I was placing my items on the conveyor belt of the express lane. The girl behind the checkout looked very bored. He name tag told me her name was Kate.

"How are you tonight, Kate?" I asked.

She looked at me through half-lidded eyes. "Fine, Wade."

"Right. The name tag," I said, glancing down at my own. "For a minute there I thought you were a genuine psychic. I was going to ask you what I had for breakfast this morning."

She rolled her eyes as she continued to slide groceries over the scanner.

"I'm going to apologize for that last joke. I have this problem where something sounds funny in my head and when they come out... well, you heard it." The corner of Kate's mouth twitched a little.

"It was pretty bad."

"I bet you're looking forward to the end of your shift."

She let out a sigh. "You have no idea."

"I think I do. I felt that way an hour ago. Must be tough working in a place that's open 24 hours."

She finally smiled. She was pretty when she smiled.

"Yeah. Over-night shifts are the worst. I'm done in an hour though, thankfully. I'm dying for a cigarette and a coffee."

"Me too. I only have to wait three minutes, though."

She laughed and threw a bag of Doritos at me. "Come on. No teasing."

I paid for the groceries, and we bagged the groceries together.

"Well, I'm glad you're night is almost over, Kate. I hope you have someone waiting to buy you that coffee. You deserve it."

"Not tonight. I'll just make some when I get home."

"That's too bad. I'm going to be at that little coffee shop a couple doors down. If you feel like stopping in there maybe I'll buy you one. Maybe."

She smiled even bigger, and I walked away without another word. I didn't need another word. She'd be there.

* * *

I sat in the coffee shop for the next hour enjoying a few cups of coffee and the silence of late night. There was only one other customer, a few tables away, and the girl behind the counter.

Kate walked in a half hour later than I thought she would. She had gone home, changed and done something different with her hair.

"Here for that coffee?" I asked.

She quickly sat down at the table, smiling. "I wasn't sure you'd still be here."

"I was just about to leave," I said, and watched a little disappointment creep into her face. "But I suddenly feel like having one more cup."

I ordered two more coffees at the counter and brought them back to the table.

We carried on with some useless small talk for a while. I hate small talk. There's nothing interesting about the weather. Two people can't learn anything about each other with small talk.

After a minute of silence, I looked into Kate's eyes. "What do you want to do?"

She opened her mouth, but couldn't speak.

"With your life," I continued.

"Oh! With my life? I don't know. I want to go to school

for something, but I can't find a career path that can hold my interest."

"I know how that goes. Have you narrowed it down to any areas?"

"No. Not really. How about you?"

"Not as far as school is concerned."

"What do you mean?"

"I know one thing about my future. I don't want to be ordinary. College offers a lot of different options, but every career path is being filled by tens of thousands of people every day. In a lot of cases, hundreds of thousands. Even the professions that impress people are overflowing. Take lawyers for example. You have to go to school for several years, dedicated to your studies if you want to make it, and once you do make it you have to put in a ton of hours. And still, there seems to be a never-ending supply of them.

"I want to do something with my life that stands out. I want to write a song that reaches the top of the charts. I want to write a book that becomes a New York Times Bestseller. I want to direct a movie that wins an Academy Award. I don't want to do something good with my life. I want to do something great with my life."

She stared at me in silence. It wasn't all a lie. I did want to do something great with my life. I just didn't have the talent to do any of the things I had mentioned.

"My place isn't far from here," Kate said, once she got her breath back. "Do you want to come over for another coffee?"

*   *   *

Coffee was never served. Kate grabbed me as soon as we were inside the door and kissed me, pushing her body against mine, trapping me against the wall. Kate was a great kisser, but we were getting bored with kissing.

There was no hesitation when I pulled off her shirt. She didn't flinch when I tugged at her zipper. I saw a soft smile appear on her face when I unhooked her bra. By then she was down to her underwear and more than willing to remove them herself.

Afterwards, Kate snuggled up to me and started to whisper in my ear. I wasn't listening. I was busy considering the rest of the night. *Should I stay with her the night, have a quick breakfast in the morning and head home with just enough time to get ready for work, or should I go home right now?* I wondered.

I was still considering my options when I turned and looked at Kate. She was still talking to me.

"I can set the alarm to give us enough time for a great morning before you have to go."

I put a big, slightly goofy, grin on my face. "Actually, I think once was enough for me."

She was so angry.

Inside of a minute she had me standing in the hall outside of her apartment, completely nude with my clothes in my arms. I couldn't help but laugh. It was my own situation I was laughing at. However, Kate, thinking the laugh was directed at her, ripped open the door and screamed at me.

"Fuck you, asshole!"

"Yeah, I know," I admitted.

Two doors down, a middle-aged woman opened her door and popped her head out into the hallway to stare at me as if I was an alien.

"Hi, there," I said smiling and waving with one hand while trying to hold my clothes in front of my crotch with the other. The woman just stood there and stared. "Fine." I dropped my clothes, exposing myself completely, and started to get dressed.

She watched for a few more seconds, until my dick was covered, then pulled back into her apartment.

I admit, I was an asshole, but it was almost 3 AM and the morning shift was already going to be hell. If I had to get up even earlier with Kate, and spend more energy, my day would've become unmanageable.

Besides, she was an express lane check out girl. Best to keep the relationship to 12 hours or less.

CHAPTER 7

The next morning I arrived at the store, mere minutes before it opened, cradling the largest coffee Starbucks is allowed to legally serve. My fellow employees were still scurrying around making sure the store was up to the company's standards of cleanliness, which it wasn't, and turning on all the demonstration products. A small group of customers were already milling around the front of the store, wanting to get in the second the doors were unlocked.

Saturday.

Most of the working world looked forward to Saturdays. Retail employees hate them.

Saturday was always the busiest day of the week. Mid-afternoon was the worst, but the morning was bad enough.

I dragged myself into the manager's room and dropped Jameson's keys on the table in front of Lewis, who was going over the sales goals for the day. I plopped down in the chair across from him letting my head loll back over the chair.

"That's a big coffee," he said. "Rough night?"

"Late night."

"You going to be good to go today? Brent asked me to join in on a sales conference call this morning. I'm going to need you to be sales lead for a bit." That was a surprise.

"You know me. I'll get it done." With some effort, I forced myself to sit up straight. "But, I should warn you, if I end up with a real shit head, and I don't mean the usual assholes and idiots, but a real feisty shit head, I'm probably going to rip his fucking face off." The way I felt, that could have been a figurative threat or a literal one.

"Well, that's always a risk with you. Here's this morning's numbers. Get out there." Lewis handed me the sales lead clipboard, and picked up the phone as I left the manager's room.

It was difficult to hide from customers on a Saturday morning. There wasn't even a point in trying. They were everywhere. Looking at things they had no idea how to use and just waiting to dump all their stupid questions on salespeople who are forced to answer the exact same questions over and over again.

I walked the floor with my coffee in hand, which was against company policy, but I decided it was a necessity this morning. Beyond that, the only manager in the building would be tied up indefinitely. I was the current ruling class.

I wandered the aisles of big screen televisions and surround sound systems, since it was the least populated for the moment.

"What are you doing on my turf, boy?" said a deep voice.

I turned to see Sawyer Thompson, the Home Theatre supervisor, doing his best to give me a tough glare.

"What's happening, Sawyer?" We clasped hands.

"Shit. What a night, man," he said, his face breaking into a smile.

"Here. I feel your pain," I handed him my coffee and he took a long drink before handing it back to me.

"Thanks, man. You up late, too?"

"Yeah. Met a check out girl. She was nice." I wasn't bragging. Sawyer would've pestered me until I told him, so it was easier to just tell him right away, even if I didn't tell him all of the details.

"Just one?" he asked.

He wasn't joking. Coming from Sawyer, that was a legitimate question. He was a tall, good looking black man who regularly left clubs in the company of two and sometimes three women.

"Yeah. Just one."

"I got with twins last night. Unbelievable."

"Just one set of twins?" I asked, walking away.

"Funny guy," he called after me.

I stopped in the middle of an aisle of televisions and stared at the video loop that every television in the store was showing. Somewhere between two and twenty minutes later a part-timer, whose name I couldn't remember, approached me with one of the store's cordless phones.

"Wade? There's a call for you. A guy named Frank." He handed me the phone and practically ran away.

Frank was my best customer. "Hey. How are you?" I said.

"Good. Wanting to place an order."

Frank was getting on in years, and didn't leave his house much. When he wanted something from the store, he would give me a call, make his order and I'd deliver it to him. It wasn't something I did often, but Frank wasn't like any other customer. He had been my best customer from the first day I started.

"Let me guess, you've got a list of movies." It was usually movies.

"Yup. Some good ones, too."

"All right, let me grab some paper."

I wrote down Frank's list and hung up the phone.

I noticed one of my favorite subordinates, Dev, standing near the front of my department waiting to attack the next customer that came in range of his sales pitch.

Dev was of East Indian descent, though he hadn't been born there. His real name was Devakeenandan, but since he had spent his entire life surrounded by people with names like Jeff and Sarah, he quickly found that most people didn't have a chance at pronouncing his name correctly. It was at that point that he got used to saying, "Just call me Dev."

"Hey, Dev. How're sales?" I asked approaching.

"Hey, bossman. Got two laptops already this morning. I'm rocking today."

"Don't get cocky. I don't want to have to step in and show you up."

Dev made a sound of pure disbelief.

"Yeah, right! Even if you resorted to getting your hands dirty by actually handling a customer, I'm untouchable."

"We'll see about that," I said as I spotted an attractive young woman looking at a laptop.

As sales lead I wasn't supposed to personally handle a sale, but a good-looking girl like this deserved immediate attention.

Secret of Retail #5: Attractive people will always get service first.

"See you in a bit, Dev."

I approached the young woman.

"Hi, there. My name is Wade," I said offering a hand and smiling.

"I'm Elizabeth," she replied, shaking my hand.

We called this a warm opening. It's where a salesmen engages a customer without just blurting out 'Can I help you?' Customers were more likely to feel a bond of trust using this method. Most of the time I preferred to blurt, but with certain customers it was worth the effort.

"Checking out the laptops?" I asked.

"Yeah. But, there's like a million different laptops."

"Are you looking to get one for college?"

"Yeah. How'd you know?"

"I don't know. I guess you just look like the college type." That, and girls fresh out of high school still made exaggerations like a 'million laptops.' Her parents were likely buying her the laptop, and probably somewhere in the store at that very moment.

"Elizabeth?" said a man walking up behind her. "Oh good. You found a salesman."

"You must be Elizabeth's father," I said, offering my hand. "I'm Wade."

"Allan. How'd you know?"

"Just a hunch." And the fact that I'd been doing the job for so long I probably knew more about their buying habits than they did.

"Did you figure out which one you want?" Allan asked.

"No. I was just going to ask Wade which one I should get."

"Right," Allan said. "She's going to need to do her school work. You know, write essays, research on the Internet. Things like that. We don't need anything fancy."

In the course of an average sale the English language was manipulated several ways. A customer who said they didn't want something 'fancy' meant they didn't want something expensive. A customer who said they didn't need something with all the 'bells and whistles' meant they wanted something cheap. When a customer said they didn't think they needed something it meant they didn't want to pay for it. Basically, everything customers said could be broken down to mean 'I'm cheap.'

The store was just as guilty. A customer who wanted a good computer but didn't have a lot of money was shown the 'economic' model instead of a 'mid-level' model. Someone who claimed to want the best, but was still a cheap ass, was shown a model that was 'best in its class' instead of 'the cheapest piece of shit on the shelf.' Items that were re-sold after being returned weren't 'used', they were discounted, put back on the shelf labeled as 'open package.'

As a salesman, or rather a customer service sales representative, it was difficult to make the right recommendation. Allan wanted a computer that could surf the Internet and type up a document. I could surf the Internet on my cell phone and type a document on a typewriter. Any laptop in the store would have done the job. The store doesn't want me to say that, though. Neither does Elizabeth.

The store wanted me to recommend the most expensive model Allan could afford. Something that would bring in a few more dollars to contribute to the sales goal.

Elizabeth wanted me to recommend a cooler model. Something that was capable of letting her have a little fun.

"I would go with this one over here. It's got everything you need, and maybe a little more, but it's a great price and it's on sale this week." I've said that kind of line so many times that it was pretty much automatic.

My recommendation seemed to please both Elizabeth and her father. I showed them every other possible thing they could buy with a laptop and gave them a break on the price wherever I could. Most people thought that being aggressive and playing games was the way to get a deal in retail. If only they knew the truth.

Secret of Retail #6: Nice people get a break. Pricks pay full price.

I began ringing through the purchase when my dream girl from the previous night wandered into view. Today she was looking at digital cameras.

"I'm really sorry about this," I said to Allan and Elizabeth. "But there's something I have to take care of, real quick."

They were more than happy to let me take off for a moment. Even if they hadn't been, I was completely willing to lose a sale to talk to this girl.

I approached her quickly, before anyone else could.

"Hi, there. My name is Wade," I said, offering my hand.

She looked at me and smiled. "Hi, Wade," she said, shaking my hand.

"Considering a new digital camera?" I asked.

"Kind of, but, I'm just having a look, thanks." She went on looking at the cameras, forgetting I existed.

I was speechless. Normally, I was relieved when a customer didn't want my help, but at that moment I was looking for any reason to keep talking to that girl.

"Well, there are some good ones here." What a dumb thing to say. I probably would have been better off running around in a circle wetting myself.

"What was that?" she asked.

"Nothing. If you have any questions," I made a motion with my hand, which I meant to indicate she could ask anyone, but all I did was point at the ceiling and walls.

"Uh, thanks."

I went back to my customers, feeling deflated. I finished processing the sale and helped them carry everything to their car. Most people looked at this as great service. I looked at it as a chance to get out of the store for a few minutes.

With everything loaded in the car, Allan shook my hand.

"I appreciate everything, Wade. You really helped us out today."

And I barely even tried.

"If I can ever help you out with anything," Allan continued. "Give me a call." He handed me a business card. He was a real estate agent.

Elizabeth shook my hand again and gave me a cryptic smile. "And I work at TSR Video, so if you ever want a movie, let me know."

"Thanks," I said. "To both of you." I looked Elizabeth in the eye. "I'm sure I'll be talking to you soon."

*   *   *

It was early in the day and the store was still busy. I walked back into the store and my eyes fell on Becky, by an arrangement of cell phones, smirking. Her department was devoid of customers.

"Hey, Wade. Busy day?" she asked, smiling.

"I guess. Not too busy to give you a hand, though. You need some help finding something in the warehouse?"

"In the east corner, perhaps?"

Security cameras covered every square foot of the store and the warehouse except for a single corner in the back of the warehouse on the east side. For security reasons, nothing was kept in that back corner except for a mop. For all those same reasons, the east corner of the warehouse was a rather popular spot for employees to meet for a make-out session, or more, depending on the time and day.

Becky was smiling, but her smile was misleading. It said she was comfortable joking around, but it also said there was no truth in her joke.

"Yeah," I said. "If it's not already taken. I'll see you later."

I continued back to the computer department wondering what kind of customers I would deal with next.

Elizabeth and her father were good customers. They recognized me as the expert, listened to what I had to say, and based their decisions on that expertise.

The next customers I would serve that day were perfect examples of bad customers. Actually, I should say they were an example of one class of bad customers.

Before I could find another cute girl to pester, I heard a shrill whistle. Out of the corner of my eye, I could see a man motioning for me to come over.

The way he beckoned me and whistled at me was common among a certain type of customer. I absolutely hated it. I couldn't stand the idea of some moron calling me like a dog. I pretended to not see him, or hear him.

He continued making gestures with his arms and whistled again. I continued to ignore him, pretending to be very interested in the store's current flyer. After a moment, he gave up and walked over to me, out of breath by the time he arrived.

"Can I get some service here?"

"Absolutely, sir! I'd love to help you out." Killing this man with kindness was the only thing I could do to prevent myself from spitting in his face. "What can I do for you?"

"I want to get a computer."

No shit, I thought to myself.

Over time, I had become a self-proclaimed expert in first impressions. Nine times out of ten I had a person figured out based on the way they dressed, their body language, their general posture and the way they spoke, which included tone of voice and vocabulary.

This guy knew nothing about computers. He looked like he could fix my car, but barely knew enough to turn a computer on. If I had to guess, I would have said he worked in a factory.

"I have my brother here with me," he said. "Hey Mark! I found a guy."

A slightly taller, slightly fatter version of the man waddled over.

"I found the one you want, Chris." Mark pointed at one of the desktop computers and we walked over to its spot on the shelf where we could stare at the demonstration model.

Mark started to run down all the specs. "It's got a 3600 processor, 640 gig hard drive, CD, DVD, a burner. Comes with a 19 inch monitor. Uh...printer."

"Do you need all those things?" I asked Chris.

"Of course he does," Mark said. "It's the best on the market right now. It's what you want to get."

"What are you going to use your new computer for?" I asked.

"E-mail, Internet, maybe download some music."

Unfortunately for Chris, his brother was an idiot. Chris didn't seem extremely bright either, but at least he knew that he didn't know computers. His brother probably knew computers better than anyone else that he knew, but it still wasn't much. Mark knew a few computer terms that he had overheard someone else say, but he had no idea what any of them meant, what they were for, or why anyone would want them. However, Chris was kind of an asshole, so I was going to let this train wreck continue.

I let Mark talk Chris into buying a far more expensive computer than he needed and pretended to be the helpful sales guy. Then they tried to haggle on the price, and when that didn't work they tried to get me to throw in something for free.

I apologetically told them there was nothing I could do and even pretended to go and ask a manager. Really, I just went and shot the shit with Becky for a couple minutes, but the brothers dim believed that I had fought to try and get them a deal.

Several hours and customer later, my shift was over and the best part of my day was about to begin. I punched my employee code into the electronic punch clock which was located just outside the manager's room. As I was turning toward the front exit the door to the manager's room opened up and Jameson poked his head out.

"Wade. Excellent. Can I see you for a minute?" he asked.

I looked longingly at the front doors of the store and sighed. "Sure. Why not?"

* * *

I entered the manager's room and sat on one side of the table. Jameson sat on the other side along with Lewis. They whispered between each other, repeatedly glancing at me, as if I couldn't tell they were talking about me.

"What's up?" I said loudly. I was tired, wanted to go home, and incapable of bullshit.

Lewis started. "You know we're going to start ramping up for the holiday season soon. So we'll be hiring new employees and getting them trained up now before the store gets busy. Our first group comes for orientation tomorrow."

Lewis acted far more excited about this kind of thing when Jameson was around.

Jameson butted in. "And we'll be looking forward to your help with all the new recruits." Mainly because he still didn't know how to properly train a new employee.

"No problem," I said. "Been a while, but I remember the program."

"Also with the holidays coming up," Lewis continued. "A lot of new products will be hitting the shelves. The company has decided to send some of our top supervisors to a technology expo to get the inside scoop."

"We want to send you," Jameson said. "It's actually a two day event. Expo on the first day and the second day will be all about training you, and the other supervisors, to give you the skills you'll need to one day become a manager!"

I already knew more about being a manager than Jameson did, but I was still glad to have the offer. Out of town conferences were like mini vacations. Meals and hotel accommodations paid for by the company and those who went usually went out to sample the night life in a new city.

The expo would be a day of sneak peeks at all the newest gadgets and free stuff the manufacturers threw at lowly retail employees in exchange for allegiance. A pen seems like a meaningless trinket, but if it was a nice pen it could sway an employee to recommend one brand over another.

Above all else was the euphoria of being paid for two days and not having to deal with a single customer.

"That sounds great," I said, trying to mask my excitement with professionalism.

Jameson beamed at me.

"Who else are you sending?" I asked.

"Sawyer and Rory," Jameson said.

"Rory? Really?"

"Yeah. Was there someone else that you had in mind?" Jameson asked.

"I guess not. You didn't consider Mike or Becky?"

"We considered them," Jameson said, turning his attention

to straightening a stack of papers. "Mike's a great guy and good supervisor, but just not quite ready for management training." He just didn't like Mike. "And Becky is still getting comfortable in her role." Becky had been in her role longer than Rory had been in his. She wasn't going because she was a woman. Jameson would never admit it, but he wasn't just a prick, he was a sexist prick.

"I tell you what," he continued. "We'll give them another look before we make our final decision."

He wouldn't, but I gave a nod. Any further discussion would be a waste of words and my evening.

"Good," Jameson said. "Now go home and get some sleep. You look like shit."

"I plan to. Just have a quick delivery to make first."

CHAPTER 8

Frank lived in a quiet suburb in a simple rancher house. He had lived there the entire time I had been working for the store. His wife had died decades before, and though he claimed to have lady-friends, Frank never remarried.

I entered his home without knocking, as he'd instructed me to do many times.

Frank was in his living room watching a movie with the sound cranked. Stretched out in his recliner he looked like he was asleep, though he motioned with one hand toward the couch when I walked in.

I sat down on the couch and set Frank's new movies on the coffee table, which he would later organize and add to his massive collection of DVDs and blu-rays. Frank even had some VHS tapes lying around.

"Wade," he said. "How are you?"

"Not bad. Bullitt?"

"Bullitt. That McQueen is good!"

"Haven't you seen that a hundred times?"

"It's a classic. Besides, my order seems to be a little late this week."

"Bull," I said smirking.

Frank loved car movies. He had been a mechanic for his entire professional life. When he retired, he bought a big TV and become a movie connoisseur.

"How's the car running?" he asked, searching my face for tells.

"Fine."

"You sure?"

"I'm here, aren't I? I didn't take the bus."

I was one of the few people Frank still did mechanical work for. He insisted I let him do whatever I needed. Tune-ups, brakes, even oil changes.

The majority of the time, I insisted he just sit, watch and tell me what to do on the car. However, on everything but a regular oil change there would come a point where I didn't know what to do and Frank would step in and make it look like the simplest thing he had done all day. He'd just shrug and say something like, "I may just be an old car guy, but I know a thing or two."

"Here's this week's cheque," Frank said.

The store didn't have any kind of delivery system. Whatever Frank wanted, I just bought for him and he paid me back, always with a blank check. He didn't care much to know how much the movies were, and trusted that I would always cash it for the right amount.

"Don't forget to add a little something on there for your trouble."

"You got it. Thanks." I never added on extra. It didn't feel right. I enjoyed visiting Frank.

"You want a beer?" Frank asked.

I didn't. I wanted to go home and fall asleep, but I knew Frank got lonely. I grabbed a beer for him and one for me, and we watched the rest of Bullitt while talking about cars and movies.

*   *   *

It was dark by the time I got home to my apartment. Frank had sent me home when he caught me nodding off on his couch.

My answering machine blinked with new messages. The first message was from some telemarketer who was trying to tell me about a great opportunity and that I should call him back before the opportunity passed.

The second message was from Sawyer. "Yo, dude. It's your boy. Look, I'm gonna hit the club tonight, I think you should come with me. I'm ready to teach you how to get to the next level."

Sawyer thought that I had a block. Mainly because I did pretty well with certain girls, but not all girls. There wasn't a girl I had ever seen that Sawyer didn't do well with. Sure, he had some skills, but he also looked a lot like Will Smith and I didn't think that sort of thing could be taught.

"Anyway, dude. Come on out and join me tonight. But, hey, if you don't, can you open up the store for me tomorrow? Thanks, kid. Later."

Unbelievable. He was such a charming guy that I actually felt special to be asked to open the store for him. It was pretty clever of him to mask asking for a favor with an invitation.

The third voice on my answering machine was an automated voice letting me know that was the end of my messages.

I texted Sawyer to let him know I'd open for him and headed straight to bed.

CHAPTER 9

Sunday.

Sunday's one saving grace was that the store closed at six o'clock instead of nine. Of course, that didn't help me much as the opener.

I got to work before the store opened and helped the home theatre guys turn on all the TVs and then gathered them for an impromptu meeting.

"All right, guys. You're fearless leader isn't here today. He's at home being a giant pussy."

"More like *in* some pussy!" said one of the anonymous guys whose name I couldn't remember. The rest of the guys had a good laugh.

"All right, all right," I said. "Just do your jobs like normal. If you do something that makes me have to come over here, I'm going to make you sing on the intercom."

They all headed to their posts, some laughing about singing, some muttering about it.

I retreated to the back of the store and sat behind the Tech Repair desk with my head in my hands.

I was thinking about what I should have been doing on my Sunday off when a shrill, obnoxious voice drilled into my eardrums. "Has fucking Rory talked to you lately?" I looked up and saw Christine standing on the other side of the repair desk, fists planted on round hips, pure bitch resting on her face.

"I just had this same type of conversation with Rory the other day."

Christine, in my simplest description, was gross. There wasn't one glaringly obvious reason, but several. She smelled like dirty laundry and cigarettes, her teeth were yellow, and she had more facial hair than most men. However, she could have been beautiful, skinny and hairless with a great scent and she still would have been gross due to her fucking personality.

"How come you looking so fucking depressed?" she asked.

"No reason. Just mentally preparing myself for another day of shit."

"Well excuse the fuck out of me," said Christine, as if I had snapped at her. "So, what did Rory fucking say about me?"

I groaned. "Why don't you two just talk to each other?"

"Just tell me what he fucking said."

"Nothing. He just asked if you had said anything about him, that you two were just friends now, and something about a stereo he thought was awesome."

"What a fucking asshole."

"I know. Who gives a shit about stereos?"

"We broke up, if that's what you fucking mean. Last week he calls me up all drunk and asks me if we can spice things up by inviting another fucking girl into the bedroom. So I tell him,

'No fucking way!' and he keeps fucking bugging me about it and then gets all fucking defensive when I ask him why he didn't want to bring another man into the fucking relationship. And then he has the nerve to say–"

"Look, I can't wait to hear the rest of this story, but I really have to head up front and help Lewis open the store."

"Fucking store. Okay, talk to you later."

"I hope not," I said, once I was out of earshot.

Lewis was standing behind the customer service desk pretending to look at sales reports and budgets and whatever else sales managers pretend to look at.

"Hey, Lewis."

"Wade. Didn't think you were in today."

"I'm not supposed to be. I didn't think I'd find you outside of the manager's room."

"Who are you in for?"

"Sawyer."

"Lucky you."

"Lucky me? He's probably in bed with a beautiful woman. Maybe two. And I'm working his shift. I'm real lucky."

"Go open the doors," he said, tossing me the keys.

As always, when the doors slid open the small group of people standing out in front of the store rushed in. One man stopped to ask me where to find a computer monitor. I hated that. The store had been open for 10 seconds. The man was had only made in two feet into the store before asking for help. Put in a little effort before giving up.

Since I couldn't say any of that, I directed him to the back of the store.

I went back to sitting behind the repair desk working very hard at looking busy.

I got away with that for about an hour when a man marched

right up to the repair desk and slammed a box down on the counter.

"This is broken. Can I return it?" He wasn't angry. Just blunt, and maybe hyperactive. He chomped on a piece of gum while his head swiveled in random directions. It was like he was trying to look at everything in the store from where he was standing, but he didn't want to look at any of it for more than a second.

The box he had brought in held a printer. A shitty printer. Apparently a broken, shitty printer.

"What's the problem?" I asked.

"Yeah. It's broken."

"Great." Most people may have questioned that response, but this guy wasn't paying attention. "Do you have a receipt?"

"What?"

"Receipt. Do you have one?"

"Oh. Sure."

He tossed a crumpled and faded receipt on the counter. It took me a couple minutes to make anything out on the receipt.

"According to this, you've had this for over a year."

"I don't know." He looked at me for a few seconds. "No?"

"Was that a question?"

"No?"

"Well, the date on this receipt says you got this printer 13 months ago."

"Oh, yeah. I guess that's right then. What's the return policy?"

"30 days."

"Well, that sucks. You have to fix that."

"The printer?"

"No. Fix your policy. I want to return the printer." This guy wasn't getting it.

"You can't return the printer."

"Why not?"

"You've had it for over a year. We don't even sell that printer anymore." I started to talk a little slower. I didn't know if it was insulting or necessary.

"So what? You've got to keep up with the other stores." This was getting annoying.

"What other stores?"

"I had a tent for a year and returned it to Wal-Mart. They took it back. No problem."

"Well, our policy–" My brain just finished processing his last comment. "Wait, you used a tent for a year and then returned it?" I asked.

He hesitated. He obviously hadn't expected to be called out. Either he was lying or he was a complete asshole. In all likelihood he was a liar and an asshole. I saw Lewis walking nearby.

"The best I can do is go talk to my manager."

"Sure. Go ahead."

I walked over to Lewis and filled him in on the situation.

"Hey, Lewis, if you just want to start shaking your head like you're really telling me 'no', I'll act like I'm really trying to convince you."

"And then I'll act adamant about my decision, and you look downtrodden," Lewis added.

Before we could finish pretending to have a conversation the customer marched up to us and started talking directly to Lewis. He broke out all the standard lines that customers like to use.

He claimed he would never shop there again and neither would any of his friends. He threatened to report the store to the Better Business Bureau. He asked to speak to someone at head office. He claimed the customer was always right. The list went on and on.

Finally, Lewis pulled me aside.

"Do you think we should do this return?" Lewis asked.

"Fuck no! Are you kidding me?"

"Here's the thing. A guy like this might actually call head office and talk to one of the district managers. District managers hate talking to customers. They're complete pushovers and they'll give this guy whatever he wants and then some. We can either take care of this now, and make this guy feel like we're doing him a favor, or he could come back a week from now and gloat over us because our boss is making us do something about it."

District.

A team of managers that resided over all the stores in the company chain, but knew very little of what it was like to work in an actual store. But their word was law. The only person that could overrule district was the president of the company, and I doubt that he cared. Counting that much money had to be time consuming.

"It doesn't seem right. The guy's an asshole."

"I know. Don't worry about it. I'll bring him up front and take care of it."

He turned back to the customer.

"Sir, Wade just convinced me to do the return for you." Lewis said.

He then walked the asshole up to the asshole service desk to make the return.

I spent the next half hour replaying the situation in my head over and over again imagining what it would have been like if I had acted differently.

What would have happened if I had simply told the customer to fuck off?

What would have happened if I had backhanded the customer in the nuts?

How would the customer have reacted if I had just smiled and nodded in response to absolutely everything he said?

What if I jumped up on the counter and punted the printer across the store?

Those were the kinds of options I liked to fantasize about after dealing with an asshole. I fantasized a lot.

At one o'clock Sawyer sauntered into the store, in full uniform.

"I'll be damned," I said. "I didn't think I'd see your lazy ass at all today."

"Nah, man, nah. Just needed a little sleep."

"I know, but you've said that before and disappeared for three days."

"Whatever. Why didn't you come out last night?"

"No reason, really. Just tired."

"Tired?" Sawyer made a noise of disapproval and crinkled up his face. "That's why you can't elevate your game, dude. Show no weakness!"

"Sure, Sawyer. Hide my weaknesses. I'll be sure to write that one down when I get home."

"I've been using this new tactic lately. It's really paying off. Not only that, it's really becoming a way of life for me."

"What is it?"

"I made a promise to myself not to lie to women anymore."

I laughed in disbelief. "You're not going to lie to women anymore?"

"Nope. It's the truth or nothing with me."

"So you're going to tell women everything about yourself? Even the parts that aren't so flattering?"

"I didn't quite say that. I said I wasn't going to lie to women. Shutting the fuck up about certain things is not lying."

"But if they ask..."

"Then I have to tell. I started doing it at the clubs and now I just do it all the time."

"But you'll still lie to me."

"Oh, hell yeah. I'll lie about anything and everything to you. Only ladies get the whole truth and nothing but the truth. You should try it."

"Well, thank you, for the stellar advice, but now that you're here to excel at your job, I'm going home," I said with a big smile and started for the front doors.

"What are you going to do there?"

"I don't know," I said. "Elevate my game."

CHAPTER 10

It was the early afternoon and even though I was coming from work, I still felt as though I had the entire day off. If I hadn't worked that morning I would have just been waking up as I was leaving the store.

On my way home, I stopped at TSR Video. If for no other reason, I went in to marvel that stores like it still existed. Aside from the various digital methods phasing out DVD rentals, the price of a renting a movie was almost as high as buying one.

I walked past a man standing behind the counter. He looked up at me with a complete lack of enthusiasm and put on a fake smile. Then he noticed my uniform shirt and relaxed.

"How's it going?" he asked.

"All right," I replied.

I was studying the back of an Angelina Jolie thriller when I heard a familiar voice from behind me.

"Come to see me already?"

"Angelina?" I said, pulling the DVD a little closer to my face.

"Very funny!" said Elizabeth, as she snatched the DVD from me and hit me on the shoulder with it.

"I didn't know you were working today."

"I'm not."

"Then what the fuck are you doing here? I don't step foot in my store when I'm off."

"Yes, but the benefits of working here include free movie rentals." She held up another DVD to show me. It was some chick flick that looked terrible.

"Really? That's the one I came here for." Hook.

"Too bad, sucker. I got the last copy."

"Well, you'll have to let me know how it is." Line.

"You really came in for this one?" she asked.

"Yeah. I really did."

"Maybe we could watch it together?" Sinker.

"That sounds like it could be fun."

"What are you doing right now?"

She followed me back to my apartment. I changed out of my work uniform while she snooped through my personal belongings.

Three minutes later we had a nice warm bowl of popcorn and ten minutes later I was bored to tears by a terrible movie.

"This movie is not what I expected," I said.

"Just shut up and watch," she replied. She leaned into me, resting her head on my chest. I stretched my arm across the back of the couch to make room for her.

I endured a little more of the movie when Elizabeth turned away from the screen and looked up at me. It didn't seem she was enjoying the movie either. She opened her mouth to speak, but I was already leaning down to press my lips on hers.

The rest of the movie passed by quickly in a blur of making

out and pelvic grinding. When we separated the movie's credits were rolling.

"I'll be right back," she said, standing from the couch and disappearing into the bathroom.

I knew what she was doing. Along with checking her hair she probably had some sexy underwear on, a nice bra and panty set. She was minutes away from opening the bathroom door and revealing her surprise for me.

Not to be outdone, I stripped down to my underwear and stretched out on my couch. When the bathroom door opened, and the beautiful Elizabeth stepped out, she was fully clothed.

She looked at me and giggled.

"I think I'm gonna go," she said, still laughing.

"You don't have to take off."

"Uh.." She hesitated, searching for something to say as she collected her DVD. "I really should."

"Can we do this again?" Asking for a second date. Sawyer would be ashamed of me.

"I've got your number in my phone. Maybe I'll give you a call after first semester."

"After first semester?"

She slipped her shoes on and stood by the door.

"Look, today was fun, but I'm off to school soon, and well... look at you. You seem nice enough, but you work in retail. I'm looking for someone with more prospects ahead of them."

"I'm not proposing marriage. Just..." I motioned to my nearly naked body.

Elizabeth laughed and shook her head. "See you later, Wade." Then she was gone.

I didn't know what to think other than she was a video store clerk, all returns must be made by midnight.

CHAPTER 11

The next morning I woke up to my phone ringing.

"Morning, Wade!" said a far too chipper Mike.

"Why are you calling me so early, Michael?"

"Oh, come on. You would've been up in the next 10 minutes, anyway."

"But the last 10 minutes are my favorite 10 minutes of the whole sleep."

"I need you to come get me this morning."

"Why?"

"My van won't start. Alternator, I think."

"Fuck. OK, I'll be there in an hour."

Monday.

Usually the slowest day of the week. With most customers shopping on the weekend, Monday brought an army of the elderly and the unemployed. Fewer customers was a poor trade off when each one wanted to take up hours of time out of desperate boredom.

An hour after my wake-up call I was parked in Mike's driveway honking the horn. He came out looking as chipper as his voice had sounded on the phone. It was very annoying.

"Thanks for picking me up," he said getting into the passenger seat.

"The price is one blow-job. Start sucking!"

"Nice to see you, too. Stop wherever you want for coffee. I'll buy."

"Dude, I had the most messed up night. I had this girl over, she starts giving me all the right signs and disappears into bathroom. When she comes out, I'm naked on the couch."

Mike burst out laughing loud enough that I had to stop talking until he finished.

"Are you done laughing?"

"Is that what you said to her?" His laughing renewed.

"Shut up. Some girls would have liked it."

"Okay. Keep telling yourself that."

"Anyway, she comes out of the bathroom, I'm naked, and she's ready to leave."

"That's what I'd do if you were naked."

"But she was ready to leave before she knew I was naked."

"Win some, lose some, huh?"

"I guess. It's weird though. I didn't really want her to leave."

"Of course you didn't. You were naked."

"Well, yeah, that too. But even if she had told me to put my clothes back on... I don't know."

I pulled into a coffee shop and Mike hopped out. I checked my cell phone to see if I received any voicemail or text messages through the night. You never could tell with friends like Sawyer. No messages. I held my phone, stared at it in fact, willing a message to suddenly appear. I gave my head a shake, feeling pathetic and pocketed my phone.

When Mike got back in the car he had two coffees and a pair doughnuts.

"Here. I got you an extra-large since you missed your favorite 10 minutes of sleep," Mike teased.

"It doesn't make up for it, but it's a nice gesture."

"How did the store do yesterday?"

I snickered. "Like you care."

"I know. I'm practicing. I want to act like I care when I talk to Jameson. Was it convincing?"

"It was good. It felt casual but genuine. Why are you always trying to get on his good side?"

"Because, I'm somehow permanently on his bad side. It would make my job a lot easier if he wasn't constantly reaming me out."

"Do you ever think about getting another job?"

"Are you telling me to quit?"

"No. Not at all. Just thinking out loud, I guess."

Mike nodded with silent understanding. "Not really. This one pays pretty well."

"Yeah, but if you went back to school you could probably find something that pays more."

"Possibly. My sister went to school for five years and still makes less than me. Either way, I can't afford to go back to school."

"Yeah, you're right."

"What about you? Ever think about heading back to school?"

I shrugged. "Once in a while. I'd burn through all my savings and still need a school loan. I'd probably still get bored after a month and drop out. That's a poor investment."

When Mike and I walked into the store we noticed nine

people in a line, all standing at attention. The store wasn't open yet, so they weren't customers. They could have been from the army from the way they were standing.

"Why are they standing like that?" Mike whispered to me. "New hires?"

"I don't know, but it's kind of creepy."

We walked to the Manager's room and found Jameson playing solitaire on his company laptop.

"Morning, fellas."

"Hey. What's with the live mannequins out there?" I asked.

Jameson chuckled a little. "They're rookies. I told them to stand at attention until their trainer got here."

"Who's their trainer?" I said.

"I was hoping you could do it," he said, not looking away from his solitaire game.

The majority of my day would be spent over explaining a simple job, watching terrible how-to videos, and wouldn't interact with a single customer. I'd be stupid to pass up the opportunity. "Okay."

As I turned to head back to the new hires I heard Mike ask Jameson how the store had done yesterday. It did sound convincing.

The new hires didn't even look at me as I approached them.

"Everyone relax. You don't have to stand at attention. That's Jameson's idea of a joke. You'll be selling DVDs, not battling overseas."

One of them spoke up. "Are you our trainer?"

"Yes, I am." They relaxed, and rubbed at sore necks and backs. "Have you all had the store tour?" They all nodded. "Good. I want everyone to head back to the lunchroom, grab a chair, take it into the warehouse, find a nice open area and sit in semi-circle. I'll meet you there."

Ten minutes later they were all huddled around a 19" inch television owned by the company. Yes, that's right. A company that sold 65" high definition flat screen chose to use the shittiest, off-brand televisions that the store had ever sold.

I made them watch the full 3 hours of training videos all at once. They were supposed to be spread throughout the day, but I preferred to get them out of the way. They were a poor substitute for real training, but I was required to show them.

It was always funny to watch people as they watched the videos. Some people actually took notes in a spiral notebook they brought from home, some struggled to stay awake, while others just watched quietly with a look somewhere between boredom and feigned interest.

"After watching those videos, who can tell me what your job will be as customer service sales representatives?" A few people stared at me blankly. "I know. It means salespeople." The blank stares were replaced with pensive nods.

A guy who had been taking notes through the entire video raised his hand instantly.

"My name is Stephen. Our job will be to understand our customer's needs, evaluate the circumstances, compare the products in our customer's price range, and recommend the right one, along with any accessories they might need with it."

"Good answer. How about you?" I pointed to one of the guys that fell asleep a couple of times.

"Uh, I'm Ron. And, I think it's my job to, like, ask questions, and stuff."

"Yeah, asking questions is definitely part of the job."

"I'm Trent," said another guy who appeared to intentionally sleep through the videos. "And I'm not 100% sure about my job description, cause I didn't pay attention to the videos, but I'm pretty sure my job is to sell stuff."

"You're not wrong." I pointed at one of the three girls of the group. "What about you?"

"My name is Megan, and I don't really know what my job is here."

"You didn't pay attention either?" I joked.

"I paid attention. But the videos didn't seem to tell the real story."

"What do you mean?" I was intrigued.

"Well, the video suggested to always do right by the customer, but also says to try selling them every extra accessory possible because there's higher profit on them. Those two concepts seem to move in opposite directions."

As she finished speaking every pair of eyes looked to me for a reply. I could have gone with the first convincing bullshit answer that came to mind, but this girl seemed to see right through bullshit.

"Sometimes they do." My eyes were locked on Megan's, and vice versa. "Let's take a break. Go wander around the store a bit. Play around with the cameras and laptops. Have a smoke. Whatever."

I stepped close to Megan and lowered my voice. "Can I talk to you for a second?"

"Of course," she said with a sigh.

Once the others had left she turned to me and said, "I understand if you want me to leave."

"Who said anything about leaving?"

"I thought you were about to."

"Why would I ask you to leave? For telling the truth? No. I've been doing this long enough that I can pretty much tell who's going to make it in this job and who's not."

"Really?"

"Yeah. That Stephen guy. He'll make it for a bit, but sometime around the three month mark he'll quit when he realizes his job isn't as important as he thinks it is, and the managers don't take anything he says seriously."

Megan laughed. She had a nice laugh.

"Ron won't make it. The store might keep him around here in the warehouse to lift heavy things for a while and give him the boot after the Christmas rush is over."

"Let me guess," she joined in. "Trent won't last a week?"

"Trent? He's cocky and brutally honest no matter how it makes him look. He'll be fine. He's probably the most qualified one here."

Megan burst out laughing.

"What about me? Am I going to make it?"

"I'm not sure about you yet."

She smiled.

I smiled back. "Don't take this the wrong way. What are you doing here?"

"What do you mean?"

"Not only can you see through bullshit, but you're confident and intelligent. What are you doing at a job like this?" I asked. I wasn't encouraging her to quit. I wanted her to stay. But I did want her to consider the job she was taking.

She didn't even hesitate before responding. "What are you doing at a job like this?"

Did that mean that she thought I was confident, intelligent and overqualified?

For the second time in ten minutes, she left me searching for words. I just stared at her. I found myself looking from her eyes to her lips and back to her eyes again. Eyes, lips, eyes, lips. I couldn't figure out which I liked more. The lips and the eyes were getting closer.

Was she moving closer to me, or was I moving closer to her? I wondered.

We were both moving.

The door of the warehouse was shoved open and the din of the rest of the training group broke the silence. Megan and I both jumped back from each other.

I pulled a card out of my wallet and handed it to Megan.

"What's this?" she asked.

"There are certain things that management is going to try to make you memorize. These things have nothing to do with the actual job itself, but they're going to insist on their memorization anyway. Every one of those things is on this card."

"Don't you need it?" she asked, offering the card back to me.

I shrugged. "Unfortunately, if you pretend to have that stuff memorized long enough, you end up having it memorized."

She took a few steps to join the rest of the group, then turned back to me. "By the way, I'm only here until I'm done with school."

If she stayed in school she was already smarter than I was.

I spent another few hours with the new employees filling their heads with company propaganda, and sent them home early. There were still a few hours left in my own shift, which I planned to spend avoiding work as much as possible.

One of my usual places to waste time was behind the customer service desk. I could pretend to sort through the pile of returns, testing and retesting, as long as I needed. After an hour of that, I heard some shouting coming from the checkout area. I left my refuge for a better look. Angry customers were entertaining when I wasn't the one dealing with them.

This wasn't a customer kicking up a fuss about having to pay taxes on merchandise, or accusing a cashier of short changing them because they couldn't count. The shouting was coming from a man with a desperate look on his face and a gun in his hand.

CHAPTER 12

The gunman continually turned, keeping an eye on everyone and everyone in fear. He repeatedly shouted, "Nobody move!"

How cliché.

I glanced over my shoulder and noticed one of the customer service girls on the phone. She looked panicked. I assumed she was on the phone with the police, and stopped worrying about making the call myself. Turning my attention back to the gunman, I noticed something very peculiar.

I never would have noticed it if my sister hadn't married a hunter. His name was Clark and he knew more about hunting than I knew about anything. He taught me to shoot a few of his guns, which was kind of cool. I got to feel like Bruce Willis for a short while, but I wasn't a very good hunter.

The gunman holding up the store was holding a 9mm pistol, which uses a clip for its ammunition. The clip is inserted into the bottom of the gun's handle and sticks out just a little.

There was nothing sticking out of the bottom of the gunman's gun. Barring the unlikely possibility that the gunman had a bullet sitting in the chamber, his gun was not loaded.

I slowly walked toward the gunman with my arms held out to show I had no weapon, and wasn't there to fight. Even without bullets, he could hit someone with that gun and spill some blood.

The gunman swung his gun around at me as I approached.

"What are you doing?! I said 'Nobody move!'" he screamed at me.

"I know, but I was way over there when you said it, and I wanted to talk to you. How am I going to talk to you from way over there? I don't want to be shouting across the store. It's rude."

"Why do you want to talk to me?"

"I want to make sure no one gets hurt."

"No one's going to get hurt. Just give me the fucking money or I'm going to start shooting!" He spun in a circle, inciting a scream from the crowd around us.

"I can help you get the money. The only problem is our security system is some of the leading technology in artificial intelligence. Through its cameras, it will have recognized you as a threat and locked these cash registers down. I know an override code, but once I put in the code, it'll take three to five minutes before the registers will open."

"Put in the fucking code!"

I walked to the closest register and punched in a bunch of random numbers. There was no code. The security system wasn't state of the art. We had a bunch of cameras, but that was about it. I was just killing time.

The gunman directed me to each register to punch in my override code.

"OK everyone, we just need to sit tight for the next three to five minutes, and then I'll be out of your life."

"You know, if you really wanted to rob this place, you should've applied for a job," I said.

"What are you talking about?"

"A store like this, with the state of the art security system, we don't usually see things like armed robbery. Most theft committed here is done through shoplifting and internal theft."

"I don't have time for that."

"But this is so short sighted. I can tell you that you might get a thousand bucks out of these registers combined. You could've gotten yourself a job back in the warehouse and set up a nice little system."

"Really?" The gunman seemed more interested in my bullshit plan than the registers.

"Sure. When the shipments come in, you're the guy who verifies the invoicing. So you claim the shipment is a few laptops short. Where did those computers disappear to? Well, the company will try to back track them through paperwork when the whole time the laptops were really in the backseat of your car. If you take high end ones you could sell them for a thousand bucks a piece. Constant revenue."

"Why aren't you doing that?" he asked.

"I don't work in the warehouse."

The gunman stared at me for a minute, thinking hard. He pointed his gun at me with new vigor. "When these registers open, put the money in a bag, and throw in an application!"

Sirens sounded in the distance and were getting closer by the second. He looked at me, eyes wide.

"I don't think they're here for me," I said, trying to keep a smirk from my face, but failing.

"I guess this is a hostage situation now!" He spun around again pointing his gun at each person for a split second. "Who's it going to be, huh?"

"Hey," I said. The gunman stopped dead in his tracks and slowly turned to look at me. I motioned for him to come to me.

He motioned back for me to come to him.

I motioned even more persistently for him to come to me.

His shoulders slumped and he came walking over. "What is it?" The sirens were right outside the store now.

I leaned close to him. "If you hand the gun to me and give yourself up, I won't tell anyone that your gun isn't loaded."

He stared wide-eyed at me for a few seconds. His eyes slipped off of me and he stared into the distance, seeing nothing and everything. I took hold of the gun and gently pulled, it came out of his hand without resistance. The staff and customers in the area applauded enthusiastically. He didn't even seem to notice.

I put a hand on the gunman's shoulder and started to walk him to the front door. I tucked the gun in the back of my pants. The last thing I needed was the cops to see the gun in my hand and think I was the gunman and I had picked a hostage.

We exited the front doors and saw four police cars scattered around the entrance. When they saw the gunman was no longer armed they ran to us and put him in handcuffs.

"Hey," the gunman called to me as they were pulling him away. "Do you think your boss would give me a job when I get out?"

"I don't think so. He's got this thing about convicted felons."

Another cop walked up to me and asked if I would give a statement. I gave him my statement along with the gun.

The cops stuck around for another hour interviewing various witnesses. A lot of those same people approached me afterwards to shake my hand and thank me for my bravery. It was tough to keep a straight face.

Matt, one of the part-time guys who had seen the whole

thing, waited until the store was nearly empty before coming up to me.

"Is that true what you said?" asked Matt.

"Is what true?"

"The whole warehouse thing. Laptops disappearing."

I looked at him, wondering after the real reason behind the question.

"Of course not. Someone might get away with it one time. But the company would be up this store's collective ass with an investigation. If it happened a second time, they'd put us all under heavy interrogation until someone cracked. They do not take theft lightly."

Most theft was done by shoplifting and internal theft. That was true.

The company never suffered either for long. Anytime they were burned by someone, a policy was implemented shortly after that to kill any similar attempts.

One time a man brought back a desktop computer he purchased, claiming he never opened it and just couldn't afford it. The man was given a full refund. When someone finally got around to opening the box, there was just a big rock inside. The next day a company-wide policy went out that we were to thoroughly check every product coming back.

A lady once came into the store claiming she wanted to return a CD. The store policy at the time said that all products being returned get a little yellow sticker at the door so customer service would know it was brought from outside the store. The lady took the sticker off of the $15 CD and put it on a $1,500 computer. Then she tried to return the computer, but since she didn't have a receipt with it, the store sent her home, with the computer. Once the store figured out what had happened, a company-wide policy was implemented which changed the little yellow sticker policy to a multi-colored sticker policy. Each color represented a specific price range.

Internal theft was harder for the company to battle. One policy that had been in place since day one was termination on first offense or attempt. No second chances. That scared the majority of the staff into not even keeping a pen they found lying around in the lunchroom.

A few people dreamed a little bigger and would steal a DVD from time to time. Most who were brave enough to try it got away with it a time of two, but it never lasted long.

One guy had a good television scheme going for a while. He, or one of his friends, would steal someone's credit card from the change rooms at their gym. Then our employee would bring the credit card into work and ring through a big purchase on it, claiming the customer was coming in later to pick up the sale. Minutes later, one of his friends would pull up with a pick-up truck and they would load the massive sale into the back.

In the case of a stolen credit card the victim does not have to pay for purchases made. Neither does the credit card company. It ends up coming back on the store. After the store had three of these come back in a month, all the managers had to do was look at who made the three sales. That guy wasn't just fired. He was arrested.

* * *

When my shift, and the parade of congratulations, finally ended I went to find Mike back at the repair desk.

"There's the store hero," he called, holding his arms out wide.

"Ah, fuck! Enough!"

"That's what you get for saving people's lives."

"I didn't save anyone. The guy had no bullets in his gun."

Mike laughed so hard he had to hold on to the repair desk to keep from falling over. "The guy was shooting blanks?"

"Yeah, and he had no bullets in his gun."

"Your secret is safe with me."

"Are you ready to go?" I asked.

"Yeah, let's go," he said, still laughing.

On the way to Mike's house I stopped off for gas. After pumping Mike and I both went into the store. I grabbed a few unhealthy snacks, none of which would survive the night.

The girl behind the counter looked like she was born with an enthusiasm deficiency disorder. She sat there, reading a magazine, supporting her head with one hand and loudly chomping on chewing gum.

"Looks like you're having a rough night," I said with a small, supportive smile.

She looked at me as if I had just told her she had chunky thighs and flabby arms and said, "Just the gas?"

"No," I said. "I would also like to purchase these items as well. The ones that I'm holding."

Her face broke and she smiled. She was much prettier when she smiled.

"I'm sorry. It has been a rough night," she said.

"Don't worry about it. I understand. Customers are the worst."

"Aren't you a customer right now?"

"Yeah, but I'm not a real customer. I'm a customer that understands. And understanding customers don't really exist. Therefore..."

"You don't exist?"

"Something like that."

"Yeah, well, customers who don't pay are even worse," she said.

"What do you mean?"

"Earlier in my shift I had a guy drive off after filling his tank."

From the back of the store Mike called out to us. "Too bad that guy wasn't here now. Wade could karate chop him in the throat!"

She looked at me for an explanation. "Long story," I said. "What's the big deal about a drive off? It's a gas station, it must have happened before."

"But my boss is a dick and that gas will come off of my paycheck unless the cops happen to find this guy."

"That's not even legal. Stores are insured for theft. He has to pay a deductible, but in the long run he gets most of his money back. It sounds to me like your boss is getting money from you and from the insurance. Prick."

"Maybe he is. Not like I can do anything about it."

"Tell your boss to knock it off. Tell him that you know he's double dipping. Tell him it's illegal and tell him that you have no problem reporting his ass to the proper authorities."

"Are you kidding me? I'll get fired. Even if he is taking my money, when I come at him like that, I'm gone. What then?"

"Don't you think you could get another crappy, part-time, minimum wage job if you had to?"

She smiled and gave me a look that I was very familiar with. "Yes, I could."

"Screw your boss. Not literally. Tell him off and if he decides to fire you, get yourself a job where you'll be better off and report him to the labor board."

"Thanks for the advice." She wrote her phone number on the back of my receipt. "If you have any more advice, I'd love to hear it. Maybe on Saturday night?"

"I'll give you a call." I gave her a smile before walking back to my car with Mike on my heels.

I slumped into the driver's seat and crumpled up the receipt and the gas girl's number.

"Why did you do that?" Mike asked. "Seems like she's into you."

Mike meant well, but had been away from the game for too long. He just didn't understand.

"I'm not looking for a date on Saturday night. We're part of a generation that is dependent on instant gratification. If she had mentioned tonight instead of Saturday, I'd still be in there."

"That's fucked up. You're fucked up."

"What can I say, Mike? I'm just not willing to pay before I pump."

CHAPTER 13

Tuesday.

Cheap night. A lot of restaurants and movie theaters have some kind of discount on Tuesdays. Things like half price movies and buy one, get one free appetizers. Whatever might bring in customers on what would normally be another slow weekday.

For some reason the same people that went for a cheap movie and meal always made sure to hit our store as well. The store had never had any kind of Tuesday special, but this group of customers felt that just by coming in on a Tuesday they were entitled to discount prices or maybe even the greatly desired freebie.

These customers were possibly the worst kind to deal with. They asked for a special price on everything and when they didn't get it, they walked. Tuesdays usually meant low sales, a whole lot of time-wasting customers, and a frustrated staff.

Fortunately, I was off that Tuesday.

Unfortunately, I was almost bored enough to want to be at work. Almost.

I spent most of the day bouncing around my apartment playing video games, checking my e-mail, aimlessly flipping through multiple channels of shitty television, then aimlessly surfing though hundreds of websites, ultimately ending up at a porno site, masturbating and having a short nap. I woke up an hour later, checked my e-mail again, put on a movie that I didn't want to watch, and finally achieved such an interminable level of boredom that I cleaned my apartment.

A second round of surfing the internet had me considering a second round of masturbating when my phone chimed from across the room with a new text message.

I tripped over my own couch as scrambled across the room. A text message from Sawyer said:

Sup Wade? I'm hitting the club tonight. Just thought I'd let you know, even though you won't come. Peace.

He was right. Normally, I wouldn't go. Clubs and bars weren't my element. The thought of trying to fill the rest of the evening had me willing to do just about anything. Besides, it was Tuesday. Maybe they would have some cheap drink specials.

I met Sawyer at a club called The Red Door. The name made no sense to me. The front door was black. The bathroom doors were green and the door to the V.I.P. section was gray. The bar was crowded with barely legal teens taking selfies and posting on the internet. It was trendy to pay more than double for a drink in a glass smaller than a Yahtzee cup.

Sawyer and I sat down at a table near the dance floor and ordered a couple of overpriced drinks from the nearest waitress.

"I'm surprised you came out tonight, man," Sawyer said.

"What the hell, right? I've got the afternoon shift tomorrow."

"I ain't talking about whether or not you gotta work in the morning, but whatever, man. You made it out. That's what's important." He quickly scanned the club and pointed out a group of young girls dancing like it was their last chance for the night. Sawyer was studying the group, eyes never staying on any one girl for more than a second. The girls looked too young to me. I expected someone to bust into the club and arrest me on some kind of perversion charge just for looking. I wasn't old, but watching girls that young dance made me feel old, and the longer I watched, the older I felt.

The waitress brought our drinks. I downed mine and ordered two more before the waitress could walk away.

"Time's wasting, my friend," Sawyer said with a smile, and strolled over to the group of young girls and began dancing with all of them.

For the next twenty minutes I sat at the table remembering why I hated bars and clubs. I was just about ready to leave when two girls came and joined me at the table. One was a gorgeous blonde and the other was an extremely cute brunette. Not only were they incredibly attractive, they were old enough to stop me from feeling like a dirty old pervert spying on high school girls.

"What are you doing sitting here all alone?" asked the blonde.

"Yeah, you should be partying." the brunette said with a smile.

"Being mysterious," I said.

"What's mysterious about sitting by yourself?" asked the blonde.

"Nothing, I guess." They looked around the bar, seconds from heading off to find someone more interesting to talk to. "So, what do you ladies do?"

"No offense, but I really don't want to talk about work tonight," said the brunette.

Small talk. There was nothing worse than small talk. I just didn't know how to do it. My eyes wandered and fell on Sawyer. He winked at me and looked down at his feet.

It was worth a shot.

"I like your shoes," I told the blonde. I might have said it to the brunette instead, but she kind of pissed me off.

"You do? I have the cutest little purse to go with it, I didn't bring tonight, though." She continued on about matching accessories, dresses, blouses and other things that I didn't care about. "What do you do?" The blonde asked, sounding like she was doing me a favor by bringing it up.

"I asked you first," I said.

"I'm a child care technician." She was beaming with pride. As far as I knew, that meant she worked at a daycare.

The brunette made a noise of disgust and left the table. I figured she either really hated her job or...

"Don't mind my friend. She lost her job. Poor girl." The blonde explained.

"Daycare, huh?" I asked.

"Yeah. It's really great. I love it there."

"Don't you hate those times when the kids won't leave you alone, though? They just keep bugging you and bugging you with stupid shit until you just want to pull out your hair and jump out the nearest window?"

"No." She looked at me like I had just devoured a kitten right in front of her. Apparently children were nothing like customers. "I'd better go check on my friend."

She left the table and I went back to watching Sawyer and the dancing girls. Although at that point most of the girls were more concerned about grinding on Sawyer than dancing.

This club was considered to be one of the hottest clubs in the city. There were plenty of hot girls around, dancing, laughing, drinking and having a great time. All the while I sat at a table all by myself thinking about how much of a loser I was.

CHAPTER 14

The next afternoon I woke up still feeling like a loser. I vowed that next time I was bored enough to go to a club with Sawyer I would just stay at home and bang my head against the wall until I passed out. It would have been just as productive.

There was only an hour until the start of my shift, so I took my self-loathing into the shower.

Wednesday.

Wednesday was the slowest day of the week and my favorite day to work. The only people that came shopping just happened to be within sight of the store with some time to kill. No one ever made a point of coming into the store on a Wednesday. If something wasn't done first thing Monday, it was pushed off until the weekend.

Becky was just getting out of her car when I pulled into the parking lot. She smiled and waved at me and my loser complex lifted a little.

"Hey, Becky. What's happening?"

"Hey, Wade. Are you coming back from lunch, or are you with me on the afternoon shift?"

"Even if I was coming back from lunch, I'm definitely with you."

As we walked toward the store I checked my phone for the first time that day. "Holy shit!"

"What?" Becky asked.

We stopped walking and faced each other.

"Mike sent me a text this morning. He said Jameson is freaking out because a bunch of money went missing yesterday."

"That sucks."

"You don't know the half of it. You weren't here the last time this happened. He'll sit everyone down one by one and grill them about where the money is."

"So, why are you smiling?" she asked.

"Because, I wasn't here yesterday."

When Becky and I walked into the store I immediately saw Mike walking towards us from the right with a half-smile on his face.

"Oh, shit," said Becky. "Jameson, ten o'clock."

I looked and saw Jameson marching towards us with his hands in tight fists, and his arms rigid at his sides. He marched with purpose and reached us before Mike did.

"Wade, I need to speak to you," he said, then spun on his heel and marched toward the manager's room. After only a few steps he stopped and turned back to me. "Now."

I followed him into the manager's room, barely keeping a smile off of my face.

As soon as the door was closed, Jameson started freaking out. "Some money went missing last night. A lot of money."

"Any ideas?" I asked. "Who did it? How they did it? Motives? Alibis?"

"No. That's why I brought you in here. I trust you. Plus you weren't here yesterday, so it couldn't have been you."

"What do you want me to do?"

"I want you to get out there and start tracking down the money. Try to get on the inside of the action. Tell people that you want in on it." He had been watching too many cop shows again. "While you're doing that, I'm going to develop a list of prime suspects and bring them in here one by one for interrogation."

"I think that's a good plan," I said. Jameson nodded. "However, while we're in the beginning stages of our search, don't you think you should have someone do a recount?"

The last time a lot of money went missing a recount wasn't done for three days, at which point they discovered there hadn't been any money missing in the first place.

"I guess it couldn't hurt. But I'd better interrogate the people that are going to do the recount first. Just to be sure."

"Good plan, Sarge. I'm going to go start my side of the investigation." I gave him an enthusiastic thumbs up.

Jameson gave me an approving nod. He probably enjoyed being called Sarge.

I had such faith in the recount that my side of the investigation consisted of me walking around and chatting to some of my favorite co-workers. I flirted with Becky, talked movies with Mike, joked around with Dev, and listened to stories from Sawyer. As long as I gave Jameson a thumbs up whenever he marched into my field of vision he thought I was getting to the bottom of things.

I was on my way back to my own department when I was ambushed by Rory. "What's up, Dub-dub?"

"Hey, Rory."

"Did you hear we're going to that product show and manager training together?"

"No, I hadn't heard that." A string of cursing started in my head.

"Yeah. You, me and Sawyer are all going. I could use the break. Change of pace, you know? I haven't been sleeping good lately. I think I got narc's epilepsy, or something."

He meant narcolepsy.

"Narcolepsy," I emphasized the real word. "is when you fall asleep all the time. Not when you're having trouble sleeping."

He chomped loudly on his gum as his eyes darted around the store. I assumed he was debating with himself whether to just move on, or to pretend to fall asleep right in front of me so he didn't look like such an idiot.

"Yeah. I know," he said. "Did you talk to Christine the other day?"

"Yeah," I said. *Unfortunately*, I thought.

"What did she say?"

"She said 'fuck' a lot, and then something about you wanting to bring a man into your bedroom when she wasn't even there."

"That's not how it happened!" Rory practically sputtered. "I wanted to have a threesome with another chick! She wanted another guy, I said 'fuck that' and broke it off."

"Right. Now I remember. Christine said that exact same thing, but called you an asshole and used 'fuck' a lot more than you did."

Rory's eyes wandered while his brain processed the information. I used the opportunity to slip away to my department.

That night I had three employees on my computer sales team. Two of them were with customers. The third was Dev.

"What's going on, Dev?" I asked.

"Nothing, bossman. Just another slow Wednesday night, you know?"

"Did you hear some money went missing last night?" I asked.

"Ah, shit. So Jameson is going to pull me into the manager's room and grill me again?"

"Probably. You're practically a terrorist in his eyes. You'd be at the top of my list too."

"That hurts, man. Brown skin still bleeds."

"It does?" I pretended to sound shocked.

"You white people don't even have your racial profiling down. I wouldn't be stealing money, I'd be blowing it up."

"How are your sales tonight?" I asked.

"Shit, bossman, you know me."

"Kicking ass and taking names, I assume."

"As much as you can on a Wednesday," Dev said.

"That's my boy." I glanced around the department. "What's this?"

"What?"

"It seems a young lady has slipped into the department without your detection. Over by the laptops."

"No problem, boss. I'm on it."

My arm sprung out to stop Dev in his tracks as I noticed it was the hot girl that I had embarrassed myself in front of twice so far.

"I think I'll handle this one, Dev."

Dev took a good look at the hot girl. "Don't worry about it, boss. I'll take good care of her."

"I said I got it, Dev."

"And I said I'll take care of it."

"Dev, I'm your supervisor."

"We've always been trained to leave our supervisors available for more important things whenever possible. I got this."

"I guess you've got me there, Dev."

Dev smiled in victory.

"However," I said, causing his smile to fade away. "As your supervisor, I'm sending you on break. See you in fifteen."

Dev couldn't argue anymore, but instead of heading to the break room he went and sat behind the repair desk where he had a clear view of the laptops.

I approached the hot girl with what felt like a goofy smile on my face.

"Welcome back," I said.

She turned and smiled at me. "Oh, hi. Did we speak last time?"

"Sort of." I wasn't sure if I was upset that she didn't remember our last encounter or not. It wasn't a very impressive display. "Are you looking to get a laptop?"

"I think so. I definitely need a computer, but should I go with a laptop or a desktop?"

"You need to ask yourself if you would use the portability of a laptop. Would you ever want to bring your computer to a friend's house? Would you ever want to work on it while at a coffee shop? Or at the very least, sit in a coffee shop and make it look like you're working on your laptop while you really just play solitaire."

We both laughed. She seemed to bring out my inner dork, but for the moment, the dork was gone.

"I'm Wade, by the way," I said offering my hand.

"Tess," she replied, giving my hand a gentle shake.

Over the next half hour I showed her what she needed to know on both laptops and desktop computers, all while dropping lines intended as bait. If she bit on any of the lines it would eventually lead to some kind of date. However, Tess didn't bite on any of them.

After heavy consideration Tess chose a laptop. I was racking my brain for what to say to her next. She deflected everything I tried. I considered simply asking her out. Straight forward with no lines. Sawyer had always warned me about that tactic, claiming its results were worse than death.

"What do I do if I have problems?" she asked.

"What do you mean? Like money problems? You don't want to come to me. Trust me on that one." We both laughed again.

"Technical issues. What do I do?"

"Just bring it in. Any one computer problem can be caused by a hundred different things. It's best if we can just look at it."

"Do you guys have some kind of 24 hour service? What would happen if I was working on something important at 3 AM and had a problem?"

"Is that common for you?" I asked. An idea sparked in the back of my head.

"It's happened before," she admitted.

"My first instinct is that any problem you have at 3 AM is because you're working on something at 3 AM."

I took a business card with the contact information to the repair department, wrote my number on the back, and handed the card to Tess.

"Here. That's the phone number for the repair desk, which you can reach during regular store hours. Anything beyond that, my phone number is on the back. If you have a problem, odds are, I can probably talk you through it."

Tess would either see through the technical support angle and realize it was just an excuse to give her my number, or I would end up trying to fix her computer someday at 3 AM.

"Thanks a lot. I really appreciate everything."

"No problem. Customer service is my middle name." What

a dorky thing to say. I tried to quickly change the subject, hoping Tess would forget I said it. "Do you want a hand to your car?"

"It's a laptop. I think I can handle it." It seemed she had not forgotten. "Thanks again." She smiled, turned and walked out of my department, out of my store, and out of my life. I watched her the whole way, wishing I had been smoother and not such a dork.

"What are you staring at?" I turned my head to see Jameson standing right beside me.

"Nothing. What's up?"

"There's a lady who wants to buy a computer. She asked for a good looking salesman, but you're the closest I've got." Jameson's idea of a joke.

"Get Dev to do it." I said, swatting at the air, as if Jameson was nothing more than a gnat.

"He's with a customer. Everyone is."

"What about my investigation into the missing money?"

Jameson turned a shade of pink. "They did a recount, and it turns out there's no money missing."

I sighed, giving in. "All right, let's go."

Jameson led me over to a woman in her 40s, despite the fact that she was trying to pull off an outfit that only the most confident 20-year-old would wear to the club.

"Thanks for waiting, Bridget," Jameson said. "This is Wade. He's very knowledgeable with computers."

She smiled widely when she saw me. When I offered my hand she took it in both of hers. "And such a strong young man, too."

"Nice to meet you, Bridget," I lied.

"I'm going to leave you two to it. But I'll be back to make sure Wade is treating you right," Jameson said.

"Thank you so much, Kevin. You're such a gentleman."

Jameson practically ran away, leaving me with Bridget.

"I'm told you're looking for a computer," I said.

"Among other things," she replied, and then licked her lips.

Sighing loudly, I led her over to a computer that I guessed would be far more than she would ever need and listed off all of its features, even though she wouldn't have a clue what any of them meant.

"Oh my! You know so much about computers, don't you?"

"Well, I am the department supervisor."

"Well, I would like to buy this machine." She made a very awkward motion with her hands. "Wrap it up!"

I put on a fake smile and tried to sound happy. "Great. I'll carry it up to the front for you, and they'll cash you out."

"Is it heavy?" she asked.

"The computer?"

"Yeah. Is it really heavy?"

I sputtered a bit. I never knew how to answer this kind of question. I've always thought that 'heavy' was a relative term.

"It looks heavy," she said. "Do you offer a delivery slash installation service?"

"We only offer delivery on big screen TVs."

Jameson walked by and decided to poke his big, stupid head into the conversation.

"Hi, Bridget. How is my good friend, Wade, treating you?"

"Excellent! I was just asking if there's any kind of delivery slash installation service I could get with it."

"Sure!" Jameson answered. "It's not something we do for every customer. My personal approval is needed, but guess what? You've got it."

"Thank you so much!" she said.

"It's not a problem. Just give your address to Wade here, and he'll be over with your computer as soon as his shift is over."

"Wonderful!"

Even though I hated Jameson, especially at that moment, I never embarrassed him in front of a customer. I should have, but I didn't.

I took Bridget up front to a cashier, got her address and then went searching for Jameson with murder on my mind. I found him in the back warehouse berating, Greg, a young kid that worked nights when shipments came in.

"Jameson! I need to talk to you," I said.

He glanced at me then turned back to Greg. "Don't let me catch you texting during work again. You're here to work. Work."

Greg walked away, looking a little deflated. I made a mental note to find him later and give him a few pointers on how to text without getting caught.

"Jameson." He turned and faced me. "What's the big idea with volunteering me to deliver a computer?"

"It's in the name of customer service, Wade. Once we do this for Bridget, she'll be a customer for life."

"You couldn't have asked me to deliver it? You had to volunteer me to do it?"

"You might have said no."

"Shouldn't that tell you something?"

"Yeah. It told me that as your boss I should make you do it."

"I've got plans after work. Plans that I can't break. You're going to have to send someone else."

I didn't have any plans. I was just pissed off. Jameson stared at me and I could almost hear the gears of his tiny brain grinding together.

"Here's what we're going to do," he said. "You leave tonight an hour before your shift ends. That way you can do the delivery, do the install, and by the time you're done it'll be the end of your shift. OK?" I opened my mouth to say something, but before I could get in one word Jameson slapped me on the back and said, "Okay!"

I spent the rest of the shift picturing Jameson with a bloody nose and a few less teeth.

CHAPTER 15

After my shift I spoke aloud, to my empty car, what I would do to Jameson if I ever met him in a dark alley. I grumbled all the way from the store to the address Bridget had given me.

When I arrived, Bridget had changed out of the outfit for women half her age and had slipped into sleeping attire that only lingerie models wore for catalog shoots. I had to admit, for the most part, she was pulling it off.

"I'm sorry about my appearance," she said. "I go to bed pretty early. Early to bed, early to rise and all that."

Bridget showed me to her den, where she wanted her new computer set up, and disappeared while I started unpacking boxes. She returned a minute later with a glass of whiskey.

"You looked thirsty," she said setting it down in front of me. Looking at that glass, I wasn't quite so mad at Jameson anymore. I thanked her for the drink and noticed she had a glass full of whiskey herself.

Once the install was done Bridget insisted that I have a seat with her in her living room until we finished our drinks.

"How do you like working at that store?" she asked.

"It's alright. The pay is surprisingly decent. Customers get on my nerves, but that's part of the job, I guess."

"I'm a customer."

I nearly choked on a mouthful of liquor. I forgot I was talking to a customer.

"It's okay." She smiled. "I know what you mean. I used to work in a clothing store. A few years ago, when I was in high school."

"Only a few years ago?"

She stared at me for a moment. I prepared to move toward the door, hoping I wouldn't have to dodge thrown objects. Her blank stare shattered as she laughed out loud. "Who am I fooling, right?"

"Not me."

She went back to looking shocked again. My tongue was getting very loose as the whiskey disappeared from my glass.

"What do you mean?" she asked.

"You don't look 20. Even 30 is stretching it." Her face fell, eyes shining. "But the thing is, you don't need to wear outfits that young girls wear, and you don't need to pretend that you are younger than you are. You are an attractive woman."

She looked away from me, elegantly touched the back of her neck and smiled. It the first real smile that I had seen on her face since meeting her. She really was beautiful.

"And I can see now that you have a great body," I continued. "The clothes you were wearing earlier today just got in the way. Made it look like there was something about your body you were trying to hide." I looked at her body from her head down to her toes and back up to her head again, and I made it obvious that

I was looking. "There's nothing about this body that you should be hiding."

She sat looking at me and studying me. She bit her bottom lip, which drove me crazy. She leaned in and kissed me. It wasn't a pathetic peck of a kiss, but it was shorter than I was hoping for.

She retrieved a bottle of whiskey from the kitchen and then grabbed my hand, leading me upstairs and into her bedroom. She pulled me by the hand until I was standing at the foot of her bed. She pressed herself close to me and kissed me again. Then I was shoved hard and fell onto her bed. I would have spilled my drink if my glass wasn't empty.

"Pour yourself some more," she said, tossing me the bottle. Then she vanished into a walk-in closet.

The closet doors blocked my view of anything inside the closet. Even though I was extremely curious to see what she was doing in there, I did what I was told and poured myself another drink.

"Are you ready?" called Bridget from the closet.

"Hell, yeah!" I called back.

She stepped into view wearing a women's business suit, which unfortunately for me, covered her from the neck down.

She held out her arms. "What do you think?"

"I think that when a woman takes a man into her bedroom and then goes to change she usually goes from an outfit to lingerie, not lingerie to an outfit."

She laughed. "I wanted to know how I look in clothes made for..." She gestured awkwardly at herself.

"A woman your age?"

She smiled awkwardly.

"Turn around," I said. She spun, with a little less confidence then she had a moment ago. "You look incredible."

I got up from the bed, intending to make a move on her, but she pushed me back down again.

"Not yet," she said.

For the next hour and a half she tried on outfit after outfit, presenting each one in turn to me. I told her honestly which ones made her look great and which ones I thought she should get rid of. We laughed, had a great time, and made out a little between outfits.

When the last outfit had been modeled, instead of returning to the closet, Bridget put on some music and began doing a slow, sexy striptease. Once she was down to her bra and underwear she grabbed a chair from the corner of the room and placed it in the middle of the room. She motioned for me to sit in the chair.

She sat in my lap and squirmed to the music. She took my hands and put them all over her body. The anticipation of sex was killing me. If there wasn't going to be sex I was sure the resulting case of blue balls would finish me.

"I know what you're thinking, but no, I was never a stripper. Pole dancing has become a popular thing to do at bridal showers."

Bridget removed her bra and underwear while still sitting in my lap. Then she crawled from my lap to the bed and motioned for me to join her.

I've never undressed as quickly as I did that night.

Bridget knew more about what she was doing than any girl I had ever been with. Then it occurred to me. Bridget wasn't a girl. She was a woman.

It was in the subtle ways she moved her hips, the speed she moved, the way she kept changing things up on me, forcing me to change what I was doing.

The orgasm I had that night was unlike any other I had had before. I thought my brain was going to explode. I felt like laughing and crying at the same time.

Then I fell into a very deep sleep.

*   *   *

When I woke up the next morning, it took me a minute to remember where I was, especially with the pounding headache courtesy of too much booze. A glass of water and three aspirin sat on the nightstand beside me. I took the aspirin and drained the entire glass of water, thirsty for more.

Normally at that time of the morning I would have snuck out of the house, leaving my number if I really liked the girl. However, I woke up alone. Bridget was already gone.

I went downstairs and found her in the kitchen.

"Morning," I said.

"Sit down. Have some breakfast," she replied.

She had made me eggs, toast and sausage, topped off with a steaming cup of coffee. I thanked her for the meal and we ate in silence.

The fifteen year age difference that didn't seem to matter to either one of us last night looked different in the morning sun.

"Thank you for last night," she said. Her words were soft, but they stiff shattered the silence.

I grinned. "It was my pleasure."

"I don't mean the sex."

We sat in silence again until the meal was over. Neither one of us bothered with the formality of saying it was time for me to go. I was dying to go and Bridget was dying for me leave.

She walked me to the door and spoke genuinely. "I really hope we meet again sometime, kid."

She kissed me deeply. It wasn't an arousing kiss. It was intimate, but felt like a kiss between friends.

There was no traffic that I could hear. No one else in the

neighborhood was awake or moving. The birds didn't even seem to be up. The scraping of my feet on the cement was the only sound.

I got in to my car and closed the door feeling like the only man on the planet. If I drove off now, I might never see another human being again.

CHAPTER 16

Thursday.

Thursdays were a little busier than Wednesdays, but not by a lot. Most people who thought about coming to the store on a Thursday ended up saying, 'Screw it. I'll go on the weekend.'

I had the dreaded mid-shift. Opening meant being at the store early, but at least there was an hour before the store opened. An hour free of customers. It was a nice way to start the day. Closing meant working late, but at least there was an hour free of customers once the store closed. It was a nice end to the day. With the mid-shift, customers were there at the start and they were there at the end. There was no reprieve.

When I walked into the store I was met with a very unusual display. Everyone was working. They weren't just pretending to work, they were really working.

People were scrambling around the store, cleaning everything within reach. Every customer was being taken care of, mostly by sales people that were still cleaning while talking. My shoes squeaked on the newly buffed floor. There was only one reason for all this to be happening. Corporate was coming for a visit.

Corporate were the bosses of the bosses. They effectively had authority over every store. They had the power to walk into any store and fire any employee for any reason.

One member of the corporate team was supposed to visit our store once a week. That never actually happened. Usually we got a visit once per month when a few of them would come together. I guess they preferred to car pool.

Jameson was standing behind the customer service desk shouting orders like he was a General in a fox hole. He saw me and ran over.

"Wade! I got word an hour ago. Corporate is coming!" He was panicking. Probably because every time corporate came they found a hundred things to point out that needed improvement.

"Do you know when they'll be here?" I asked.

"90 minutes. Maybe less. I need you to make sure this place looks spick and span."

"Has anyone cleaned behind the repair desk?" I asked.

"I don't think so."

"It's disgusting back there. But don't worry. You can count on me to take care of it." I gave him a big thumbs up.

"Wade, you're a lifesaver."

I walked away smiling. The repair desk was always clean, but Jameson didn't know that.

The smile on my face only remained until I walked by the Audio section.

"What's up, Dub-dub?" said Rory, practically jumping out from behind some shelves.

"Why do I always come this way?"

"Did you hear corporate was coming for a visit? They're going to be so impressed. My department is emacalite."

He meant immaculate.

"That's fantastic. I should really go. I have to..."

"I hate to keep dragging you into this, but you've been talking to me and to Christine, and I just don't know what to do. She calls me in the middle of the night, so I just don't answer. But when I call her back at a sensible time, she refuses to answer."

"What the fuck is going on here?" demanded Christine. She approached us from the video game section, with a look of disgust on her face. I had never been happy to see Christine before, but this was going to give me the perfect opportunity to get away. "Are you talking shit behind my back, again?"

I started to back away from the two of them.

"No, Christine. Wade and I were just talking about corporate coming for a visit. Weren't we, Wade?"

I stopped dead in my tracks. "Yeah. We were..."

"You know what, Wade?" Christine said. "No one was even talking to you, so shut the fuck up."

Insubordination aside, I was glad to shut the fuck up and walked away from two people that needed psychiatric evaluation.

Mike was already behind the repair desk by the time I got there. He was sitting and looking bored.

"Great. Now what am I going to do?" I asked.

"You can do whatever you like. I opened this morning, and I'm just hoping that my shift ends before those corporate morons get here."

"When is your shift done?"

"Fifteen minutes."

"I think you'll make it. Are you in Saturday?"

"Yeah. Noon to 8."

"I'm closing. You want to meet for a beer or two after?"

"Sure. Why the hell not?" Mike said and got up from his stool. "Until we meet again, you may continue my work here." He motioned toward the stool. "I was going to spend fifteen minutes getting my coat on anyway."

I took Mike's place sitting behind the repair desk looking bored. An hour later, even from the back of the store, I watched Brent Baker walk in through the front doors.

Brent Baker was the district manager for District 4, commonly known as D4. Our store was one of twelve in the district, but at the time three more stores were being built. Brent's office was at the center of D4's 800 mile radius and our store was at the very edge, just under 400 miles from his office. That meant we were the longest drive out of all his stores. He hated visiting us and was usually a little harder on us for it.

Brent walked with a cockiness that only came to men who had more money than they would ever need and hundreds of people under his boot that he could crush at any time. Even with all that going against him I still liked him better than Jameson.

Brent stopped the first employee and launched into a lecture. It could have been about anything. Cleanliness, customer service, world politics and their effect on the stock market. Corporate loved to remind everyone that they knew more, even if they didn't. There was only one way to avoid having Brent talk down to me, and that was secret #3.

Secret of Retail #3: Managers of any level won't bother you when you're with a customer.

It was hard to believe that helping customers was more desirable than talking to managers, but within seconds I was approaching every customer in the area whether they were looking to buy a desktop computer or a mouse pad.

Jameson met up with Brent and they started walking the floor together, cornering employees whenever they came across one. They were slowly making their way toward me. I looked around for a customer, but I had done my job too well. There wasn't a single customer in my department. Jameson and Brent were getting closer. I felt desperation take over.

I practically ran over to a guy looking at the movies.

"Hey, man. Can I give you a hand with anything?" I asked.

Jameson was about to move on, but Brent stopped him and crossed his arms, watching me intently.

"No, man. I'm good," said the customer.

Damn.

"Actually, I do have a question," said the customer.

"Oh, thank you!" I said.

"What?"

"Nothing. What was your question?"

"You're selling this for twenty-five bucks, but they're selling it for eighteen at Wal-Mart. Will you price match it?"

"Sure. No problem."

Normally with a small purchase I would have sent the guy up to a cashier, but I handled the transaction myself hoping Brent would move on and take Jameson with him. However, after the customer turned for the door with his purchase in hand I turned around and found Brent Baker right in my face.

"Hello, Brent," I said, backing up a few paces.

"Hi, Wade. The department looks great," Brent said with a warm smile.

"It really does," Jameson said. He wore his yes-man smile and nodded like a bobble head.

"Thanks," I said, putting on a sincere tone.

"I wanted to be the first to let you know about the exciting news." He paused for dramatic effect, smiling at me like a moron. "Are you ready?"

"Yeah, I'm ready."

"Pop sensation Brianna Hill is going to be making appearances at all the stores in district 4. She's going to do a concert or anything. Just an autograph session at each store, but that's still pretty big to me. It's going to be great."

"Yeah. I love her," Jameson added. "Her music."

"Brianna Hill. I think I've heard her before. Doesn't she sing that song that's all about oral sex?"

"I'm not too sure," said Brent with a nervous laugh.

"Probably not," said Jameson.

"Either way," I said. "I guess that's cool."

"Can I ask you a question about that last customer?"

"Of course."

"What was going on there? Was it some kind of price match?" This was such an odd tactic. I had done something he considered wrong, and although he knew what it was, he still felt it necessary to ask me leading questions until I admitted what he already knew I did. Probably so he had verbal evidence against me.

"Yeah. I price matched a movie."

"And the customer was happy?" Brent asked.

"Yeah. Left with a smile on his face."

"That's good. High five."

Oh, yeah. High fives. It was one of the company's initiatives to help with employee morale. Reward them with high fives, it's exciting!

Not really.

Brent stood there expectantly with his hand up in the air. I gave him the high five just so he'd put his hand down.

"Let me just get in there for one, too." Jameson held a hand up toward me.

Jameson hadn't given anyone a high five since the last corporate visit, but I gave him one anyway to move things along.

"How much was the price match?" Brent asked.

"Seven bucks. Twenty-five down to eighteen."

"OK. Seven bucks. Not a lot of money to make a customer happy, is it?"

"No. Not at all," I said.

"What if we did that for a thousand customers? How much would the company be out then?"

"Seven thousand dollars."

"Right. So, now you see that we can't always be so free with our price matching."

I nodded slowly, acting like I was letting his words sink in, while I considered whether I should leave the conversation at that.

"Can I throw a question your way?" I asked.

"We don't really have time," Jameson said.

"No, no. There's time," said Brent. "What's on your mind?"

"If I decided not to do the price match for that customer and he decided to go to Wal-Mart, how much are we out in sales?"

"Twenty-five bucks."

"And if a thousand customers head down the road and shop at Wal-Mart? How much then?"

"Twenty-five thousand. I get it," Brent said smiling.

"Wrong," I said.

"Twenty-five multiplied by one thousand is twenty-five thousand."

"True. But if I sent that guy away to go buy a movie at Wal-Mart, something else is going to catch his eye and he's going to get that too. So, instead of spending twenty, he spends fifty. Then the next time he wants to go shopping, he remembers that he got a better deal at Wal-Mart and that we wouldn't price match. So, he doesn't even bother coming here. And over the span of a year, being an average man, he spends a little over a thousand dollars there that he could have spent here." Brent Baker was now considering every single word I said. "So, you see Brent, we don't stand to lose twenty-five thousand in sales. We stand to lose one million."

Brent stared at me for a long time after I was done talking. Either my words were really sinking in with him, or he was really good at pretending.

"That's a," Brent started, but hesitated. "An interesting point of view." Then he walked away with his head down. Jameson did a double take between me and Brent, then spun on his heel and ran to catch up to Brent.

Either I had just made a really big impact with upper management or I had signed my own pink slip. It was tough to tell. I kept an eye on Brent and Jameson for the rest of the day, looking for any kind of indicator. Odd glances, dirty looks, staring during long conversations. Any of which could have meant an involuntary career change was coming my way. However, I didn't see any signs at all.

Soon after that I watched Jameson walk Brent Baker to the front doors. They spoke for a minute, shook hands, then parted ways.

After a few minutes of considering my options, I laughed at myself. I'm still not sure what seemed more humorous to me. The fact that I could have been on the chopping block for being right, or the fact that I was concerned about losing a job in retail.

When my shift was over, and Jameson still hadn't come out of the manager's room, I went in after him.

Jameson jumped as I barged into the room. "Jesus Christ, Wade!"

"You know what? If you're going to fire me, let's just get it over with. Don't wait until the end of the day. Don't wait until the end of the week. Let's just do it right now."

Jameson stared at me in utter shock. "Fire you? You're one of my best people. Why would I fire you?"

"Brent Baker doesn't want me gone?"

"No. If he does, he didn't say anything to me about it."

"Oh." Super heroes had super strength. At that moment, I had super stupidity.

"I thought you had some pretty interesting things to say, though."

Uh-oh, I thought to myself. If Jameson is agreeing with my theory, it can't be good.

"Uh, thanks," I said.

"Yeah. You know what? I think you and I should go for a beer on Saturday and discuss some business. What do you think?"

Normally, I would never agree to spend time outside of work with Jameson, but I was caught off guard. I fumbled for an excuse in my mind, but nothing was there. Feeling stunned and unsure of myself, the only words that came out of my mouth were, "Yeah, sure."

"Great. I'll meet you at, uh, how about The Greenhouse? You know the place, right? 10 o'clock?"

CHAPTER 17

I drove to Frank's house, with another stack of movies, still disgusted with myself for agreeing to hang out with Jameson.

When I entered the house, Frank didn't even turn to see who it was. He just held up a hand in greeting and said, "Put them on the table. I'll sort them later."

After putting down his stack of movies I grabbed a beer for Frank and one for myself and took my usual seat.

"What's happening?" I asked.

"I don't know."

"What's this?" I said motioning toward the television.

"You can't tell?"

"Not everyone has time to sit around and watch movies all day."

"Too bad for you."

"No kidding."

"Your check is on the table there. Don't forget to add a little something for yourself. How are things?"

"Weird."

"That's not much of an answer."

"Corporate was at the store today."

Frank gave a low whistle. "Big dogs, huh?"

"Yeah. Well, I proved the big dogs wrong today. Then I yelled at my boss and told him to fire me. Then I agreed to go out with my boss, who I hate, for a beer."

"Sounds like you got hit in the head," said Frank.

"It feels like I got hit in the head."

"There's aspirin above the sink."

"Thanks." I got up to grab some of the little white pills while continuing the conversation. "After I proved the corporate guy wrong, I got the impression that he was embarrassed, and figured a man with his power would strike back by canning my ass. So, instead of taking it lying down I went and yelled at my boss."

"That makes sense." Frank spoke with just a hint of sarcasm, but I knew he intended his statement to be brimming with it.

"I know. After I tear a strip off of him he tells me I'm crazy and no one wants to fire me and in the same breath asks me if I want to go for a beer."

"Sounds like he likes you."

"I was so taken aback, I actually said yes. It was like I left my brain out of that conversation."

"Sounds to me like you spent too much time thinking about what was going to happen instead of finding out what was really happening. I love this part." Frank said pointing at the television screen. He hadn't taken his eyes from the TV since I walked in.

"OK. I still don't know what to think about the corporate guy. What if he really is embarrassed and sends word to have me fired?"

"Do you know for a fact that he's embarrassed?"

"He looked embarrassed, but no."

"And is there anything you can do about it right now?"

"No."

"Stop worrying about it. Watch a movie. You'll accomplish the same damn thing, but the movie's more entertaining."

"It's not that easy to stop worrying."

"I know. But if you can make yourself stop, you'll be all the better for it."

I sat there on Frank's couch in silence and watched the movie that I still couldn't recognize. Slowly, I let the care slip away until it was gone.

"That's good advice," I said after some time.

Without looking away from the television, Frank nodded. "I may just be an old car guy, but I know I thing or two."

I stayed and watched the rest of the movie with Frank. He fell asleep ten minutes before the movie ended. I turned his TV off and headed for home, leaving Frank to sleep in his favorite chair.

CHAPTER 18

I hated buying things that my store didn't sell. Not because I had some kind of private pride in my place of employment. I hated shopping at other stores because I didn't get an employee discount. I always felt like I was taking a step back on the evolutionary scale. I had to shop like one of the 'common folk.' It made me feel like such a customer.

There were a lot of pros to shopping during the week. No large crowds to fight, lots of parking spots available, and sale items were usually in stock since the crowds wouldn't attack for another few days.

There were also some big cons. The majority of the people that shopped with me during the week were elderly people. A group of five old bags could be in the way as effectively as a group of eighty regular people.

Old people walked slowly and always in the middle of the aisle so there wasn't enough room to pass them on either side. If

I tried to squeeze by with an, "Excuse me," they either didn't hear me or pretended not to.

If I got in line behind an old person it meant extra waiting time as they started some kind of pointless conversation with the cashier because they didn't have anyone else to talk to except other old people. Not even old people want to talk to old people. The conversation would always go on far too long cause the old person would make a joke they thought was funny and the cashier would have to repeat herself thirty-seven times due to a hearing aid with a failing battery.

If all these things weren't bad enough, stores had less cashiers working during the week. So the lines of old farts were longer than they should have been.

On my way into the store a young girl, about 13 years old, stepped in front of me wearing a big goofy smile.

"Good afternoon, sir!" she shouted at me. "Would you like to make a donation to the Junior Cadets of the 4th division? Every dollar you give goes toward..."

"I feel really bad for you," I said.

"Why?"

"It must really suck to ask for donations these days."

"What do you mean?"

"Two reasons. Store fronts probably used to make really good areas for donations a few years ago. People are going in and out spending money, why can't they give a little extra, right?"

She nodded, listening intently.

"Only now, very few people carry actual cash. All the stores accept credit cards and debit. Those people that used to have a couple bucks to throw your way haven't been to a bank in months."

The young girl nodded slowly, as if she finally had reason

to why she wasn't getting more donations. "What's the second reason?"

"Most people are like me. And all I really want is to be able to get from my car to the store and back to my car without some annoying do-gooder asking me for a damn handout."

She was speechless. I must have been tired. Dressing down a thirteen-year-old girl?

Even though there were fewer people in the store, they seemed to be spread out. Every item I needed, every shelf I wanted to look at had a few people standing in front of it. Every item in my basket represented me having to wait on someone else's indecisiveness or finally getting frustrated enough to rudely reach in front of them.

On my way to the checkout, I passed a thirty-something woman, holding a list in her hand. As I passed, her eyes wandered and ran over every item I had in my basket. This wasn't the first time this had happened. A lot of women did this. It was puzzling. Was I being judged for the contents of my basket? Was she hoping something in my basket would remind her of something she needed? Or was the sale she missed out on and she wanted to know if I got it. If I did would she resort to trying to get it away from me? It wasn't Black Friday, but a sale's a sale.

At the checkouts I got into a line four people long. Ahead of me were two elderly women, an old man, and a middle-aged woman.

The two elderly women were together but made separate purchases. That would have sped things up except they forgot who was buying what and took a few extra minutes to sort it out.

When the old man had his turn he placed his items on the conveyer belt and smiled widely at the girl running the till.

"Working hard, or hardly working?" asked the old man.

Why the fuck did people still think that was funny? It was a little funny the first time I heard it, at age five, and then it became as trivial as saying 'hello,' but far more annoying.

When it was time for the old man to pay, he held his money in hand but kept chatting with the cashier. She was kind and humored his conversation, repeatedly reminding him of his total, which kept reminding him of a story he had to tell her.

The lady in front of me turned to me with a smirk on her face, but when she saw me the smirk disappeared and she snapped back around.

"Oh, come on. I want to hear it," I said.

"Excuse me?" she said without turning back around.

"Your witty comment. You had one all ready."

"I think you're mistaken."

I wasn't mistaken. She would have told another middle-aged woman, but not a man of any age. We waited in silence until the old man ahead of us finally paid for his purchase and started shuffling toward the door.

When I started placing my items on the conveyor belt, the woman ahead of me instantly grabbed a divider and slammed it down between our things as if the cashier might accidentally put some of my things on her bill. Once she's paid for some of my stuff, I will somehow find a way to get it back from her and laugh all the way home with a pair of socks and a tube of toothpaste that I didn't have to pay for.

When it was my turn the cashier only scanned a few items before stopping at the sound of a musical chime. "Just a second," she said.

A hand came from her pocket, cell phone attached. She smiled and began hammering with her thumbs at the onscreen keypad. I stared in disbelief as she took her time composing a text message in front of me, a customer. I hated my job too, but I had never ignored a customer tweet something. Not yet.

"Are employees here allowed to text while they're on duty?" I asked.

"I don't know," she lied.

"Cause that manager-looking dude doesn't seem too happy about it."

The phone disappeared and she quickly scanned two more items before daring to glance around.

"What manager-looking dude?" she asked.

I made a show of looking around. "Huh. I swear he was there a second ago."

She gave me a sigh and a dirty look while she finished ringing my purchase through.

"Would you like to apply for our in-store credit card and save ten percent on your purchase?" she asked.

"I know you're supposed to ask that, but I think I can handle $23.17 without resorting to major financing."

"I'll take that as a no."

"You do that."

"Would you like to donate a dollar to the School Supplies for Orphans fund?"

Someone else looking for a hand-out. They were everywhere. I remembered the girl outside the store and how terribly I had treated her.

"Fine. But only because I don't want to see another generation of annoyingly forceful squeegee kids."

After handing me the receipt she spoke the words, "Have a nice day," but her tone told me to run head first into the nearest wall.

When I left the store, the young girl was still standing by the doors. I avoided making any kind of eye contact with her, but shoved a ten in her direction. I still felt bad, but didn't know what else to do.

I was halfway to my car when she called out to me.

"Hey, mister!" I stopped and looked at her over my shoulder. "Eat a dick!"

I smiled and thought to myself, *Now I don't feel so bad.*

CHAPTER 19

"This is your final test," I said, standing in front of my three trainees, Stephen, Trent and Megan, in the back warehouse. They weren't all going to be in my department, but they were assigned to me for sales floor training.

"This is Saturday, our busiest day of the week. I'm dropping you out there in shark infested waters and you're going to swim or you're going to die."

Stephen's hand shot up in the air.

"You don't have to raise your hand, Stephen. If you have a question, just ask it."

"What happens if the customer asks a question that we don't know the answer to? Like a product specification or something like that."

"Good question." Surprisingly. "I'll be keeping an eye on you while you're out there, but there's also a massive force of co-workers on the floor with you. No matter how long you work here there will always be another employee who's been here longer and has more answers than you. Use them. There's also computers everywhere. Google is your friend. Don't be afraid to tell the customer they've asked a good question, bring them to a computer and find the answer. One thing I highly recommend you don't do," I looked directly at Trent. "Is try to bullshit your way through every question you don't know."

"I get it," Trent said. "What if I get a customer who's being a real dick?"

"Look for me. Bring me into the conversation somehow and I'll help you out. I've practically got a Ph.D. in handling dick customers."

"Any other questions?" I asked. Stephen and Trent were both passively shaking their heads. I looked specifically at Megan. "None?"

Megan gave me a look that made my legs want to shake. My mind was transported back a few days when it seemed like she wanted to kiss me. "Maybe later," she said.

It felt like it was getting really hot in the warehouse.

"All right, let's get out there and put up with some customers." That was as close as I could get to motivational.

The first few hours were pretty standard for trainees. I bounced between the three of them, listening into their sales, answering questions about how fast a processor was, or what resolution a television supported.

Each time one of them made a sale they showed a happiness and excitement that I could no longer remember. I knew there had been a time when I felt like that, but it had been a long time.

Stephen was the first one to get a really interesting customer. I was listening in on Trent's sale when I saw Stephen waving his arms at me like he was in mortal danger.

"What's going on, Stephen?" I asked.

"This guy. I've got the sale, I think, but he's asking all these questions about the price and what I'm going to throw in. There was nothing in the video about this."

"All right, calm down. Let's go talk to him."

Stephen led the way to a guy who looked a little like he had to take a shit. His face was a shade of red that wasn't normal and he pursed his lips oddly. He flicked his head upward at Stephen as we approached.

"Sir, this is my supervisor, Wade. He's going to help you out."

"Hi, Wade. I'm Corey."

"Hi, Corey. What can I do for you today?"

"First off, let me just say that Stephen has done an excellent job. He's been very helpful, he's very knowledgeable. He's been great."

"Good to hear."

"You see, it's like this, I'm buying this computer package from you guys today. That's a computer tower, an LCD monitor and an inkjet printer." He listed all the items off on his fingers.

"Right." Like I didn't know what a computer package was.

"When I'm buying so much stuff from you, spending all this money, I guess I just kind of feel like I should get a little something back."

How about a computer? I thought to myself.

"I see," I said, pretending to think about it. "What is it that you're looking for? A discount?"

Corey breathed in through closed teeth, making a hissing sound. "Now, I didn't say that. I know the prices are the prices for a reason. Maybe something could be thrown in?"

"A freebie?" I asked.

"It's a possibility, right?"

I made of show of looking hard pressed to make Corey feel like he was asking for the world, instead of some free crap.

He was probably hoping for blank CDs or DVDs, maybe some screen cleaner, a cordless mouse. But after I was done putting on my little show, he would have been happy with a free mouse pad.

"I'll tell you what I'm going to set you up with," I said. Corey was listening very intently. "Three months of high speed Internet service, absolutely free. What do you think?"

Corey smiled widely. "That's awesome. Thanks a lot, Wade."

"It's my pleasure, sir. Stephen and I are going to go get the voucher for your free internet. We'll be right back."

Corey was still smiling as we walked away. He was proud of himself.

Stephen and I walked into the back warehouse and I handed him one of the Internet vouchers.

"I don't get it, Wade," Stephen said.

"What's not to get?"

"The free internet is free to everyone who buys a computer."

"Yeah, but he doesn't know that."

After listening in on another of Stephen's sales I noticed Megan talking to a couple of guys in suits by the digital cameras. Her brow was crinkled and she kept getting cut off each time she opened her mouth.

"Hello! How is everything going here?" I said, opening it up for either Megan or the customer to fill me in.

Megan started. "These gentlemen are here to look at a digital camera, and I was just trying to show them..."

"I don't want to look at anything yet," said the shorter of the two. His tall companion looked like he wasn't even listening to the conversation. I profiled the short guy as some kind of ruthless businessman and the tall guy was his either a protégé or an assistant. Maybe he carried the money.

"What are you here to look at then?" I asked.

"A digital camera."

"Megan is fully qualified to show you our best digital cameras."

"I'm not looking at anything yet," he repeated.

"I don't understand."

The short man stepped in front of Megan and turned to face me, completely shutting her out of the conversation. It was one of my top ten rudest things I've ever seen a customer do.

"What I want to do is..." The short man started. He stopped when I held up a finger, silently asking for a second. I took a step to the right and pulled Megan beside me so she was back in the conversation. The look on Shorty's face said he didn't like that, but he continued. "Before I look at a single camera I want to know what kind of discount I'm looking at."

"We guarantee the lowest prices. It's part of our price guarantee." The short man was pissing me off and a mocking tone was starting to slip into my voice, as if I were trying to explain something to a 10-year-old. The short man either didn't notice, or didn't care.

"So, what kind of discount do I get?" he said, as if he didn't hear what I had just said, or as if I hadn't even said it.

"You know what? Maybe once you choose a camera we can look at doing something for you, but generally speaking, our prices are what they are and we've already set them as low as possible."

"Fuck that," said the short man. "I don't pay full price for anything."

There it was. Not only was the guy a rude, obnoxious prick, he was a rude, obnoxious prick who thought he was special.

"Why is that, sir? Do you have some kind of discount card that I'm unaware of?"

"No, but it doesn't matter what store I go to or what I'm buying. I do not pay full price. Ever."

It was time to end this conversation. "Sir, we're not running a flea market."

The short man looked at me in pure disbelief. "A flea market? Come on." He snapped in front of the other man's face and headed for the door. The taller man followed him out, staying as close as possible.

Megan turned away from me with a hand on her forehead. "Oh my god!" she said. "What an asshole!"

"You can't let it get to you. You're going to run into customers like that all the time."

"No, I meant you! You ruined my sale."

"Nice. See if I help you again."

"I'm going to have to deal with guys like that all the time?"

"No. That guy is probably going home to polish his lifetime asshole achievement award. It's rare to get one that bad. The worst is probably over. For a week or so, anyway."

She laughed and I found myself admiring her smile.

"Thanks," she said.

"Get back to work." Blunt words, but there was no harshness in my voice.

I strolled over to the home theatre department where Trent was approaching a middle-aged couple inspecting a large screen television.

"Hi, folks. My name is Trent. Can I help you with anything?"

The man spoke first. "Yeah, we're looking for a good TV. Can you show us a really good TV?"

"Sure," said Trent. "Follow me."

Trent led them to one of the best models in the department. "This one here. Sixty inch, highest definition on the market."

"That's a pretty nice TV," said the man. The smile fell from his face when his eyes rolled over to the price tag. "Do you have anything a little less expensive?"

"Sure," said Trent. He led them to the next model. "This is basically the same thing, but it's fifty-six inch instead of sixty."

"It's great, but do you have anything a little cheaper?"

"Of course." He led them to another TV. "This is also fifty-six, but one step down in resolution. Still high definition, though."

"These are all nice TVs. Do you have anything that doesn't have all the bells and whistles?"

'Good' was a very subjective term. Some people measured quality to be the best on the market. These people gauged the quality of the television by the price tag. In their eyes, the lower the price, the better the television.

It would have been best to walk them directly to the cheapest television in the store. I could have stepped in and told Trent that, but it was better to let him learn that on his own.

As I watched Trent lead the couple to a fourth television, I felt someone tapping me on the shoulder. I turned around to see a scrawny guy in his twenties with a cocky smirk on his face.

"There's currently no available help in the computer department. Can you get someone for me?"

I glanced around and saw that the nerd was right, everyone was busy. As much as I was enjoying Trent's torture, I was going to have to help the nerd.

"I'll help you out. What are we looking at?"

"There's a tower over there, and I just had a couple questions about the processor."

"Lead the way."

The nerd led me to one of the high-end towers and motioned to it with an attempted elegance that came off as awkward.

"This is the one I was looking at. Can you tell me what the front side bus of the CPU is?" he asked emphasizing 'front side bus' and 'CPU'.

He didn't care about the front side bus. He just wanted to

drop a little computer lingo on someone and feel like a computer genius.

"Not off the top of my head, but if you want we can jump online and find the answer for that."

"Wait a minute." The look on his face turned arrogant. "You mean to tell me that you work in the computer department and you don't know the front side bus on this machine's processor."

"Not only that, I'm the supervisor," I said with a goofy smile.

"Let me get this straight. You're the supervisor of this department, and you don't know the front side bus of the CPU in this machine?"

I wore my goofy smile for a few seconds longer before letting it disappear. "Listen, guy. I stock over 100 models here and just about every model has a different processor in it. Front side bus is something that is so rarely asked about that I haven't yet had the time to memorize 100 different processors."

"But people like me who want a high end machine need to know that kind of thing. I come here expecting some expertise but all I get from you is the same thing I could read off your website." His words were brimming with self-righteousness.

"If you were really looking for a high end machine, and were that concerned about the specifics, you wouldn't buy it from here. You'd research and order each piece separately and build it yourself. You sure as hell wouldn't be buying a Dell."

"That sounds like the standard line of the sub-standard employee who doesn't even know what a front side bus is or that computers even have one," he said.

"The front side bus is measured in clock speed and connects the CPU with the northbridge, which accesses the RAM and graphics card, as long as the graphics card isn't on-board. The back side bus, if the computer has one, connects the CPU with the cache. Most commonly the northbridge is connected via internal bus to the southbridge which controls the rest of the machine."

The nerdy guy tried to hide his shock. "Well, any idiot..."

"I'm betting you just learned what a front side bus was earlier today and you wanted to bust someone's balls about it. You don't have any real friends and all your online friends already knew what it was. So, you came here to bust the balls of the first salesmen you could find."

The nerd's eyes filled up with water. He stared at me with a frustrated rage. After a moment, the rage faded into acceptance and he hung his head in shame. I felt bad, after my outburst, but he needed to be put in his place. He'd probably be better for it.

"Thank you for your help." His were quiet and careful. He turned and walked toward the front exit like a man heading to a death sentence.

"Hey," I called.

He stopped and turned to look at me.

I didn't know what to say. "A lot of people don't know what a front side bus is."

He smiled politely and continued on his way to the door, staring at the floor.

I wandered back over to the home theatre department just in time to see Trent showing the cheap couple another television.

"This one is a forty-two inch projection television. It's not even close to high definition." The usually confident and chipper tone in Trent's voice was gone, murdered by frugalness.

His customers smiled when they saw the price.

"Now this is a great TV!" exclaimed the man.

"It really is nice," said the woman.

"Hey, this is a good one, right?" the man asked Trent.

That was the most frustrating part about really cheap customers. You could show them all the good models first, but they don't want you to show them the good models. They want you to show them the shitty models with the cheapest price and then they want you to lie to them and tell them how good it is.

Trent saw how much this couple admired the television, then he smiled and said, "It's great."

Megan approached me from behind. "Wade, can I get your help?" Her face looked pained and she was holding one of the store's portable phones.

"Sure. What's going on?"

"I answered the phone and the guy on the other end is really angry and I have no idea how to handle it. He won't talk to me. He just keeps screaming for me to get him a manager."

"No problem." I took the phone from her and took a step away. "Thank you for holding, my name is Wade, how can I help you?"

"Are you a manager?" asked a harsh, angry voice.

"Yes, I am."

"Well, I want to know what the hell is going on down there!"

"OK, fill me in on your situation."

"My name is Davidson and I want to know what the hell is going on down there."

"I'd like to help, but I'm going to need a little more information than that."

"You got my name. What the hell else to do you need?"

"How about you start by telling me the situation? The one that makes you wonder what the hell is going on down here."

"My wife came into your store and needed a printer cartridge, and your idiot salesman sold her the wrong one."

"Well, I apologize for that." I hated apologizing to customers like that, but I took solace in the fact that I didn't really mean it. "If you or your wife would like to bring the cartridge back we'd be more than happy to exchange it for the right one."

"Exchange?" For some reason that made him angrier. "You should be giving us our money back!"

"Fair enough. If you'd prefer a refund, I have no problem with that."

"It's too late," said the angry man.

"How so?"

"My wife already went back to the store and got an exchange for the right one."

"And does that cartridge work?"

"I haven't put it in the printer yet, cause you don't deserve our money since you sold us the wrong one in the first place."

"So, you would like to return it?"

He gave an angry laugh. "I'm not coming back into your store!"

"I don't understand. You have the right cartridge, but you don't want it because we made a mistake, but you don't want to come back to the store to return it?"

"That's right."

"I still don't understand."

"You don't deserve to have our money."

"How do you want me to fix this for you?"

"You're the manager, you need to figure out a solution."

"If you're not willing to come back to the store to return it, here's what I suggest. You keep the cartridge and I'll give you store credit for the price of the cartridge. It'll be like getting a free one."

"I'm not driving all the way to your store to pick up a store credit."

"You don't have to. It'll be waiting for you the next time you come in. It works around your schedule."

"I have no reason to come to your store anymore. You don't deserve our money and your salesmen are fat."

"I don't see what the weight of my salesmen has to do with anything."

"They're stupid, too."

"You can yell at me all night long. But if you insult my salesmen again I'll end this call promptly."

"You don't deserve my money."

"You've mentioned that." I sighed extra loud so Davidson would hear it. "It sounds to me like the only thing that will make you happy is if I took your money out of the cash register, personally drove out to your house, gave you the money, let you keep the cartridge and head back to the store feeling deeply ashamed of myself."

"Are you kidding me? I'm not letting you come to my house!"

"Then I'm done helping you."

"You can't do that! I'm the customer!"

"Sure I can. I've exhausted every avenue, presented every option, and you've shot them all down. Therefore it is impossible to help you and now I'm just wasting my time. I'm still willing to leave a store credit here at the store for you, but if that's still not good enough for you maybe you should go yell at your wife since she's the one who did the exchange instead of the return."

I waited for an enraged retort to come through the phone. There was silence on the other end. I waited a full minute before speaking again. "Sir?"

"You don't deserve our money." He must have had an old fashion telephone, because the sound of him hanging up on me was loud enough to make my ear ring and cause a headache.

I brought the phone back to Megan and noticed her department was dead. The whole store was starting to die down.

"What did that guy want?" Megan asked.

"I have no idea."

"You were talking to him for 15 minutes."

"And I still have no idea."

I looked around for my other trainees. Even though customers were getting scarce Trent was talking with another couple and Stephen was showing a computer to an old man.

"You want to take a break?" I asked Megan.

"Sure. Let me just ask that customer if he needs any help."

I looked where Megan had pointed and grabbed her arm before she could walk over.

"No, no. Don't talk to that guy."

"Why not?" she asked.

"That's the lonely man. He's in here all the time. If you offer him any help he'll talk to you for an hour and then he'll leave. He never buys anything. He is a one hundred percent waste of time. The good news is that if we leave him alone, he leaves us alone."

She shrugged and we headed to the break room at the back of the store. It was empty except for Sawyer who was sitting at one of the tables trying to look busy except that his eyes were glued to the television when we walked in.

"Oh, shit. What up, Wade?"

"Hey, Sawyer. This is Megan. She's training today. She's going to be in digital cameras."

Megan and I sat across from Sawyer.

"Nice to meet you, Sawyer."

"It's nice to meet you, Sweetie. How are you doing?"

"Don't be fooled by this man," I said. "The second you walked in here he was picturing you naked."

"No, I was not, Wade," Sawyer fired back.

"Megan, go ahead and ask Sawyer if he was picturing you naked," I said.

"Were you picturing me naked, Sawyer?"

Sawyer sighed. "Yes. But it's only because you're so beautiful, I just couldn't help myself."

"Now ask him how often he uses that line on women," I said.

"Sawyer, how often do you use that line on women?"

Sawyer let out a frustrated cry in my direction. "Daily."

"Now ask him..."

"Please," Sawyer pleaded to Megan. "No more questions."

"All right, you're off the hook. For now." Megan said.

"How's my new boy doing out there?" Sawyer asked.

"Trent? He's learning the tough lessons, but he's going to be fine."

"Yeah, I heard he was good. I'm glad to hear it too, man. I'm going to get out of here before I get grilled with any more questions."

Sawyer headed straight for the door, but before he couldn't escape before Megan called out to him, "Hey, Sawyer!"

"Yeah?"

"What cup size do you think I am?" she asked, sticking her chest out a bit. I knew Sawyer must have been staring, but that was just an assumption since I was too busy staring to check.

"A solid C. Later."

"What was that all about?" Megan asked once the door was closed.

"He's got this thing about not lying to women. I don't know why he does it, but it's fun to mess with him."

She laughed and I found myself admiring her smile again. I gave my head a shake.

"So, we're done in about an hour, right?" Megan asked.

"Well, you're done. I've got a few hours to put in once you three leave. What do you think about your first day on the floor?"

"It's not as bad as I thought it was going to be."

"So, you're going to stick it out, then?"

"Yeah, there's a couple perks to the job. I might stick around for a bit."

We sat in silence stealing looks at one another like a couple of pathetic teenagers. I felt the magnetic force taking hold again. The same magnetic force that took hold in the warehouse on Megan's first day of training. Just like the first time, I couldn't tell if I was moving closer, she was moving closer or if we were both moving together. The silence was unbearable.

"Was Sawyer right?"

"What?"

The magnetic force stopped pulling.

"Your last question. Was he right?"

The magnets kicked in again, and stronger than ever before.

"What do you think?"

The break room door burst open and I stood right out of my chair. It was Mike.

"Hey, Wade. Hey, new girl." Mike opened his locker and grabbed his coat. "You're starting in digital cameras, right?"

Megan cleared her throat, trying to compose herself. "Yeah."

Mike walked to her and extended his hand. "I'm Mike, the repair desk supervisor."

She shook his hand and smiled. "I'm Megan."

"Mike," I said. "I can't believe it, man. I was so busy today that I didn't get a chance to talk to you the entire shift. I haven't kept that busy in months."

"Don't worry about it, man. We'll talk later."

"Have a good night," said Megan.

Mike waved as he headed out the door. "Bye, Megan. Wade, I'll see you later."

"See ya," I called after him.

Megan remained sitting and I stepped closer to the bulletin board posted in the break room and pretended to be very interested in a memo that was months old.

"Well," I said without looking away from the memo. "I'd

better head back out there and see how Stephen and Trent are doing. The store seems pretty dead. I'll probably send you guys home early."

"Sounds good," Megan said, avoiding eye contact.

Trent and Stephen were pretty happy about getting off an hour early. Megan was quiet. I walked the three of them to the front doors telling them how great they were on their first day.

Megan walked out the door and looked over her shoulder at me. I smiled and gave a friendly wave. She turned away. I could only imagine what she was thinking. Probably that there was something wrong with her or there was something wrong with me.

There wasn't anything wrong with me, and there definitely wasn't a thing wrong with her. She was undeniably attractive. She was fun with a good sense of humor and really smart. There was something else getting in the way.

After the store was closed I moped around. My thoughts kept drifting to Megan, then to Bridget, Elizabeth, and finally to Tess before it started all over again with Megan.

Before any of them I claimed to know a lot about women. I knew nothing.

That wasn't even the worst part of my night. *Beer with Jameson*, I thought to myself. *Maybe a workplace accident will happen to me and I won't have to go.*

CHAPTER 20

When I arrived at The Snapping Turtle Jameson was already sitting at a table near the back of the place, beer in hand. I walked past the long bar filled with the bar's regulars. They looked like they hadn't left the barely padded stools in months. Each man's stool bore his signature in the form of a permanent butt print. They looked at me, a stranger, with unfriendly gazes, daring me to turn around and leave.

Jameson looked up as I approached the table.

"Hey, Wade! You made it."

I took the seat across the table from Jameson and never wanted to go home so badly in my entire life. "Yup."

"You want a drink?"

"Yeah." I was going to need one.

Jameson raised an arm until the waitress looked our way, then he pointed at me. I felt bad for the waitress to be beckoned that way.

The waitress got to the table two painful minutes later in which Jameson babbled on about soccer. She stared at me with a look of intolerance. I knew the feeling, but didn't like being on the other end. I stared back waiting for her to say something, but she didn't. I still wonder how long we would've stared at each other if I hadn't spoken up.

"Beer?"

"What kind of beer?"

"What kinds do you have?"

"We serve Canadian, Budweiser and Coors Light, but we're all out of Canadian and Coors Light."

"I guess I'll have a Bud then, won't I?"

She left the table and Jameson called after her, "You might as well bring me another one while you're at it, darling."

Without turning around she raised a hand making a gesture that said both 'I heard you' and 'I hope you die.'

Jameson kept rambling on about soccer until our waitress had finally returned with a beer in each hand.

"Thanks," said Jameson. "Can you bring us each of shot of Jack Daniels? It feels like that kind of night."

"Are you going to order something every time I come to this table?" she asked.

Jameson started laughing. "Don't ever lose your sense of humor, Mary." I could tell she wasn't kidding, but I wasn't surprised to see that Jameson couldn't.

"Whatever," she said, and walked away.

"So, what business are we discussing tonight?" I was hoping to steer him to the point before he started talking about professional tennis or golf or whatever he was going to talk about next.

"I was really interested by the conversation you had with Brett."

"Has he said anything about it?"

"No. I haven't talked to him at all since then."

Damn. I was hoping to find out if the corporate suit was embarrassed and if I should be expecting some form of retribution.

"So," Jameson continued, "you really think that pleasing the customer each time is the way to go?"

The manager of a store built on customer service was asking if pleasing the customer was the right thing to do.

"Yes, I do."

"Even if you're going to lose a little money on the sale?"

"You can't always look at that isolated sale. If you do right by them, they're going to come back. A lot. You piss them off and they might never come back."

Jameson was nodding slowly. I couldn't believe this was the first time he heard this kind of theory. I didn't know if that spoke poorly on Jameson or on the upper management that would have trained him.

"What did you learn in your manager training?" I asked.

"To look at the sale price versus the cost, factor in whether the product is clearance or not, and how much of an impact that sale is going to make on your daily budget."

"But never the actual customer?" Was I actually standing up for customers?

"No. But in the end, even if one customer leaves pissed off we just have to work that much harder on the next one."

"What about the customers you just pissed off that weren't even in the store?"

"What are you talking about?"

I should have been running the store, not him.

"A person who has a good retail experience will go and tell four of their friends. A person with a bad retail experience tells ten to fifteen of their friends. You piss off one customer, you may have lost sixteen customers."

Jameson was speechless as the concept began to sink in.

He may have come from outside of the company, but he still came from another customer service business. The idiot should've known that shit.

During our short bout of silence Mary came back to the table, set the shots down and practically ran from the table before Jameson could order anything else.

"From now on, we're going to be all about the customer," said Jameson.

"We already are."

He looked at me, confusion obvious on his face.

"I already think like that," I said. "That's what I've taught my team. Most of the other supervisors use the same theory."

I neglected to tell him that we also hold onto the theory of 'screw the customers who are assholes.'

"Well, I'll bet we can do it even better under my guidance," said Jameson.

The only good ideas that Jameson ever heard came out of his own mouth.

"Tell me something, Wade. What's your ultimate goal with your career?"

This was a tough question to answer. A guy like Jameson always asked pointed questions. It was one question on the surface, but there was another question beneath that, and that was the one Jameson.

In this case, he was asking me about my career, but what he truly wanted to know was if I planned to stay a store employee or not.

"You can be honest with me," Jameson added.

"I really don't know. Does anyone ever really know?" I said hoping he would buy the bullshit.

"Good point. I'm twice your age and I still don't know." He gave a laugh that he intended to sound genuine.

"Since we're being completely honest with each other, let me ask you something."

"Sure."

"How come you didn't choose Mike to go to the conference?"

Jameson sighed loudly. "I think Mike's a great guy." Lie number one. "But Rory is more qualified." Lie number two.

"More qualified? Mike knows more about technology and manages a team twice the size of Rory's."

"I don't think Mike knows more about technology than Rory." Three in a row. "And personally, I just see a little more potential in Rory." That made it four. "How come you're always sticking up for him anyway?"

"He's a good friend of mine. Why wouldn't I?"

"When we show up to work each day, we're there to do business, not play friends."

That was probably true since Jameson didn't have a single friend at the store.

We sat in uncomfortable silence for a moment before Jameson began jabbering on about what a great connection he had with Brent Baker.

I spent the next half hour telling my ideas to Jameson. Jameson spent that time shooting down my ideas only to bring them back up worded differently as his own.

My cell phone chirped with an incoming text message. I jumped at the opportunity to turn my attention away from Jameson. "I'd better get this."

He waved a hand at me indicating he didn't care, and made another hand motion toward Mary.

The message was from Mike.

Wade, where the hell are you? I've been waiting for 45 mins. We said 10, right?

"Oh, shit!" I said aloud.

"What's the matter?" Jameson asked.

"I forgot something I was supposed to do tonight."

"That's too bad. Maybe it's not too late, here's our bill."

Mary was back at the table. She dropped the bill on our table and walked away. Jameson examined the bill then looked at me.

"Your half is 27 bucks, plus tip."

"27? I had a beer and a shot that you forced on me."

"I don't know what to tell you. We had basically the same, and that's half."

I knew he had three more beers than I did, and I was pretty sure he had a plate of nachos before I got there. Rather than argue, I put exactly $27 on the table.

"Could you throw down a fiver for me? I'm a little..."

"Short?" I finished.

He closed his eyes and winced. The word almost seemed to physically hurt him. "Yeah."

I threw another five bucks on the table. "Well, thanks. It was... fun?" I said.

"No problem. Glad you came out. Have a safe drive, I'm going to take a shit before I go."

He clapped me on the shoulder and headed straight to the men's room.

I walked toward the exit when I saw Mary standing behind the bar counting her tips, shaking her head and muttering to herself. Once I got a little closer I could make out a few of the things she was saying.

"Lazy fucking customers. Bring me this, bring me that. I'll

have another round. Bring me some ketchup. Bring me my bill. Do you have change?"

I walked right up to her and waited until she looked up at me. After a few seconds of silence I bellowed out, "IT'S YOUR JOB!" and headed for the door.

All the regulars sitting on their bar stools stared at me as I walked by. I messed with their regular waitress at their regular bar. The only thing that stopped them from kicking my ass was that fact that they had been sitting for so long their legs had fallen asleep. That, and they all knew that Mary really was a bitch.

Once outside I called Mike on his cell.

"Hey, Mike. I'm on my way, man."

"What's the hold up?"

"I completely forgot about tonight. It's been a long day." I laughed to myself. "Some shit went down at work and before I knew it I was having a beer with Jameson and..."

"Hold on. You're hanging out with Jameson? What the fuck?"

"He caught me off guard, and our plans just slipped my mind."

"Yeah. You conveniently forget about me to go hang out with our boss. Did you figure it would help your chances of getting that manager spot?"

"It wasn't like that in the slightest—"

"You know what would really help? Going for beers with your boss and bashing the one guy your boss really hates."

"Come on, Mike."

"No, no. Hear me out. You sit with him and he starts talking about all the things about me that he can't stand and all the reasons he thinks he should fire me and then you can add in things about me that he doesn't know. And you can tell him about all the things I call him behind his back, letting him add insubordination to his list."

"Is that what you think happened?" I laughed, hoping Mike would join in. "Just hang out there another few minutes. You and I will have a couple beers and I'll tell you every single word that was said."

"Don't bother," Mike said. "And the next time you want to go out for beers, don't bother calling me. Call your buddy Jameson." The call disconnected and Mike was gone.

I had never heard Mike react like that. It reminded me of a girlfriend I had once. In high school.

At the time I thought it would blow over after Mike slept on it.

Jameson picked this moment to walk out of the bar, stretching and holding his belly.

"You still here?" he blurted. "Thought you had something to do."

CHAPTER 21

That Sunday I drove to the store parking lot with my suitcase in the trunk. I was meeting Sawyer and Rory then we'd all drive four hours together to our hotel in the city. Management training was the next day.

Rory was already there, standing near his car with his stereo cranked and his windows down while he pretended to play hacky sack.

"Is it still hockey sack when you miss hitting it every time?"

"Oh, shit! What up, Dub-Dub?" he said as I got out of my car.

"Sawyer not here yet?" I asked.

"No. I don't even know where he is."

"He texted me an hour ago. He's probably still picking up the rental car."

"Oh, shit! We get a rental car?" Rory dropped the hacky sack and jumped into in the air, twisting his feet.

"Yeah. It's cheaper for the company than paying one of us mileage."

"I hope he gets a Camaro or a Corvette!" Rory said giggling to himself.

"How many seats are in a Corvette, Rory?" I asked as though he were a child.

"There are some models with four seats."

"No, there aren't."

"I think the 1999 model had..."

"No, they didn't."

Rory missed his hacky sack again in silence.

"Well, I hope it's something a la critic." said Rory.

He meant alacritis.

"With Sawyer behind the wheel, anything is fast."

After a few more minutes of Rory failing at hacky sack, Sawyer squealed into the parking lot with a disrespect every person reserved exclusively for rental cars. He sped toward us and we started to back up. Sawyer whipped the car around came to screeching halt mere feet from vehicular manslaughter.

"Come on, hurry up. Get in." Sawyer called. "I want to get there early. Hit the mall, check out a club. Let's go!"

Sawyer popped the trunk and I threw my bag in as Rory ran to shut his car off. I climbed into the passenger seat and shook hands with Sawyer.

"Hey, come on!" Rory called from outside the car. "Who says you get shotgun?"

"I'm already sitting here. It's not my fault you're so slow."

"I get it on the way home," said a five-year-old child with Rory's voice.

"Rory!" Sawyer said through gritted teeth. "Get in the damn car. Now."

Sawyer's driving was fast, aggressive, inconsiderate and even a little reckless, but I felt surprisingly safe sitting in the passenger seat of the two-ton steel trap streaking down the highway.

Less than three hours later Sawyer pulled off the highway. Instead of going to our hotel, Sawyer drove to the closest mall.

Sawyer circled around the parking lot while rapping along with a song on the radio.

"Oh, shit!" said Rory from the back seat. "You made good time, nigga!"

The car wasn't traveling very fast, but it still screeched to a halt.

"Rory, don't you ever call me that shit again!"

"You were just saying it like a hundred times in a row!" Rory held his hands up in defense.

"I was rapping along with a song, plus I can say it a million fucking times in a row with no words in between and it's still cool! You know why? Cause I'm fucking black! You don't get to say nigga. And you know what? You don't even get to say n-word. Nah, fuck that. You don't even get to use words that start with the letter N."

"What? That's crazy!" Rory said.

"That's the way it is now. Instead of night, you say evening. Instead of nuts, you say balls. For example: This evening my balls will be in your mouth."

"I can't use words starting with N?"

"Nope. Not anymore."

"Not one?" asked Rory.

"You said not," I said.

"Shut up, Wade. This doesn't concern you," Rory said.

"He's right, though. You said not."

Rory spoke with a deliberate pause between each word. "OK, OK. I'll try to watch what I say."

"You're lucky I don't remove the letter N from you

completely." Sawyer faced front again and continued his search for a parking spot.

Fifteen minutes later I was in the mall watching a true artist at work. The artist was Sawyer and his medium was fucking with people.

Sawyer sat on one of the benches when a couple walked close by, hand in hand. Sawyer looked directly at the girl and said, "Hey, girl! Why didn't you call me last week? I thought we had a good time."

The couple kept walking without responding, but before they were ten feet away the couple released hands and began arguing in whispers. Sawyer watched and laughed.

"That was mean, man," I said. "Funny, but mean as hell."

"Ah, they'll be closer than ever before once they talk it out."

"And if they're not?"

"Then they'll probably break up, and their relationship wasn't that strong in the first place. Either way, I'm doing them a favor."

Sawyer stared a guy who was walking out way. He stood up and stepped in front of the guy.

"Hey, man," said Sawyer. "Did you steal my wallet?"

Fear washed over the man's face. "No. Why would I steal your wallet?"

"Oh, I don't know. Maybe because that's what pickpockets do."

"I'm not a pickpocket."

"This guy says he saw you steal my wallet," Sawyer said pointing at me.

"What? That's ridiculous. I did not. Is this some kind of scam?" said the man.

"Nope. I don't know you, and I don't know this guy, but what I do know is that my wallet is gone and this guy says you took it."

The man turned to me for an explanation of some kind. It was fun watching Sawyer mess with people, but I didn't want to be involved in the games.

"I don't know. Maybe this guy just looks like the guy I saw," I said to Sawyer.

Sawyer stared at me with a look that said he was appalled by my performance.

"Fine," Sawyer said to the man. "Get out of here. But just know that I've got my eye on you. Until I find my wallet you're still a suspect."

The man walked away shaking his head and muttering.

Once the man was out of earshot Sawyer turned on me. "What the hell, dude? I thought you had my back."

"Yeah, and thanks for the warning."

"Improvisational skills are key."

"Why is it so important to mess with people while we're here?"

"Because, this isn't our city. Don't no one know us here. And you need to be prepared at all times because I might need you again."

"We'll see about that." I hoped my terrible performance would deter Sawyer from bringing me in again.

"Seriously." He looked around the mall. "Where's Rory?"

"Probably at the food court. As soon as we were in the mall he practically ran from you."

"Can you believe that fat fucker called me a nigger? He's lucky I didn't pull him out the car and beat his ass."

"I hate to defend Rory, but you know he didn't mean anything by it. Rory may be a moron but he's not malicious."

"Yeah. You're right." Sawyer looked around the mall again. "This place is dying out. Let's go get something to eat."

I texted Rory to meet us at the car and we headed toward the parking lot.

"You know where we should go?" said Sawyer as we walked. "Hooters. I haven't been to a Hooters in a long time. They got some good chicken wings there, man."

"Yeah, cause you're thinking about chicken wings right now."

Sawyer shushed me, but before I could curse him out for being a dick I noticed his eyes were locked on another happy couple walking our way.

"Hey girl," he called out. "Why didn't you call me last week? You said you had a good time."

The man stopped mid-stride and stared Sawyer in the eye. "This is my wife, bro."

Sawyer's games depended on most people's desire to avoid confrontation. His targets aren't supposed to say anything to Sawyer, they're supposed to argue between themselves as they walk away.

Sawyer had come across a man who didn't want to avoid confrontation and was willing to fight for the honor of his wife. His aggressive stance and stocky frame said he could have been dangerous.

I knew Sawyer wouldn't resort to fighting, especially with a guy like that. I also knew that despite the situation, Sawyer wasn't about to drop his game either.

"Oh, my bad. How long have you two been married?"

"Four years," said the man. His stare dared Sawyer to throw out a dispute.

"No," Sawyer said. "It can't be that long. She was just hanging out with me last week."

The man took a step forward.

"Whoa, whoa!" Sawyer said. "Don't be getting all aggressive here. We're just talking."

"I don't like what you're implying about my wife, bro."

Sawyer stepped away from the man to take a better look at the girl. "Melanie, will you tell this fool we were hanging out last week?"

"Her name's not Melanie."

Sawyer stopped mouth agape, in an award-winning performance of surprise. His face broke into heavy laughter. The man still looked ready for a fight.

"My bad, my bad, man. Your wife looks so much like this girl I know." Sawyer offered a hand to the man, still smiling.

The man reluctantly accepted the handshake and slowly switched out of his aggressive mode.

"I can see why you were ready to fight for her, dude. You've got yourself an amazing woman there," Sawyer continued.

The man smiled for the first time. "Thanks, bro."

"Yeah. I'd be ready to fight if anyone implied what I was implying. Just look at the way she looks at you. You can tell she's so in love with you, I'll bet she'd never cheat. Ever."

The man's smile faded and he avoided eye contact with Sawyer.

"Anyway," Sawyer continued. "Sorry about the confusion. Have yourselves a nice night."

Sawyer and I continued to the parking lot.

"Did you see that guy's face? She's cheated on him before, at least once."

"Maybe. Maybe he only suspects that she's cheated and you just deepened his suspicions."

"See? I'm still helping couples. I'm like a goddam saint."

* * *

"I told you I'd find one," Sawyer said with a grin.

"Sawyer, I'm so hungry you could have pulled into a DMV and I'd still try to order some food," I said.

It had taken Sawyer two hours of turning down random city streets to find a Hooters. Our GPS turned up nothing but Sawyer told us he had a feeling in his gut. Despite all begging, pleading, and threatening he persisted.

A twenty-something girl walked up to us with a huge smile on her face. She wore the mandatory Hooter's uniform. One pair of short orange shorts, a tight fitting tank top and a large pair of breasts. Fake or real, didn't matter.

"Hi guys!" she called. "How are you tonight?"

"We're doing a lot better since we got here," Sawyer said, looking her up and down.

She gave and embarrassed giggle that she probably practiced and perfected in front of a mirror. "Come on, guys. I'll show you to a table."

All three of us stared at her ass as she led us to a booth, our heads snapping up to meet her eyes as she turned around.

"Your server, Natalie, will be with you shortly."

"Did you see that chick's rack?" Rory said. "Nice!"

Sawyer pointed a finger in Rory's face. "What did you just say?"

"I...uh..." Rory pulled a small book out of his pocket and flipped through the pages, and then looked back up at us with a refined look on his face. "I said they're illustious."

"Do you mean illustrious?" I asked.

Rory looked back at the book and the back at me. "Whatever, dude. It doesn't start with N. That's all I know."

"That's good," Sawyer said.

"Sawyer, how long do I have to keep this up?"

"I don't know. I haven't thought about it."

"Can you think about it... presently?"

"Sure." Sawyer began stroking his chin and making a real show of it. "Depends."

"On what?"

"On how much you piss me off. The more you piss me off the longer you will be unable to use N-words."

"Fuck!" Rory replied.

"Wade, it's your show now, man. Get ready."

"What show?" I asked.

Sawyer made an impatient clicking sound with his tongue and looked up at the ceiling. "Man, this is Hooters. After we order our food the waitress is going to come back to our table and talk to us. She's going to try to make us feel like we're the only table she's paying extra attention to, therefore, we're special, therefore, we feel like leaving a bigger tip. If she's going to try to play us like that, we're going to play her first and you're gonna lead. Got it?"

"I don't want to lead. You lead."

"I'll lead," Rory said.

"No. Wade's going to lead."

"Why do I have to lead?"

"Two reasons. One, I know you can do it. You have the capability. And two, our waitress is a woman. I can't lie to her." He paused and pointed a finger at me. "But you can."

"Fuck off," I said pretending the study the menu.

"Let's figure out what you're going to say. What are we going to be? Doctors? How about dentists? We can say we're here for a molar conference."

I said nothing.

Another girl, spilling out of her uniform, came to the table with a practiced smile.

"Hi, guys! I'm Natalie! What are a bunch of good looking guys like yourself doing here on a night like tonight?"

"Hi," Rory said with a big smile. He risked a quick look at Sawyer, who was staring back with a furrowed brow. "Atalie."

"Pardon me?" she said.

"I said 'hi...Atalie.'"

"Did you call me Atalie?"

"Of course n...I didn't." Rory said with a snort.

"It sounded like it."

"Oh, you must be hearing my speech impediment. Sometimes it sounds like I don't pronounce certain constants."

He meant consonants, but she didn't seem to know the difference.

"I'm so sorry," she said with a look of concern, which was gone in an instant and replaced with canned happiness again. "What can I get you guys to drink?"

"How about a pitcher and some frosted mugs?" I suggested. Sawyer and Rory both nodded.

"Coming right up," she said, darting away from the table.

"All right. You got it figured out?" Sawyer asked me.

"I'm not doing it."

"Wade, listen. Did you see the way she tried to play our man Rory over here? Acting like she was all sympathetic to his condition." He turned to Rory. "By the way, that was some quick thinking with the speech impediment, I'm kind of proud of you."

"Thanks!" Rory beamed. "Can I use N-words again?"

"Not that proud." Sawyer turned back to me. "She's going to come back to this table with a pitcher of beer and she's going to try to play us all in turn. Are you going to let that happen, or are you going to turn the tables and mess with her?"

Sawyer had a way with words. I was a good salesman. Sawyer was the Six Million Dollar Salesman. I continued staring at the menu.

"You know she's a customer to guys like us, right?" Sawyer asked.

Damn, he was good. Natalie was already on her way back to the table. I leaned in and told Sawyer how I wanted him to act. He nodded with a curious smile.

When Natalie arrived, she dropped off our beer and asked for our food orders. Rory went first, then I ordered. She asked Sawyer what he wanted. He leaned toward me and pointed to something on the menu and I told Natalie what he wanted.

She gave us an odd look, but kept a smile on her face and walked away from the table vowing to check on us in a few moments.

"What are you planning?" Sawyer asked.

"You'll have to wait and see."

"What do you want me to do?" Rory asked.

"Follow my lead, and don't fuck it up. Say as little as possible."

"I can do that," Rory said.

Natalie was back at our table in under a minute.

"OK, guys. I put your order in, so that'll be ready in a bit, but I have a few minutes to kill, so I wanted to come and talk to you three." She emphasized 'you three.'

"What are you guys up to tonight?" she continued.

"Tonight?" I said. "Tonight is all about rest. Gotta rest up for tomorrow, right big guy?" I said to Sawyer.

Without looking at me or the waitress Sawyer began calmly nodding.

"What's tomorrow?" she asked.

"Try-outs," I answered.

Her plastic smile melted into a real one.

"What kind of try-outs?" she asked.

"You don't recognize this man?" I said pointing at Sawyer.

She looked at him again, really studying his face. She didn't recognize him. To her credit, she had no real reason to. "He looks a little familiar. I just can't put my finger on where from."

"This man is about to be the biggest thing to hit the NBA since LeBron. You do know who that is, right?"

She nodded enthusiastically, and gave an embarrassed smile.

"That's what try-outs we have tomorrow. The GM said the try-out is just a formality, but the big man here wants to give them a good showing anyway."

"Wow, I had no idea."

"Now you do," I said. "Years from now, you'll be able to tell people how you served this man before all the championships."

Sawyer very calmly turned his head to look at Natalie. He let his eyes slowly fall all the way to her feet and then back up to her eyes.

"You could do more than serve me," Sawyer said.

She giggled.

"So, who are you two?" she motioned to Rory and me.

"I'm his personal trainer and this is his assistant."

"Oh my God. Oh my God. I'd better go see if your food is ready, but maybe when my shift is over I could grab a couple of the other waitresses and hang out with you guys."

"Maybe," Sawyer answered.

She smiled at Sawyer and backed away from the table to check on some other customers.

"Wade, you're a fucking genius," Sawyer whispered. "We start out just messing with this bitch's head a little bit and now it looks like you might have scored me a little head."

"That's great for you," I said.

"Don't be mad. You could have said you were here for pro hockey try-outs or something. You're the one that made me the celebrity."

We ate our meal in character, talking only a little for fear of our waitress or one of her friends overhearing something that would destroy our story. When the meal was over we left cash on the table along with the address of our hotel.

We waited in the hotel lounge for Natalie to show up and ordered some drinks. One round turned into two. Two rounds to four. We were ordering round six when Natalie walked in with two other girls.

"Hi guys!" she said, bouncing with excitement. "These are my friends Amanda and Kristen."

We moved from a small table to a larger round table with long curved benches. Natalie sat beside Sawyer, cuddling up to him. Rory and I each sat on either side and looked at Amanda and Kristen.

They were both brunette and both gorgeous. They could have been sisters. Standing close to one another, they studied me and Rory while whispering to each other. I got the feeling they were arguing over which one was going to sit with me and which would sit with Rory.

I prayed that they were arguing over which one got me, but I honestly didn't care which one came to sit with me.

Amanda ended up sitting with me while Kristen went to sit with Rory.

We ordered drinks by the tray, talked loudly and laughed even louder. The other people in the lounge overheard every conversation. Some of them gave us dirty looks and left the lounge while other people started getting infected by our rowdy nature and added to the noise. Before long a middle-aged man in an expensive suit approached the table sheepishly.

"Hi, there," he said with an awkward wave.

"Hello," I replied. Sawyer, maintaining his character, looked at the man but said nothing.

"My name is Dan, I'm the hotel manager here. I just wanted

to come over and say that we're very happy to have you staying in our lovely hotel."

"It's our pleasure, Dan," I replied, trying to hide my surprise. I thought we were going to be told to leave.

"And I've informed the waitress that your drinks during your stay are on the house, so enjoy!"

"We appreciate that, Dan," I said.

Sawyer offered a hand to the man, which Dan shook enthusiastically.

"One more thing," Dan said. Sawyer raised an eyebrow. "Could I get an autograph?" he asked producing a pen.

Sawyer signed a hotel napkin with an illegible scribble and the hotel Manager left the lounge with a smile on his face.

"Gentlemen," said Sawyer, "I believe it's time for another round."

Pints and mixed drinks turned into pitchers and shots.

Sawyer was charming and charismatic enough that Rory and I didn't have to say a word and the girls were falling in love with all three of us.

He really had become quite an artist. No matter what question was thrown his way throughout the night, he didn't lie once.

Questions about how good he was at basketball were deflected with answers like, "I'm the best player I know," and "I've always had a natural love for the game."

Questions about his upcoming contracts and how much money he was going to make were handled with replies like, "No one can say for sure how much money is in my future," and "I really like the way things are going right now."

The night flew by. Just as we were about to order another round the waitress told us that the bar had closed, but that the manager had approved some complimentary wine to be sent to our rooms.

Natalie almost ran with Sawyer back to his room. Amanda and I walked to my room with our arms around each other, laughing over something that wasn't all that funny. Rory seemed to be dragging Kristen toward his room.

By the time Amanda and I reached the door to my room she was leaning on me so heavily that when I let go of her to look for my room key she nearly fell to the ground. She hit the wall, laughing, and I caught her before she slid to the floor. Barely.

Still laughing, I propped her up against the wall beside the door and went back to digging in my pockets. Amanda began kissing my neck and fiddling with my belt. Though she meant to take my belt off, she only managed to clumsily and repeatedly yank on it, throwing me off of my already delicate balance.

I pressed my body against hers to still us both and produced the room key from my jacket pocket.

Once inside the room we made out like the world was ending. Clothes came off in a blur. I was down to my boxers when there was a knock at the door.

I yanked the door open. "What?!"

A hotel employee was standing there with two bottles of wine in a large bucket of ice. I laughed, mainly at myself. I had just yelled at the poor man for doing his job.

"I'm sorry about that. Bring it... there." I pointed randomly. The man placed it on a small table and walked back out to the hallway.

I started to close the door in his face when I remembered some of my manners. "One second, sir!" I said to the hotel employee.

I grabbed a handful of change that had spilled out of my pants pocket when Amanda had pulled my pants off and pelted the poor man with the coins. "There you go! Goodnight!" I called and slammed the door on the man wearing a look of shock due to the currency assault.

Like a couple of alcoholics fresh out of rehab, Amanda and I each grabbed a bottle of wine and drank straight from it. We continued drinking straight from the bottle between spats of violent kissing and pelvic grinding.

Amanda slid her hand inside of my boxer shorts and wrapped her fingers around my dick. Another knock came to the door, louder this time.

"Ignore it," Amanda commanded. I was more than willing to obey.

The knock came again, even louder. Someone was pounding at the door.

"Amanda!" came a woman's voice.

Amanda pulled away from me. I tried to pull her back to me, but she pushed me away and opened the door. Kristen was standing on the other side half dressed and angry.

"What's wrong?" Amanda asked.

"We're leaving! These guys are a bunch of liars. They're register jockeys."

Amanda had a confused and unconvinced look on her face, but she gathered up her clothes and joined Kristen in the hallway.

I stepped out of the room just in time to see Rory running down the hallway wearing nothing but a thong.

"This little worm," said Kristen, pointing to Rory, "told me everything. They work in an electronics store."

Rory looked at me and shrugged. "Chicks are supposed to dig honesty."

"You're an idiot," I said to Rory before turning back to the girls. "So what if we work in a store? You work in a restaurant."

Amanda still looked dazed and nearly fell over while trying

to put her pants back on. Kristen pointed her finger so close to my face that I went cross-eyed trying to look at it.

"We didn't lie about who we are or what we do. Now tell me what room your other buddy is in."

"My buddy probably wouldn't appreciate the interruption. I know I didn't." I looked directly at Rory.

"I don't care. Either you tell me what room he's in or I call the cops and they make you tell them what room he's in just before arresting your ass for attempted rape."

I put my hands on my face and said, "Fuck," to no one in particular. "Room 313."

"Thanks for nothing," said Kristen. "If you two are still horny, you could always fuck each other."

"It would probably be more fun," I said. Kristen and Rory both gave me a puzzled look. I motioned toward Rory. "Doesn't he look like a cuddler?"

Kristen grabbed Amanda's arm and pulled her down the hallway.

Despite my blood-alcohol level, the situation sobered me. I dashed back into my room and threw on my clothes. Rory walked into the room after me.

"What are you doing?" he asked.

"Down to Sawyer's room. Somebody's going to have to calm him down. I don't feel like helping him bury your body tonight."

I walked to the door and turned back to Rory. "By the way, you are not pulling off that thong."

By the time I got to Sawyer's room Natalie was standing in the doorway talking with Kristen. Amanda was slumped against the wall trying to stay awake.

"...so come on and let's get out of here," said Kristen.

"I think I'm going to stay," Natalie said.

"What do you mean you're going to stay?" Kristen asked.

"It doesn't matter. I'm just going to stay. I'll call you tomorrow."

Kristen started to protest again, but Natalie closed the door with a soft click.

I practically ran back to my room just in case Kristen turned around, saw me and felt like taking her aggression out on me.

Back in my room, Rory was sitting on my bed, still wearing nothing but a thong.

"I'm sorry, man. She said she trusted me, and it just felt like I needed to tell her the truth."

"Seems pretty stupid now, doesn't it?"

"In readyspeck, yeah it does."

He meant retrospect.

An eerie silence filed the room. Rory sat on my bed staring at the floor and I stood in front of him, repulsed but unable to look away.

"Why the fuck are you still here? And sitting on my bed, in a thong."

"I'm bored. I won't be able to sleep for a couple of hours. Not after that little confrontation."

"Yeah, I'm wide awake now, too," I said. "We can hang out and finish this wine, but not until you put some clothes on."

"OK." Rory walked to the doorway and stopped before exiting. "I've got some weed in my room. Should I bring that back with me?"

"Yes, you should," I said.

"OK." Rory shuffled out of the room and shuffled back in ten minutes later fully dressed holding a bottle of wine he brought from his room and a small plastic bag with half a dozen joints.

We spent the next few hours smoking weed, drinking wine, and laughing at late night television shows that weren't funny.

Rory fell asleep on the floor and although I didn't want him staying in my room, I was too high, drunk and tired to care. I dropped a hotel towel on top of him for a blanket and then crawled into bed. I was still trying to do the math on how much sleep I was about to have when I passed out.

CHAPTER 22

"Wade! Get your ass up. We gotta be there in an hour."

I opened the door and squinted at Sawyer. "How did you do that?" Sawyer raised a confused eyebrow at me. "You were up as late as I was, maybe later, yet here you are standing outside of my door, fully dressed and wide awake."

"Don't worry about it. You just need a little of my magic day after juice."

"It doesn't include any of your bodily fluids, does it?"

"Man, don't be stupid. It includes coffee, though. I'm gonna go get some. Be showered and ready by the time I get back."

Sawyer moved to leave, but did a double take when he saw Rory passed out on the floor with a neatly folded hotel towel on his chest.

"What the hell happened last night?" Sawyer asked.

"I'll tell you later."

"Did you guys have an orgy?"

"No. No sex at all. With anyone."

"Shit. Those bitches actually left?" he asked. "When Natalie said she was staying I thought the other two would go back and finish fucking you."

"Go get coffee. Lots of it."

"I'm out. Get ready."

Sawyer disappeared down the hall. I retreated into my room and prodded Rory with my foot.

"Rory. Wake up." He didn't move. The prodding got stronger and stronger until I was kicking him. He began to moan and I gave him a few more kicks for my own satisfaction.

"Get up," I said. "Grab a shower. Coffee's on the way."

I walked into the bathroom, but when I turned to close the door I found myself face to face with Rory.

"In your own room, Rory!"

"Right."

I waited until Rory was out in the hall before stripping down and jumping into the shower. I stood there, letting the hot water cover me. I kept turning on the spot so my back and chest got equal coverage with warmth. I began thinking about the shower I would design if I was rich. Multiple shower heads and an artificial rain system entertained my mind until the shower curtain was ripped open.

Sawyer stood there holding a cup of coffee in each hand. Normally I would have yelled and covered my package, but I was just too tired to care. Instead I pointed at him. "You homo."

"Here. Custom made for you," he said, handing me one of the cups. "And I ain't no homo. Not bad, though. For a white dude."

I drank from the cup. It wasn't coffee. It was disgusting. I opened my mouth wide and let it fall out. I watched it to make sure the water rinsed it down the drain and away from me.

"Hey!" I called out. "What the fuck is this? It tastes like you combined coffee with wine, and beer and," I paused. It was important to articulately communicate the thought. "Ass."

"Yeah. That's pretty much what it is." Sawyer called back. "Except for the ass. You couldn't get ass even when it's handed to you on a silver platter."

Instead of leaving, Sawyer sat on the toilet and made himself comfortable. "You homo," I said.

"Whatever, dude. Listen, that drink right there has coffee to wake you up, aspirin for the headache, antacids for your stomach and alcohol cause you know what they say about hair of the dog. I know it tastes like shit, but I promise if you down that shit you'll be good to go in a half hour." He got up and walked out of the bathroom. "Your choice."

I stared into the cup, weighing my options. "It can't make me feel any worse," I said and forcibly chugged the entire cup.

It tasted worse than an ashtray, mop bucket, urinal and sweaty underwear combined. I scrambled out of the shower, desperate to taste something else. Anything else. There weren't many options in a hotel bathroom. I grabbed the miniature bar of soap and looked at it closely. It was strawberry scented. I was still considering washing my mouth out with soap when I spotted the mini bottle of mouthwash.

I swished the first half of the bottle around my mouth and spit into the sink. I swallowed the second half.

Despite the taste, Sawyer was right. Twenty minutes later I was dressed, in the car, and on the way to the technology expo and feeling a lot better. Rory was lying in the back seat looking much worse. He refused to drink Sawyer's drink, claiming he'd do just as well with coffee and energy drinks.

Inside the expo a woman with an unnaturally large smile sat

behind a registration table. She took our names, gave us name tags and told us to have a 'really fun day.'

The expo was a joke. It was nothing like the larger, televised shows like E3. The hall looked more like a dark, dingy basement. The walls were packed with booths from various manufacturers, each one looking exactly the same. Large poster with images are their product, a stack of color brochures, and a guy in a suit waiting to tell us why their company was better than all the other ones at the expo.

Not even the free shit made it worthwhile. Each booth gave away some kind of pens, key chain, notepads, or t-shirt, all shamelessly covered with some company logo.

We did our part and took every free thing we could get our hands on. However, if any of these companies thought we were going to recommend one brand over another because of a free pen, they were delusional. Especially since the free pens always went dry halfway through writing any word longer than six letters.

My cell phone vibrated with an incoming text message. I hoped that Mike had come to his senses and realized I wasn't plotting against him.

It turned out to be a text from Jameson. He asked about our drive down, how the hotel was and how the expo was going. I replied with a single word: *Fine.*

I quickly hammered out a new message to Mike before pocketing my phone. I didn't want to bring up the other night, or tell him how stupid I thought he was being so I just sent a casual message asking him how things were going back home and told him the expo was lame.

At lunch the employees of the conference centre provided pre-made sandwiches that sucked by any standards.

I sat and talked with a supervisor from another store while

we tried to choke down the triangles of soggy bread and thin meat. We shared stories about our respective managers and debated over who worked for the bigger douchebag. I thought I was winning.

Sawyer came from one of the other tables and sat in the empty chair beside me. "All right, Wade, it's on tonight. I just talked to one of the local guys. He told me which spot we should hit tonight."

"Tonight? Are you kidding? I'm already exhausted. I'm going to be asleep by seven."

"Nah. You'll be good. I got a magic evening drink, too. Besides, we didn't get to go out last night, and I'm not mad at that cause it turned out all right, but we gotta hit the town tonight."

"All right, but I don't want to go to some club where the music is too loud to talk to women, even though they don't want to talk to me. I can do that at home."

"We're not going to a club. We're going to a strip club."

"I'm there." The words left my mouth before I realized I was saying them.

Sawyer laughed and slapped me on the back. "That's my boy."

The rest of the day passed by without any real excitement, except when I got into a debate with a rep from a no-name laptop company. I walked by several booths at once when this rep decided he wasn't going to let me walk any further.

"Hi, there!" He looked at my name tag. "Rory."

"Hello," I said, not slowing down.

"Whoa. Where you going?"

"Not sure yet."

"What you need to do is get a little info on our line of products."

I stepped a little closer and looked at the three laptops he had set-up on his booth.

"We already have two of these at the store. This one looks like it's the same thing with a little more RAM."

"We can talk stats all day. If stats are the only thing we were to look at, most laptops would be exactly the same. Am I right? There'd be no reason to buy one over the other, but in reality there are good reasons why people should buy one computer over another. We're talking quality of product and quality of service."

"I hear ya," I said. Being in sales as long as I had I knew he was just feeding me bullshit. By being agreeable I was hoping the conversation would end quickly.

"I'm not sure you do. If you had to recommend a computer to a customer, which one would you recommend?"

"The one in their price range."

"OK. Let's assume there are several in their price range."

This guy was starting to get on my nerves.

"No," I said. "Let me assume that you're asking me all these leading questions to get to some kind of point."

He paused, and gave me a sharp look. "Your computer breaks down tomorrow and you need that computer. There's no way you can be without it. Let's say your business, and therefore your job, depends on having a computer. How are you going to decide between all the available brands?"

"Simple. I'm going to buy a Mac."

"You're a bad example."

"You asked."

"All I'm trying to say," he said, almost pleading with me at this point, "is that there are some reasons you should impress on your customers to go with a machine like ours over the others. Quality and service in order to have the best experience possible." He looked at me with a hint of pain in his face. "Don't you want your customers to have the best experience?"

I paused and shook my head.

"Most of the time, I don't care about my customer's experience. Do you know why? The customer doesn't even care about the customer's experience. Sounds odd, right? Customers don't want to hear which computer is the best quality. Customers want to hear which computer has the best price or which computer is on sale that week. If I show 100 customers a pair of computers, one with superior quality, and one that's fifty bucks cheaper, 95 of them are going to take the one that's fifty bucks cheaper. They'll all trade quality for a bit of money without a second's thought."

"My god," he said, taking a step away from me. "You're damaged."

I shrugged. He was another guy who worked closely with retail, but knew nothing about how things worked in an actual store.

I walked away while the rep stared at me with his eyes wide. I wished the expo had an open bar. Or a cash bar. Any kind of bar, really.

For dinner, we all had room service delivered to Sawyer's room and ate together.

"What the fuck?" I said entering his room. Sawyer had been given a room three times the size of mine. It had a full size dinner table, a leather couch in front of a big screen TV, a full kitchenette and a bed that looked like two king mattresses side by side.

"How did you get a room like this?" I asked.

"They gave me a standard room when we first got here. That Dan guy hooked me up with this suite."

"Shit," was all I could say.

"Yeah, I know. I'm going to make one of my energy drinks you want one? Guaranteed to make you last the night."

"Absolutely. Your morning drink worked as advertised."

"Always does. I better make one for Rory too. Where is he?"

"He'll be here in a few. Probably grabbing a nap."

"Or jerking off," Sawyer said.

"Or jerking off and then napping."

Sawyer finished mixing the drinks, in the blender the hotel provided for him, and set a cup in front of me. It was a dark purple, bordering on brown. It didn't look better than the morning drink, but at least it smelled better.

"What's in this one?"

"Pretty much the same stuff. More alcohol than before, and some Red Bull."

Rory arrived just after the food. He had pillow creases all over his face and looked like hell. Sawyer offered him one of his drinks, but he smelled it and refused. Even when Sawyer offered to let him start saying N-words again.

"Nope," Rory said. "I'm going to last just as long as you guys, but I'm going to do it the natural way."

He was so tired, he didn't catch himself using N-words and he wasn't trying to use any new dictionary words.

"All right," Sawyer said with a shrug. "Hurry up and eat. We gotta bounce."

*   *   *

We walked into the strip club with high expectations, which were promptly smashed to pieces. The place was dead.

There was a large stage in the very center of the place, surrounded by stools. Stripper's horseshoe tables were all around the floor near the stage. Finally booths lined the walls of the club, except for the back corner where to bar was located and a lounge area that had a few couches and arm chairs.

It looked like a cool place, but none of that mattered. The place really was dead. There was a girl on stage putting very little effort into her dance, and a few people seated at a few of the tables.

A bouncer was escorting a tall, lanky dude with glasses from the VIP section on the second floor, to the door. I heard the dude pleading his case as they walked by. "I know she said she did four dances, but she only did three. I counted."

"Yeah, yeah, yeah," said the bouncer.

"Sawyer, are you sure this is the place?" I asked.

"This is the place," he said.

"This looks," I took another look around, "terrible."

"No, no. This is good. Trust me. The guy who told me about this place said it doesn't get hot til later. Right now they got their B or C squad on stage, but in a couple hours it'll change over to the main line-up. I guarantee it."

"We shouldn't have come so early," I thought aloud.

"Have faith, Wade. This is a good thing. You'll see. Go join Rory, I'll grab some drinks."

Only then did I realize that Rory wasn't standing with us. He was sitting on one of the stools surrounding the stage right in front of the girl on display. He was staring and smiling like a man in a trance.

I took a seat beside him, watched the girl for a few seconds, then looked at the menu.

She finished her dance, and a few people applauded, but none louder than Rory. The girl came right over and sat beside Rory without putting any of her clothes back on.

"Hi, sweetie," she said. "My name is Taffy."

I used to have a dog named Taffy.

"Hi, Taffy. I'm Rory."

Taffy pulled a cigarette out from a small purse she was

carrying along with her bundled up clothes. Rory fumbled his lighter out of his pocket and offered to light it.

"Thanks," she said.

Taffy looked like she was one of the club's hottest attractions five years ago. It also looked like she hadn't aged well over the past five years, nor had she really taken care of herself. Still, I couldn't blame her for staying in her line of work. As long as there were guys like Rory around, there would always be money to be made.

Rory blabbered on about useless shit while Taffy pretended to listen and watched Rory's purse strings get looser.

A waitress walked up, set a beer in front of me and smiled. She had a very pretty smile. You could say she was a step up from Taffy, but it would more accurate to say she was an entire staircase up from Taffy.

"Thanks," I said, reaching for my wallet.

"Your friend sent it over," she said. "Would you like to have a shot?"

"Maybe a little later."

"Your friend already paid for that too."

I looked over at the bar where Sawyer was leaning and talking to a pretty bartender. He thrust his drink in my direction and smirked.

"I guess I'll have it now."

She selected a shot from her tray and handed it to me. I took it but looked at her.

"Aren't these hooter shooters?" I asked. "I can't help but notice there's no hooter with my shooter."

"Sorry, I don't do that. And before you ask, I don't do private dances," she said and then walked away.

I was speechless. Had I just offended the shot girl at a strip club? Beside me, Rory continued to blabber on as Taffy began adding subtle suggestions of private dances into the conversation.

Once again, Sawyer was true to his word. A few hours, the club was full and gorgeous women occupied the stage. By that time he had charmed enough waitresses and dancers, and laid down just the right amount of money to earn permanent use of the lounge area. We must have smelled like money, because were surrounded by gorgeous strippers, and Taffy.

Sawyer was in an arm chair with two blondes on his lap. Every half hour he bought them each a vodka martini and they seemed content.

I conversed with a few different girls. A blonde would hang around for a while until she had to head to the stage for her turn to dance, at which time a brunette would take her place.

Rory had the opportunity to talk to a few other girls, but he refused to pay attention to anyone but Taffy.

"Did you miss me, Wade?" A brunette named Amy said as she came back to the table.

"Sure did. Have a seat."

"Where were we?" she asked.

"I was asking you deeply personal questions and you were answering them without batting an eye."

"Right. What's the next question?"

"What's the creepiest thing a guy's ever asked you to do?"

"Here at the club?"

I almost choked on my drink. "How often do you have creeps hitting on you?"

She laughed.

"There's a guy who comes in just about every Thursday. He always gets a private dance and pays an extra twenty bucks if I slap him across the face when the dance is over."

"A slap in the face?"

"Yeah. As if I was accusing him of being a pervert or something."

I laughed. "Do you slap him hard?"

"He insists. The harder the better. One time I slapped him so hard his mouth bled a little."

"How did he react?"

"He gave me an extra twenty."

I laughed again. "That's a little creepy, but really not that bad."

She playfully shoved me. "That's pretty creepy! What were you expecting to hear?"

"I don't know. I thought maybe you'd have a story about a guy who wanted you to shit on him, or something."

"Oh, gross!" she said, laughing. "I gotta go for a bit. If I stay at one table too long the boss gives me shit."

"OK," I said.

Sawyer was whispering in the ear of one of his blonde friends while the other was on stage with her eyes still locked on him.

The waitress who gave me my first shot approached the table.

"Do you need anything?" she asked.

She still looked upset.

"Why don't you have a seat? Take a load off."

She looked around the club.

"I really shouldn't," she said, but sat down anyway. "A few minutes couldn't hurt."

"I'm Wade," I said offering a hand.

"Amanda," she said shaking my hand.

I laughed to myself.

"What's so funny?" she asked.

"I just met a girl named Amanda last night."

"I don't know if that's a good thing or a bad thing." She giggled a little.

"Hey, I offended you earlier with hooter shooter thing, I'm sorry. I didn't mean anything by it."

"No, no. I'm just having one of those nights. Don't get me wrong, I like this job. It's really good money, the hours aren't terrible, but sometimes I get fed up with customers. These guys think they're allowed to grab my ass just because it's a strip club and they tipped me a buck. Sometimes I just want someone else to get me a drink."

"Is that all?" I asked, standing from the table.

She smiled as I grabbed her serving tray and laughed as I walked to the bar.

I asked the bartender for a beer and slipped her some money. Placing the beer on the serving tray I walked back to the table and delivered the beer.

"Beer. How'd you know?" she asked as I sat back down.

"You just seem like a beer girl."

She looked me in the eye and said, "Thank you."

"Don't mention it."

"No, really. Thank you. That was very sweet."

"You're welcome."

We looked into each other's eyes and had a whole conversation without saying a word.

"So you really don't do private dances, huh?"

"No. I really don't."

"That's a shame. Cause I'd keep you busy for the night."

She smiled a little.

"I should get back to work. Will you finish my beer for me?"

"Sure."

She walked away from the table just as Amy came back from dancing and sat back beside me.

"Did you miss me?" she asked.

"Sure. Do you know, Amanda? The waitress," I said pointing her out across the bar.

"Yeah. She's cool, a little weird though. Our boss has given her like a million offers to be feature dancer, but she always turns him down."

I watched Amanda bounce from table to table taking drink orders and dropping off drinks.

"We should go have a private dance, honey. What do you think?"

"Sure," I said, though I was still staring across the club at Amanda.

Amy kept my busy for the next half hour providing dances and lame conversation that only served as filler between songs. She kept hinting that there was more than lap dances if the money was right. I played dumb.

What I really wanted was a conversation with Amanda. A dance to go with it would have been nice, but I could tell that would never happen. The conversation would have been enough.

Once back at the table, I looked around for her, but I didn't see Amanda anywhere.

I walked up to the bar and asked the bartender if she knew where Amanda was.

"Home for the night, hun," she said.

Fuck.

I ordered another couple of beers from the bartender and skulked back to the table.

"Wade, what's with the face?" Sawyer asked.

"Nothing. That waitress is gone. I was just," I thought better of telling Sawyer I kind of liked her. "I was going to get a few more hooter shooters from her."

"Don't worry about it, Wade. This place has got plenty of

shooters and even more hooters." Sawyer laughed, and went back to putting his attention on the blonde duo on his lap.

I sat and watched Sawyer perform his magic for a bit. He hadn't moved the entire night. Most girls left if they weren't taken for a private dance once in a while. He just kept whispering into their ears and buying them drinks. What could a man say to make a pair of strippers give up most of their potential earnings for the night?

"Is one of those beers for me?" said a voice from behind me.

I looked over my shoulder to see Amanda out of her trashy waitress outfit and into a pair of jeans and a nice, feature-hugging sweater.

She sat down beside me and I slid one of bottles in front of her.

"I'm off duty," she said with a nervous laugh.

"I figured as much. I guess that private dance is definitely out of the question now."

She hit me playfully in the arm and smiled. "Would you settle for a private booth?"

We left the table to find a booth. Sawyer didn't seem to notice and Rory was off getting his hundredth dance from Taffy.

We found an available booth, sat close to one another with our drinks and talked quietly. As quietly as two people could in a strip club.

I couldn't believe that I was in a strip club, talking with an attractive woman who wasn't busy looking around for someone more interesting to talk to. However, Amanda was a waitress, and although it wasn't exactly a retail position, there were a lot of similarities.

We shared stories about customers from hell, crazy co-workers and asshole bosses. I told her all about the trip that I was on with Sawyer and Rory. I thought I saw a hint of sadness in her face when she found out we weren't staying past the next day. It could have been the booze.

Before long Sawyer and his two friends joined us in our booth and the five of us talked and laughed together. Even Rory and Taffy stopped by the booth once every half hour or so, in between private dances.

It was getting close to last call when a man walked over to our booth on legs made of jelly and pointed at Amanda.

"Get me a drink, bitch," he slurred.

"Mick, I'm off duty."

"And don't call her a bitch," I said.

"Was I talking to you?" the drunk said.

"I don't give a shit." I got out of the booth to stand face to face with the drunk. "You're talking to me now."

"Me too," Sawyer said, standing on the other side of the man. A nearby bouncer saw the situation developing and walked toward us. Sawyer saw the bouncer coming and stretched his hand out to the bouncer. "We got this."

No more words were exchanged. Sawyer and I just calmly looked at the guy. We both towered over the shorter drunk. After a minute he dropped his gaze to the floor and shuffled away.

"You know that guy?" I asked Amanda.

"Yeah, he's a regular," she replied.

As we sat back down the mood between Sawyer and his blonde duo had not changed, but there was an air of awkwardness around Amanda.

"I think I should go," she said.

Sawyer's head snapped to me, then looked at Amanda.

"Hey, Wade. I forgot to tell you, but, everyone's welcome to continue this party back at my suite." Sawyer looked at Amanda. "That's includes you, sweetie."

Amanda smiled, then looked at me. She looked like she wanted to go, but something wasn't right.

"Thanks, but I should really go."

On the outside, I smiled and said, "I'll walk you to your car." On the inside I could only think, *Fuck, fuck, fuck, fuck, fuck, FUCK!*

We walked to her car while I told a couple of bad jokes to try and lighten the mood. It didn't really work. I had no idea what to do. Sawyer probably knew what to do, but he didn't tell me.

She turned to face me, leaning against the driver's side door of her car.

"It was really nice to meet you and talk with you," she said.

"Yeah, yeah. Same here. I had fun."

"Good. Me too."

Awkwardness evolved from an emotional feeling to a sticky coating, and I was covered in it.

"Have a safe drive home tomorrow, okay?" She was waiting for me to say something. Not just anything. Something specific.

"Hey, maybe I should get your number. You know, in case I'm in the area again." I whipped out my cell phone.

"I don't know if that's such a good idea."

"Oh..." I was confused, or drunk, or both. "Of course." I put my phone away.

"Well, I guess I'll hit the road."

"Drive safe," I said. Behind my polite smile I was cursing myself for not being able to stop her. I couldn't even say anything to try and stop her.

When she opened her car door, I heard feet shuffle on the pavement behind me. Pain erupted across the back of my head.

Amanda gasped. I dropped to a knee and put a hand on the back of my head. Mick, that fucking drunk, shuffled away into the darkness, laughing madly to himself.

Amanda took my head in her hands and turned my face away. She gently coaxed my hand away from the back of my head.

"You're bleeding, but it's not too bad," she said.

"Really? Cause it feels incredible."

Amanda laughed, despite my grunts of continued pain.

"I'm sorry about that," she confessed. "I feel like it's my fault."

I touched my head again to see how much blood came back on my fingers. It really wasn't much.

"Don't feel bad," I said. "I shouldn't have confronted him the way I did. I just didn't like the way he treated you."

"Does it still hurt?" she asked.

"I'll be fine."

She gently touched the back of my head.

"Does that hurt?"

"Only a little."

She stepped close to me and pressed her lips against mine.

"Does that hurt?"

I grinned. "Not enough to make me stop."

We made out by Amanda's car until Sawyer, his two blonde friends, Rory and Taffy came out of the club.

They stood staring at us for a minute before we realized they were there. I turned slowly and Amanda started giggling.

"I guess I'll join you after all," she said to Sawyer.

But we didn't join them. As soon as we were back at the hotel Amanda and I went to my room.

Hotel management left more booze in my room. Two more bottles of wine and a bottle of whiskey sat on the table with a couple of wine glasses and some assorted candies.

Pretending I wasn't already way too drunk, I made a drink for Amanda and one for myself.

As I handed her the drink, she downed it and poured herself

another. I tried to pull Amanda close to me, but she pushed me away with a smirk.

"Just a minute," she said.

Amanda pulled a chair into the middle of the room and turned the TV onto a dance music station. She looked at me and motioned for me to sit down in the chair. I practically ran to sit down.

I've only had a few lap dances in my life. Other than the one that Bridget gave me, they never seemed that appealing to me. Sure, there was a naked chick all over me, but touching wasn't allowed so what was the point?

On that night, Amanda gave me the best lap dance I'd ever had. Probably because she let me touch once in a while, and she touched a lot.

She was grinding in my lap wearing nothing but her panties when my cell phone started to vibrate in my pocket.

Amanda gave a little "ooh," at the sensation.

Normally, I would have either taken my cell phone out and thrown it on the table beside me, or just let it ring so she could keep getting a kick out of it. My state of advanced drunkenness caused my logic and intelligence to have a traffic collision in my brain. There were no survivors.

I answered my cell phone.

"Hullo?"

Amanda didn't seem to notice, or she just didn't care.

"Hi, Wade. I'm really sorry to bother you, but you said I could call if I had an emergency."

I stood straight up out of the chair, causing Amanda to fall to the floor laughing.

It was Tess. I was nearly speechless as my pants fell down around my ankles. Amanda must have undone them at some point.

"Are you there?" Tess asked.

"Yeah, sorry. It took me a second to recognize your voice."

"I know. I probably woke you up. I'm so sorry!"

"Actually, believe it or not, you didn't."

"Really? Party night, or what?"

"No. Not really. It's kind of a work function." I was trying desperately not to slur my words, but had no idea how well I was covering.

"Are you busy right now? I could really use a hand."

Amanda was back with the bottle of whiskey, pouring another drink. Was that three or four?

"Yeah, I have a minute."

I stepped out of my pants and lay down on the bed.

"Thank you so much. I have a paper due tomorrow and my computer's acting up."

"What's it doing?"

"Nothing."

When I heard an answer like that, I immediately thought she meant nothing was wrong and she was just using her computer as an excuse to call and talk to me.

"It completely frozen," she said, to my disappointment. "I can't even get it to turn off."

"How long ago did it freeze up?"

"Half hour ago. Maybe more."

"OK, it's not coming back, then."

"What?! It has to!"

"I just meant it's not going to work itself off. Out. It's not going to work itself out."

"Oh."

"Press and hold the power button. Keep holding it."

"How long?"

"Until you see something happen."

A few seconds passed in silence.

"The screen just went black."

"Good. The computer's off now. Give it a couple of minutes before turning it back on."

"Can you stay on the line until it comes back on?"

Amanda came over to the bed, draining another glass of booze. I have no idea how many that made. She hopped onto the bed, bounced off the mattress and landed on the floor. She lay still.

"Sure."

"Thanks so much, Wade. Computers!"

"Didn't you just buy that thing?"

Tess laughed. "Yeah."

"If I were you I'd take it back to the salesman you bought it from and say 'Listen, buddy!'"

She laughed again, a little harder. Her laugh wasn't meant to be sexy, but it was. It was at that point that I realized I was touching myself.

"So what do you like to do when you're not writing papers at three in the morning?" I asked.

Tess laughed again. I couldn't resist anymore. I sunk my hand into my underwear and started pleasuring myself.

"I don't know. Regular stuff, I guess."

"Oh, yeah? What kind of regular stuff?"

"Um... I like movies. I like hiking and fishing. I like a lot of outdoor stuff, actually."

"That's great."

"Should we try the computer now?"

"Oh, yeah."

"Are you all right?"

"I'm great."

"You sound like you're out of breath."

Only a drunken idiot would think he's not going to sound different to someone while he's jerking off.

"I know, I know. I banged my shin while I was walking around my place here."

"Ouch," Tess said sympathetically.

"I know. It hurts. Ooooooooooh, it hurts."

"Oh, hey my computer is back on. Everything seems to be working! Wade, you're a genius."

Hearing the excitement in her voice and her saying my name brought me close to climax.

"It sounds like you're in real pain there, so I'm going to let you go and take care of that shin. Thanks again, Wade."

"No, wait. Just a few seconds!"

She was already gone.

I sat up and looked at Amanda, now asleep on the floor. I picked her up off the floor, put her into the bed and crawled in with her.

I kissed all over her body and let my hands roam wherever they pleased, but it was no use. She was comatose.

I sighed the way a person sighs when they want someone in the room to notice and ask, "What's wrong?" Only there wasn't anyone else in the room. No one else that could hear me.

I had given up sex with a hot waitress who worked at a strip club to take a phone call from a chick who wanted nothing more than her computer to be fixed. I didn't know what the technical definition of loser was, but I thought it must be something close to that.

I made a mental note to look it up in the morning as I stumbled to the bathroom to finish jerking off.

CHAPTER 23

I woke up the next morning lying on the bathroom floor with my dick in my hand. I had passed out before I was even able to close the deal with my own hand.

I showered before leaving the bathroom, hoping Sawyer would bring another cup of his magic hangover drink or whatever the hell he called it.

Amanda was still asleep in the bed when I walked out of the bathroom. She looked far more comfortable than someone who slept on the bathroom floor. I got dressed slowly. Not because I wanted to keep from disturbing Amanda's sleep, but for the fatigue, headache and nausea.

Amanda woke up as I shuffled around the room. She smiled at me.

"I thought I'd end up here," she said.

"You certainly did."

"Do you remember much about last night?"

"Yeah." Unfortunately, I thought to myself.

"I don't. Please don't be offended though. It has nothing to do with you."

Like a drinking problem? I thought. I was far from offended. I actually felt a little bit better.

"It was a good night. You had a great time."

"Did we..."

"Have sex?"

"Yeah."

I hesitated for a second, but only a second. "Yes, we did."

She smiled to herself, looking a little embarrassed.

"I wish I could remember."

"Well, you have nothing to worry about. I'm clean, we used protection and you said that I was phenomenal."

"How about you show me a little of that phenomenon right now?"

Everything from the previous night that made me feel like shit lifted as I walked back over to the bed, but came crashing down on me twice as heavy when there was a loud knock at the door.

"Wade! Let's go!"

It was Sawyer.

I ripped the door open and gave Sawyer one of the meanest looks I've ever given another human being.

"We don't need to go right now, do we?" I asked.

"Yeah, actually, we do. We only have 15 minutes to get there."

I looked back at Amanda. "Can't we be a few minutes late?"

"If it was just the tech expo I'd say okay, but today's our training session, which is run by the corporate team. Do you really want the whole corporate management team to see us walk in late?"

"Fuck," I said. I turned to Amanda and held my arms out and mouthed an apology.

She got up from the bed wearing nothing but the bed sheet, walked over to me and kissed me. It probably looked very romantic, but she had really bad morning breath. My stomach turned and I fought the urge to vomit into her mouth.

She wrote her number down on a sheet of hotel stationary and stuffed it into my pocket before Sawyer grabbed me by the shoulder and pulled me out the door.

Before closing the door behind us, Sawyer leaned back into the room and said, "We're supposed to check out this morning, sweetie, so help yourself to anything in the fridge but they might ask you to leave at 11."

He smiled again and closed the door.

One of Sawyer's blonde friends was waiting in the hallway with a coffee cup in each hand.

"Here's your juice," Sawyer said taking a cup from the blonde and handing it to me.

"You're a saint." I gulped deeply from the cup. It tasted just as bad as the day before, but knowing of its healing powers I forced it down as quickly as my stomach would allow.

As soon as we stepped out of the hotel our rental car came to a stop right in front of us. Dan, the hotel manager, got out from the driver's side and scrambled over to Sawyer to shake his hand.

"Good luck in the upcoming season." Dan's smile couldn't have been wider.

"Thanks for your hospitality, sir." Sawyer smirked and climbed in behind the wheel.

I jumped in the passenger side. Rory was passed out in the backseat. His neck was covered in hickeys and I absently wondered where Taffy was, but stopped caring before I could finish the thought.

Ten minutes later we were back at the convention centre.

A few signs directed us to a small room filled with long tables and fake leather business chairs. A sign above the door labeled it The Maple Room. It was very generic and uninspiring, but it had to be better than having a training session in an actual store. There were about a dozen other store supervisors sitting in the chairs, chatting idly.

"There's the man I wanted to see today!" said a voice from behind me.

I turned around to see Brent Baker smiling as he entered the room. He had two men with him, Gary Reicht and Jeff Vale. They were both powerhouses of the corporate level. I couldn't remember exactly what their fancy job titles were, or even what their actual positions were, but at the level they were at they could make up any job title they wanted.

Brent strode up to me and laughed as he shook my hand. "Gary, Jeff, you might remember Wade from store 449."

They both said something along the lines of, "Of course!" and shook my hand.

"I made a visit down there recently," Brent said. "This young man and I had an amazing conversation about customer loyalty. Didn't we, Wade?"

I cleared my throat. "Yeah, it was a pretty good talk."

"Didn't you basically say that we should be willing to cut our prices for our customers or else they might not come back to our stores?"

Brent, Jeff and Gary were all looking at my expectantly. Their facial expressions gave nothing away about what they were actually thinking. My answer could do great things for career or kill it completely. I thought about giving a bullshit answer like 'there's no way people would stop coming to out stores, cause we're the best, rah, rah, rah, bullshit, bullshit, bullshit, but I just couldn't do it.

"Like I said before, if we're unwilling to sell lower than our competitors, customers will buy from them instead of us. If we set a precedent of being the expensive guys, people won't even bother to come into our stores anymore. But, if we do the opposite, and set a precedent of having lower prices than everyone else, people will automatically come to us."

Gary and Jeff both continued to look at me as they considered my words.

"Well, of course," Gary said, after an eternity. "It seems so obvious now that you say it."

"I told you it was great," Brent said, slapping me on the back. "We're going to roll out a company-wide memo later this week outlining this theory of yours. But for now, why don't you guys go and have a seat, we're going to begin in a few minutes."

I sat down and checked my phone before the training began. No missed phone calls and no text messages. I quickly hammered out another text message to Mike telling him about how dumb corporate was acting and told him I'd be home tonight if he wanted to go for a beer.

The training session was a bunch of bullshit. It was just a chance for the corporate managers to hear themselves talk while they spewed concepts at us that we were already using on a daily basis. People like Jameson needed this training session, not me.

Seven boring hours later, we were dismissed.

"Good job everyone," said Brent as everyone gathered their stuff. "Wade, can I talk to you for a minute before you go?"

With a giant smirk on his face, Brent led me out of the room and away from the other supervisors and corporate cronies.

"I gotta know. What did you think of the training?" he asked.

"There were a lot of great concepts and ideas." I was proud

of myself for that comment. I didn't lie or get myself in trouble for being too honest.

"I'm curious about something. If a manager's spot became available at your store, what would you do?" He folded his arms across his chest and waited for my reply, like a scientist studying a test subject.

"I don't know. I never really thought about it."

"Think about it now."

I thought about it and wondered exactly what it was Brent wanted to hear.

"I'd probably apply for it."

"Right now, you've got Kevin as your general manager and Lewis as the assistant, right?" I nodded. "Well, I don't want to get you excited, but with the results your store has been putting in, there are talks of adding a second assistant manager to that team. If that happens, I really hope you'll apply. Think about it. Have a safe drive."

Brent slapped me on the back and walked away.

Sawyer and Rory were leaning against the car waiting for me when I walked out of the convention centre. Actually, only Sawyer was leaning against the car. Rory was lying on the hood, sleeping.

"What was that all about?" Sawyer asked.

"He said he wanted me to apply to be a manager."

"Why? Who's gettin' fired?"

"No one. He said I should apply if a position ever opened up."

"I'll bet he wants me to apply, too."

"I'm sure he does," I said, giving him a thumbs down. "You ready to hit the road?"

"Yeah." Sawyer reached over and slapped Rory on the leg. "Hey, go fall asleep in the back seat."

The ride home was slow and quiet, especially compared to the previous two days. I was tired, and had never partied so much in such a short time.

"Hey, Sawyer, what do you say we hit the town again tonight?"

"Nah, man. Once we get back, I'm not leaving my house for at least 24 hours."

"Come on, man. You can make us some of those energy drinks and we'll hit a club. I'll even let you pick the place."

"Wade, some days you party and some days you rest. Today is a rest day. Besides, you can only keep going on those energy drinks for so long. The record is four days."

"Is that your record?"

"Shit, no. That record belongs to a friend of mine. He tried to go for a fifth."

"What happened?"

"He died. Doctors said he had a massive heart attack. The guy was a soccer player, in the best shape of his life. He was 24 and suffered a more severe heart attack than 80-year-old chain smokers have."

"Brutal."

"Yeah. So, I stick to a two day maximum rule."

"That sucks."

"Don't worry about it, man. Give yourself a couple days and we'll hit the night scene again."

"Whatever."

"What's with the 'tude, dude?"

Sawyer wasn't the guy I liked to admit weakness to, but at the same time, I felt like I had to talk to someone.

"A girl called me last night, and I kind of blew it with her."

"You didn't ask her out, did you?"

"No. I gave her my number a while ago and told her it was for customer service."

"Good job, man."

"No. Not good. She called me for actual customer service."

"Ouch. What did you do?"

"Fixed her computer."

"That's it?"

"I kind of jerked off while she was on the phone."

"Damn! Was she into it?"

"She had no idea I was doing it. At least I hope she didn't. Oh, shit. What if she knows I was jerking off?"

"You were having one-sided phone sex?"

"I was drunk!"

"All right, all right. You're not the first guy this happened to. I mean, I don't know anyone else who did it, but someone must have done it before. Anyway, fuck all that. All you can do is ride it out and wait 'til you see her next. You'll know if she knew by the way she acts."

"I thought you'd be more help than that."

"What can I say, man? I got answers for days, but no one has them all."

"Whatever."

I leaned my head against the window and spaced out for the rest of the drive.

CHAPTER 24

I lay in bed until three in the afternoon the next day and still felt like I hadn't slept in a month. Sawyer was right.

For the first time in years, I had a bath. I relaxed in the tub with the lights off and my eyes closed, trying to push the crappier events of the past couple days out of my head. When that didn't work I tried to stop thinking all together. When that didn't work I got out, ordered a pizza for dinner and watched three movies in a row.

Even though I had just crawled out of bed, and hadn't really done anything while I was out of bed, I got ready to get back into bed. When I found that comfortable groove, my cell phone rang. The excitement I felt rivaled that of a ten year old's on Christmas morning. My mind quickly flashed with possibilities of who it might be. Mike? Elizabeth? Tess?

The last thought worried me a little.

"Hello?!"

"You sound chipper," said Jameson. "How was the training?"

"Enlightening," I said, not bothering to hide my disappointment.

"Excellent. I'm glad to hear that." The man was incapable of sensing any kind of sarcasm. "You're opening with me tomorrow, right?"

"No. I've got a mid-shift tomorrow."

"Right, right, right. I knew that."

No, he didn't.

"Listen," Jameson continued. "I need you to make sure you come and see me first thing tomorrow. Before you do anything else. There's something important that I need your help with."

"What is it?"

"I can't talk about it now."

"Right. Someone could be listening."

"What? Who?"

I shook my head. "No one. It was a joke."

"I don't get it."

"I can tell. You know spy movies? Whenever people talk on the phone they say they can't talk because the line may not be secure. No? Nothing?"

"Oh, now I get it."

No, he didn't.

"I'll come see you when I get in tomorrow."

"Awesome. See you then."

"Bye."

Thursday was already off to a bad start and it was still Wednesday.

*   *   *

Jameson and I sat in the manager's room minutes after my shift started. He looked a little worried.

"Is there more money missing?" I asked.

"No. This is worse."

"What is it?"

"When I called you last night I had just been on the phone with corporate. The company is starting to suffer due to economic reasons."

That sounded bad. When retail companies didn't do well they closed down stores.

"There's nothing to worry about," Jameson continued, almost reading my mind. "However, we are going to have to trim a little fat around here."

"So, what do you want from me? Suggestions?"

"No. Selections have been made. I need you to help me inform the employees that are being let go."

"What? That's not right."

"Yes, I can see why you'd feel that way. But we all have to do what we have to do. The needs of the few and the many and all that."

"Why are you asking me? Isn't this a managerial responsibility?"

"When I talked to corporate they said they wanted you to do it to further your training."

"Is that so?"

"Well, they suggested it, and I think it's a good idea."

In other words, he doesn't want to do it, and corporate gave him a way he could pawn it off on someone else. I folded my arms and stared at the wall feeling bitter.

"This room will be yours tomorrow. I'll be here for the first half of the day to help you out, and Lewis will be in for the rest of the day. Any questions?"

"Yeah."

Jameson looked at me optimistically.

"Can we install metal detectors by tomorrow morning?"

* * *

The next day I found Jameson standing behind the customer service counter, smiling. He seemed to enjoy the fact that we were about to fire people.

"Good morning, Wade."

He pushed a stack of files toward me.

"All these people?" I asked, looking at the stack.

"I know it seems like a lot, but in the grand scheme of things it's not that many. Take your time. I don't want to rush you, so you can start whenever you're ready. Just go find them, ask them to step into the office, and inform them of the cutbacks."

"All these people are here today?"

"Yeah. Most of them were scheduled for today. I had to call a couple people in to cover a shift," Jameson said making stupid little quotes with his stupid little fingers. He slapped me on the back and walked away.

I opened the top file to see who my first victim would be. It was one of our cashiers, Julie. I didn't know her very well, but I didn't think that was going to make my job any easier.

Desperate for some procrastination, I took a walk around the store. I was actually glad to see Rory standing by the MP3 players.

"Hey, Rory," I said.

"Hey, Dub-dub. What's with you?"

"Nothing. Rough day. How are you feeling?"

"Super relative!"

He meant superlative, I think.

"What's got you so pumped?"

"You remember Taffy?"

"How could I forget?"

"She's moving in with me!"

"Are you fucking shitting me?!"

"I know. I can hardly believe it myself. She's going to dance at that strip club by the airport for a little while, but she's also going to go back to school to be a software developer."

"Well..." I had no idea what to say next. It seemed like the kind of thing Rory should have finished off with, 'just kidding.'

"Good for you, Rory."

"Thanks, Dub. Hey, do me a favor? If you see Christine, tell her you haven't seen me. I have a feeling she's going to fucking kill me."

"I thought you two were just friends."

"Yeah, I told her that, but she doesn't seem to want to accept the just friends thing. Before we left for our trip she told me we were back together."

"Told you?"

"Yeah. I always thought it took two people to have a relationship, but she told me I was wrong."

"I guess not always."

I cruised by the service desk to talk to Mike, but he was with a customer. I tried to get his attention, but he wouldn't even look in my direction. Normally he would have made a face at me when the customer wasn't looking. The man could hold resentment better than girls I dated back in high school.

A put my hands over my face and let out a big sigh. No more stalling. I found Julie near the front of the store and asked to see her in the manager's room.

I told Julie all about the company making cutbacks due to the poor economy and that it had nothing to do with her performance. I thought she took it pretty well. She was disappointed, but realized losing a retail job wasn't that big of a deal. That gave me hope for the rest of my day.

Next on my list was Terry from the Home Theatre department. He didn't take it nearly as well. He cursed me and cursed the store. Once he got to yell at me for a bit, he seemed to feel a little better and stomped out of the store.

The third file belonged to Sam from digital cameras.

Before talking to Sam I went and found Jameson who, without his beloved manager's room, was hiding out in the warehouse. I waited until we were alone before talking freely.

"Everyone you've got me letting go so far are permanent employees."

"Yeah, I know. Everyone in that list is. So what?"

"So what? We just hired a bunch of new employees. They're all probationary. We don't even need a reason to cut them loose."

"Maybe, but these cut-backs give the company just cause to let go contracted employees and then we can let the probationary ones go later, after the holidays. If we don't get rid of the contracted employees now, we won't be able to get rid of them later, since we'll no longer have the cut-backs excuse."

"At least you're admitting it's an excuse."

"Come on, Wade. You shouldn't be taking this personally. No one should be."

"Yeah, tell that to the ones losing their jobs." I walked out of the warehouse before Jameson could say something else stupid, and found Sam.

Sam was kind of happy to be let go. He said he hated his job for a long time, but didn't know if it was the right time to quit. This just made the decision for him.

A smile grew on my face when I opened the next folder.

I walked over to the audio section and found Rory having a strip torn off of him by Christine.

"You go out of town for two fucking days and now you're going to move in with some whore!" Christine was right in Rory's face, poking a finger into his chest.

"Listen, you and I were already through. I told you that, and I'm sorry, but she's a stripper, not a whore."

"Not as sorry as you're going to be, you mother fucker."

Rory saw me watching and smiling.

"Dub, can you help me out here?" he asked.

"More than you know, Rory." I turned to Christine. "Christine, can I see you in the manager's room, please?"

She pointed a finger at Rory, "I'll be right back."

Once inside the manager's room, Christine sat with a sour look on her face and her arms crossed. I had to make a serious effort not to smile.

"Christine, as you may or may not know, the economy isn't doing very well."

"Of course I fucking know. I watch the fucking news."

"Companies everywhere have no choice but to cut back a little."

"Just get to the fucking point."

"You're fired." She wanted it to the point.

"Fuck you," she said.

"Seriously, I know it's your favorite word, but can't you say anything else?"

"Fuck off. Asshole."

"You should actually consider yourself lucky."

"What the fuck for?"

"Officially, you're being laid-off due to cut backs and not fired due to your performance. Or rather your lack of performance."

"What do you..."

"Or for swearing at your co-workers all the time."

"I don't always..."

"Or for swearing at customers when they ask for help?"

"That only happened a few..."

"It doesn't matter. Time to grab your shit and go."

For the first time since meeting her, Christine was speechless and wore a helpless expression. She almost looked human. I almost felt bad for her, but a few seconds of humbleness doesn't make up for years of being a bitch.

Just like the others, I walked Christine back to the staff room so she could collect her stuff and then walked her to the front doors to make sure she didn't grab an armful of DVDs as a final farewell.

"I can't say I'm upset to see her go," said Lewis from behind me.

"Hey, Lew. What's happening?"

"Not much. How was the training and expo thing?"

"Oh, shit. They were great."

"Sure they were." Lewis knew I was lying. "Jameson told me he passed the layoffs onto you."

"Yeah. Spineless bastard."

"Even so, if you ever apply for a manager's position the fact that you've handled this kind of thing will really help."

"Whatever."

"I know it sucks. Why don't you head to the manager's room and I'll bring the next one in for you."

"Sure."

As I headed back to the manager's room Mike walked past me with a customer. He looked at me for a second, but he didn't look like the laid-back friend I was used to. His face was accusing and mistrusting. He must have suspected what I was spending my shift doing.

After a few minutes of sitting in the manager's room with my head in hands my next victim slowly opened the door and I mentally prepared myself to be empathetic. What I was prepared for was the guy who walked in.

It was Dev.

He sat down across the table and grinned at me.

"What's up, boss man? Lewis said you needed to see me."

"You?"

"Me."

I stared at him. I was shocked and angry at the same time. Jameson had lined me up to fire my best employee. Realization washed over Dev's face as I continued to sit and stare with my mouth hanging slightly open.

"Cutbacks, huh?" Dev said.

"Dev, I didn't..." I struggled with my words as if I was just learning to talk. I knew what I wanted to say, but no idea how to say it.

"Dev, the economy... The company has been taking big hits."

"So, that's it, huh? I'm fired?"

I looked at Dev in disbelief. Hearing him say the words pushed me back into shock again. The room felt like it was getting smaller. I stood from my chair.

"No, Dev. You're not fired. Wait here."

I stormed out of the room and almost knocked over Lewis, who had been standing just outside the door.

"Is everything all right?" he asked.

"No! Everything is not all right!" I wasn't yelling, but I was close. "That's Dev in there, man. Dev! He's one of our best. One of my best. And you want me to fire him? That's not happening. Not today, not ever!"

Lewis held up his hands defensively. "Listen, I don't like it either. Kevin made these picks."

"Call him. Right now."

"Wade, trust me, there's no changing his mind. For what it's worth, I tried to argue on a few of his choices. It's no use."

"I haven't tried..."

"Wade," he interrupted. "I hate to say it, but either you go in there and do this or I will. And I think you'll be a little nicer about it than I would be."

I was furious. I didn't want to go back in and face Dev, but I couldn't let Lewis go in there to be cold and blunt.

When I walked back into the manager's room Dev was already standing.

"You don't need to say anything," he said. "Just know that you and Lewis and Jameson can all go fuck yourselves." He turned on the spot and left the room muttering.

I left the room and found Lewis.

"I'm going home. The rest are on you." I didn't wait for his reply. I wasn't done with the task I was given. I wasn't even done with my shift, but I stormed out as if I was the latest person fired.

I went straight home. I didn't eat. I didn't watch TV or play video games. I just sat on my couch and fantasized about telling Jameson off. When I grew bored of that I fantasized about physically beating the crap out of him.

I stayed up half the night figuring out exactly what I was going to say to him and thought of every rebuttal I would need for anything he could say in return. My mind was still considering comebacks when I passed out from exhaustion.

CHAPTER 25

I woke up in the morning lying awkwardly on my couch, still in my store uniform. I felt like I had only slept a few hours.

My eyes were gritty and puffy. I sat for a long time, my brain struggling to put thoughts together. Did I have to be up? What time did I work? What day was it? Then I remembered the firings and added anger to my condition.

It was Saturday and I had the morning shift.

I went in as I was. I didn't eat breakfast. I didn't shower. I didn't change my clothes. I didn't brush my teeth or comb my hair. I just went in.

Jameson had traded shifts with Lewis, which meant all the rehearsing I did the previous night and on the drive to work was for nothing.

The store wasn't open yet, so I took the opportunity to head back to the repair desk and confront Mike without any customers around. I knew he was scheduled for the morning, but there was no sign of him around the desk.

I ran back to the front of the store and barged into the manager's room where Lewis was pretending to go over the previous day's numbers.

"Did you fire Mike?" I demanded.

"What?"

"Mike. Did Jameson have you fire him?"

"No. Mike called in sick today."

I felt embarrassed. Lewis didn't deserve to be yelled at. Jameson did. But it was a relief that Mike still had a job.

"Do you think Jameson switched shifts with you just to avoid me?"

"I really doubt it, Wade." Lewis stopped paying attention to me and went back to his numbers. As angry as I was, I wasn't going to take any more of my anger out on Lewis.

I sent a quick text message to Mike telling him to feel better.

For the first time in a long time, I started stocking shelves. Stocking shelves wasn't fun, but customers were a little more reluctant to bother someone arms full of product. It was just what I needed to keep my mind occupied.

I stocked shelves like it my only purpose in life. After a few hours I had stocked all the shelves in my department and I moved on to the shelves of other departments. No one seemed to mind. Not only was it keeping my anger from erupting, not one customer had approached me.

That never could have lasted.

I was shelving memory cards in the digital camera department when a short twenty-something girl walked up to me. She didn't say anything to me, she just walked up to me while talking on her cell phone.

"I know. I know. I know. I told her if she's embarrassed to

admit that she was out with him, she probably shouldn't be out with him in the first place. I know. I know."

I looked at her for a few seconds, but when she didn't ask for any kind of help I turned to walk away. She snapped her fingers and starting motioning toward the cameras and then toward the cards, all while continuing her phone conversation.

"I know. She's totally lying to herself. I was like, whatever, bitch. Please. I know. Totally. I know."

"Do you need help with something?" I asked.

"Can I call you back, or something. The guy here isn't getting it. K. Bye."

"I assume I'm the guy," I said.

"What guy?" she asked, dripping with attitude.

"The guy who's not getting it."

"Obviously. I was saying that I need a memory card for my camera. A bigger one. One that holds like a zillion pictures."

"A zillion, huh? That's a lot. What kind of camera do you have?"

"A digital one."

"As opposed to the film cameras that take memory cards. Do you remember what brand it is or what kind of card it takes?"

"I don't know. It's silver and the card that goes in it is really small."

"Congratulations. You just described every camera and every type of memory card." The combination of sleep deprivation, my shitty mood and dumb customers disabled all my mental editing equipment. In a situation like that I could end up saying just about anything.

"Um... I think it's an LG," she guessed.

I sighed heavily. LG didn't make digital cameras. Unless you counted the little camera integrated into some of their cell phones.

"Look," I said. "I gotta go, cause you're just not getting it."

"What's your fucking problem?" she said sounding like a whiny high school girl.

"In general? A lot of things. More immediately, you and how much of a bitch you think you can be to people because so far in life you've been spoiled by your parents and you were the hot girl in high school. Guess what. Your parents aren't going to spoil you forever and you're looks are going to fade. From what I can see, they're already fading. No offense."

I had never seen someone look so offended in all my life.

"How the hell am I supposed to not take offense to that?"

"I don't think there is a way not to be offended. It's just one of those things I felt like I had to say."

She stormed off without another word. I watched her march up to the customer service desk and freak out on Lewis while pointing at me.

I went back to stocking shelves.

It was 15 minutes later when Lewis came and found me.

"I just got a pretty big complaint about you."

"I know."

"Was it warranted?"

"Yeah, I'd say so."

"I can't remember ever getting a complaint about you."

"There's a first for everything."

"She wanted you fired."

"Too bad. Firings were yesterday."

Lewis sighed.

"Go home, Wade."

"I'm fired?"

"No, but you're going home for today. You're burnt out. I've seen it before. I've had it myself. Take the day off, and if I were you I'd consider calling in sick tomorrow. You need some rest."

For all his faults, Lewis really was a good guy.

On my way home I stopped to fill up my car with gas. The dude behind the counter reminded me of Jack Black, except he wasn't funny. He was just short and fat.

He looked at me for a few seconds, nodding.

"How's your day going?" he asked.

I slapped my money down on the counter and said, "I didn't sleep worth shit last night, I had to fire a bunch of people that I really like yesterday, and my best friend hates me. I hate my idiot boss, I hate my bullshit job, and I hate my fucked up life." I walked out without another word.

On my way out the door I heard the Jack Black look-a-like mutter, "Holy shit."

*　　*　　*

Despite being the afternoon, I went straight home and crawled into bed, falling asleep within seconds.

I dreamed I was working. It wasn't lucid dreaming. If it had been I would have spent the dream kicking over store shelves and punching customers.

In my dream, Tony Danza wanted to buy a computer and was asking all kinds of ridiculous questions. Questions that didn't make any sense. Questions about hardware that didn't even exist in computers.

Fear has been known to wake someone from a dream, if their terrified enough. Sad dreams can cause the dreamer to wake when they start crying hard enough. For the first time in my life I had woken up from a dream out of frustration.

The clock on my nightstand said I had only been sleeping for half an hour.

I closed my eyes and transported back to the store.

"Oh, there you are." Tony Danza was still there, waiting for me.

I immediately woke up. Not even five minutes had passed.

I sat up in bed, forcing my eyes to stay open, waiting for the dream to completely dissipate.

Whenever I had a great dream, like making out with Kate Beckinsale, once I woke up it was over. There was no going back, even if I was able to go right back to sleep.

When I fell asleep a third time the store and Tony Danza were still there.

"Oh!" I wailed. "Tony Danza, what do you want?"

"Eh, oh! Oh, eh! I told you, I just want a computer."

I woke up again. I would never enjoy an episode of *Who's the Boss?* for the rest of my life.

Half stupid with sleep, I moved from the bed to the couch. As if the dream would stay in the bedroom if I moved to the living room.

"Where do you keep going?" asked Tony Danza.

"Away from you. It's not working."

"So, listen. This computer that we're looking at here, does it have a flux capacitor?"

"A flux capacitor? You weren't in *Back to the Future*."

"No. But, it's within my six."

"Your six?"

"Yeah. I was on Taxi with Christopher Lloyd, and he was Doc Brown. So it's okay if I borrow."

I looked around my dream world to see if there was anything I could stab myself with. Urban legend always said dying in a dream meant waking up or dying in real life. I was willing to accept either.

"So, kid, does it have one, or not?"

I woke up and punched at the air. It was still early afternoon.

"Fuck this."

Half an hour later I stood in my local drugstore comparing brands of sleep aids.

I had never resorted to sleep aids before, so I had no idea what I was looking for. I laughed a little at the directions they had printed on the box.

Step 1: Remove tablets from package. Step 2: Take tablets orally. Step 3: Sleep.

The only difference was that each brand had its own way of injecting the brand name into step 3. Sleep EZ said, Step 3: Sleep EZ. Good Night brand said, Step 3: Say Good Night! It was all a little ridiculous. I decided to go with something I trusted and grabbed a bottle of NyQuil.

On my way up to the counter I noticed Sawyer standing in one of the aisles. He was wearing dark sunglasses and had the hood of his sweater pulled up, but he generally wasn't the type of dude that went unnoticed.

"Who are you hiding from?" I said, walking down the aisle.

"Wade. Ain't you supposed to be at work or something?"

"Yeah, but I got the day off for telling off a customer."

"You told off a customer?"

"Yeah. It was kind of funny."

"Damn, man. You better watch it. Messing with a customer is one thing, but straight out telling them off? That shit can get you in trouble, man."

I tried to look at what Sawyer had in his hand, but all I could see was a corner of a blue box. Sawyer had the rest of the box casually hidden behind his back. I looked at the shelves we were standing in front of and scanned for blue boxes. There were only two. Either Sawyer was fighting off a nasty yeast infection, or...

"You're buying a home pregnancy test?" I said.

"Dude, keep your voice down."

"Are you going to be a daddy?" I whispered.

"Nah, nah, nah, man. I don't know. I hope not."

"I never thought..."

"If you mention this to anyone, I'll make you regret it."

"Don't worry about it. I'm just here for something to make me sleep."

"That's NyQuil."

"Works, doesn't it?"

Just then I caught a glimpse of an attractive Asian pharmacist who was watching me and Sawyer. When our eyes met she smiled.

"Maybe I should take her home, too."

Sawyer turned and looked at the girl.

"No, man. You don't want to mess with that. I know that girl. She gets around a little too much. Not real clean, if you know what I'm saying."

A second woman appeared at the counter beside the first and was a mirror image.

"Her twin isn't any cleaner, if you're curious," Sawyer said.

I stared at the twins before busting out laughing uncontrollably. Sawyer looked like he wanted to step away from me and pretend we were strangers.

"What's wrong with you, man?" he asked.

With considerable effort I stopped laughing long enough to say, "Take two and don't call them in the morning." I erupted with more laughter. Even Sawyer cracked a smile.

Based on Sawyer's advice, I didn't even go and talk to them. I wasn't about to give myself the gift of genital warts for a one-nighter. Besides, I was too tired to please one woman. Two would have killed me.

Once I got to my apartment and still felt like sleep was going to be difficult. I stared at my cell phone for a while, trying to will it into receiving text messages from someone. Anyone.

I thought about Elizabeth and wondered if she would ever call. She was smart not to give me her phone number. I would have called her right then. I didn't have numbers for any of the girls I wanted to call. I felt like talking to someone. I scrolled through my contact list considering who to call when the names started going blurry. The NyQuil I had taken was starting to kick in and I stretched out on my couch just in time to fall into a black hole.

The store wasn't there. Tony Danza wasn't there. No one was there. Nothing was there. Of course, I didn't realize any of that until I woke up later that night and smiled at not being able to remember any dream at all.

CHAPTER 26

I slept for more than 12 hours. I was starving when I finally woke.

There were a few options in nearly bare fridge, but they required effort and minor cooking. I wasn't willing to put forth either one.

It was too late for any restaurants to be open. Even late night drive-thrus were closed. I resorted to the only place you can in such situations. 7-11.

I knew I wasn't going to find a nutritious and satisfying meal at 7-11, but I didn't care. I grabbed bags of Doritos, bottles of pop, chocolate bars, and then I came upon the freezer section. They had Pizza Pops, burritos and oven pizzas, all at ridiculously high prices, but who was their competition at 4 AM?

I brought a mountain of junk food up to the counter. The girl behind the counter gave me a look that I could only describe as disgust.

"It's grocery day," I joked.

"I'll bet." She humored me with a forced smile.

Even with the bitchy look, I could see she was attractive. She was tall, skinny and didn't have a lot of curves, but still enough for me to look at. Her height alone that made her appealing to me. I had always wanted to be with a girl who was taller than me, like being with some kind of Amazonian woman.

"Are you all by yourself tonight?"

She stopped dead in her tracks. "Listen, buddy, we've got security surveillance and I've got all kinds of self-defense classes under my belt."

"Calm down. I'm not here to rob or rape or anything like that. Just weird to see a lady working the graveyard shift alone."

She made a sound of pure disapproval. "Tell that to my manager. Company policy says two people at night, for safety, but he puts extra people on during the day so he doesn't have to lift a finger."

"Sounds like a manager."

"Speaking from experience?"

"Yeah. Not convenience store experience. Real retail." As soon as the last two words left my lips I shut my mouth and closed my eyes tight.

"Real retail, huh?"

"I didn't mean it like that, but come on."

"Whatever. Your total is forty-seven fifty."

"I just spent fifty bucks at 7-11?"

"Yeah. How's that feel?"

"Hey, if you need to wind down after your shift I could meet you somewhere. Maybe have a drink or something?"

She seemed to look at me for the first time. Before she had just been looking through another asshole customer. Now she was seeing an actual person.

"Even though I am done in a couple hours, where the hell are we going to get a drink at this time in the morning?" she asked.

"My place is still serving. I won't even ID you."

She laughed and handed me my bag of groceries.

"Give me your address, and save me that Snickers bar."

* * *

While I waited for the 7-11 girl, whose name I didn't know, I marveled at how well the direct approach had worked. I sent a text message to Sawyer telling him all about it. He replied back that he was proud of me but I shouldn't expect it to work ever again.

The 7-11 girl showed up as the sun was rising, still wearing her uniform. I handed her the Snickers bar as she walked into the apartment. She smiled and tucked it into her purse.

She wandered around the apartment, snooping, touching whatever she pleased. When she reached the bedroom she took off her clothes and lied down on the bed.

"Your clothes. Off," she said, pointing at me.

I stripped down and got onto the bed with her. I tried to kiss her, but she put a hand over my mouth.

"I don't want to kiss right now." This chick was strange. I started to wonder if she was a hooker and thought I had contracted her services.

"OK. What then?"

"Just fuck me."

This was the kind of thing I had only read about.

"Don't kiss me unless I say so," she warned.

It turns out sex with an Amazon isn't that hot. She lay there giving me orders on how to move, how fast to go, how to hold her legs. It was like having sex with a robot. A really life-like robot. Except this robot didn't have an off switch.

After we finished, or rather after she finished and told me to 'hurry up,' we fell asleep for a few hours. That made me pretty sure she wasn't a hooker. I had never hired a hooker before, but I always imagined they would leave afterwards.

When I woke up again it was almost noon.

I checked my cell phone. Mike hadn't called or returned a single one of my messages. Despite feeling a little bitter about that, I dialed Mike's phone number and waited. I even intended on apologizing, even if I wasn't the one at fault.

The phone rang three times before the call disconnected. I dialed the number again. It rang four times, then went dead.

"Who are you calling?" asked the 7-11 girl.

"A friend of mine."

Re-dialing, the phone rang three times before I heard the call connect. No one spoke, but I head background noise.

"Mike?"

The phone went dead again.

"Shit," I said. I turned and looked at the 7-11 girl. "He hasn't been talking to me. Now he keeps hanging up on me when I call."

"So, you pissed him off. Who cares?"

This poor girl just wanted some simple sex after work and now she had to suffer my bottled up rage.

"Get out!"

"What?"

I stood up and looked down at her.

"GET THE FUCK OUT OF HERE!"

She scrambled to get her clothes on while moving toward the door, all while I yelled, "Get out! Get out! Get out!"

I didn't care how much I was upsetting her. The 7-11 girl was much like her place of employment. Convenient, but not great.

Once I was able to slam the door with her on the other side of it, I poured myself a drink. 'Drink' is a loose term in this case. It was whiskey. In a glass.

I emptied the glass in a swallow and the second wasn't far behind the first. Halfway through my third glass I called in sick to work. I was supposed to close, but I was going to be too drunk to go anywhere or do anything.

I hung out with the bottle all the night. The emptier it got the less I cared about women I didn't understand, friends who were mad at me or my soul-destroying job. I hadn't stopped caring completely, but I was determined to keep trying.

It didn't seem that long ago that my life seemed pretty okay. What happened? What changed? Did I change or was it the circumstances around me that changed? Whatever changed, I wanted to change it back. I needed to change it back. I looked at my bottle of whiskey wondering if I had enough to change it back.

I woke up, thought I didn't remember falling asleep, sitting on my kitchen floor. Bottle still in hand I put it to my lips and tipped it back.

Wasn't that full? I wondered to myself.

It was minutes before midnight. It should have been obvious that I was too drunk to go anywhere, but I decided to leave my apartment anyway. And like a drunken idiot, I was convinced that I was fine to drive wherever I was going. Thankfully, I was too drunk to find my keys.

I left anyway and began walking. I had no destination. My feet decided where I was going. I followed the sidewalk and when I needed to turn, I turned. When I needed to cross a street, I crossed.

When I eventually stopped to take notice of my surroundings I found myself standing in front of the store.

"Fuck," I said.

Then I remembered the bar across the street and practically ran to The Draft.

A blaring car horn snapped me to attention. I was in the middle of the street, a car had stopped a few feet from running me down. Despite being the one at fault, I displayed my middle finger before continuing to the bar. I was lucky I didn't get my ass kicked.

I walked into the bar and tried to look sober. By the look on the bartender's face, I wasn't doing a very good job.

"OK, pal. Hit the road."

"No. I want a drink."

"There's no way I'm serving you tonight."

"Has Mikey been in here tonight?" Even I could hear my words running into each other.

"I don't know who you're talking about, but I think you need to go home and sleep it off."

I got into the bartender's face and slammed my hands on the bar top.

"I said I want a god damn drink! Do your fucking job!"

The bartended pointed a finger at me.

"Either you leave now on your own, or you leave in 10 minutes with the cops."

"Ricky!" a woman called from another part of the bar. "Rick!" The voice was getting closer.

Soft hands were laid on my shoulders, but I could only stare at the bartender with my newfound rage.

"Ricky, can you bring some black coffee? Please?" the voice pleaded with the bartender.

"This guy with you?" the bartended asked.

"He's a friend. He's not normally like this."

I turned to look at the woman who the voice belonged to. The voice that was defending me. Becky was standing behind me, soothingly stroking my arms and talking to the bartender over my shoulder.

"All right. He can have some coffee, but another outburst like that and friend of yours or not, he's out of here."

Becky led me to a booth off to the side of the bar.

"What the hell, Wade?" she said. "What's going on with you?"

"Hi, Becks. Thanks for helping me out with that asshole back there. He new here or something?"

"Wade, I saw the whole thing, and you're the asshole."

"Shit, whatever, Becks. Hey! You got any of your hot friends here tonight?"

"I heard you called in sick tonight," she said. "I'm guessing you don't have a cold."

"I was sick. But it turns out whiskey is the cure."

"Says who?"

"I read it."

"Where?"

"I read it online."

"Where online?"

"At... home remedies dot... org."

"You're lying."

"You gotta put the www first."

"Wade, stop it."

"All lowercase."

"Wade!"

I stared at her. Anger flashed across her eyes. Who could blame her? She was probably having a good night before her drunken idiot of a friend burst into the bar picking a fight with the bartender.

Ricky came over with a pot of coffee and two mugs. He watched me, waiting for any reason to grab me by the collar and toss me out the door.

"Hey, buddy," he said. "Whatever it is, it's not worth doing this to yourself."

I couldn't believe that this man who didn't know me, and had just been in a yelling match with me, was showing me sympathy. In my drunken state I felt like crying and giving him a hug.

"Let me know if you need more," he said to Becky before returning to his bar.

"Oh," I groaned. "I am an asshole."

"Told you. What happened? I've never seen you like this."

"I don't know."

"You don't know or you don't want to talk about it?"

"Both, I guess. I think I'm too drunk to tell."

"Here." She poured a cup of coffee and pushed it over to me. "Drink that then I'll take you home."

*　　*　　*

I made jokes about Jameson as Becky drove me back to my apartment. She smiled, but didn't say much. She walked me into my apartment building and right up to my front door.

"Thanks, Beck," I said. I felt my face grow hot and I couldn't look her in the face.

"Don't mention it. Get some sleep."

"I will. Back to work tomorrow afternoon."

"Glad to hear it."

I thought I saw something familiar in her eyes.

"Can I have a hug?" I asked.

"Of course." Without hesitating Becky stepped into my outstretched arms and wrapped her own around me. It felt great. It felt like I was in love.

When she began pulling away from me I leaned in and kissed her. She gently shoved me away.

"Wade," she said, shaking her head.

I forced my way back to her and kissed her again. She pushed me a little harder this time.

"Wade, stop it."

One more time, I forced myself on her, this time wrapping my arms around her as I went in for the kiss. She shoved me hard and punched me on the chin.

I hit the floor and watched Becky stomp away, muttering about how much of an asshole I was. Ten minutes passed before I was able to force myself to my feet and open my apartment door.

The place was trashed. Even more than I had left it.

When I had been unable to find my keys, I left anyway. Without my keys I had had no choice but to leave the door unlocked. I didn't even remember closing the door behind me.

I knew I was robbed by two guys because they were still there when I stumbled into the apartment. They stopped in the middle of putting some of my movies into grocery bags when they noticed me standing there.

"Grocery bags?" I said. "Can't you criminals afford duffel bags? Or those brown sacks that have the little dollar signs on the side?"

They tensed, eyes flickering from me to the doorway. All three of us stood there not moving and not saying anything. It was actually kind of awkward.

Finally, I broke the silence with, "I'm going to kick both your asses."

I took one step forward before turning and running to the bathroom. I slid to my knees in front of the bathtub and puked until I was bringing up stomach bile. I lay on the bathroom floor panting, my head swimming and my vision fading to black.

I heard one of the burglars say, "Get more bags. We got time," before I passed out.

CHAPTER 27

I woke up on the bathroom floor with a variety of pain. I was stiff from sleeping in an awkward position, my stomach hurt from sleeping on top of a toilet brush, my head hurt from the hangover that got up a half hour before me, and my jaw hurt from Becky's wicked uppercut.

When I left the bathroom and surveyed my apartment I was somewhat shocked to see it had been burglarized. "Shit. I thought I dreamt that."

I filed a report with the police over the phone and was told an officer would be over to my apartment shortly.

Until then I walked around my apartment and tried to get an idea of what was missing.

I wondered if the crooks even bothered to see if I had choked to death on my own vomit. It was the least they could do.

I stood in the kitchen sipping water and trying not to throw up when an officer arrived an hour later. He slowly walked around my apartment examining things.

"Do you know what's missing?" he asked.

"Not a lot. Video games. Movies."

He started to nod.

"We've been seeing a lot of that lately. Approximately when did it happen?"

"Late last night." I stopped and considered what I was saying. "Technically, early this morning."

"Why didn't you report it earlier?"

"I walked in on them last night while they were still burglarizing the place. I tried to stop them, but I was drunk. Really drunk."

"That's no way to spend your life, son."

"You're right. But it's not a bad way to spend a couple of days out of a life, right?" I joked. The smile quickly faded from my face when I saw the officer didn't think it was the least bit funny.

"I see," was his only reply.

"I was out cold until about an hour ago."

"I can assume then, that they're the ones that gave you that bruise on your chin?" he said tapping a pen on his own chin.

I raised an eyebrow and felt at my chin. I hissed at how sensitive it was. Rather than explaining how I really got the bruise, I nodded.

He walked over and looked closely at the door.

"Your door looks fine, how did they get in?"

"This is embarrassing," I said, hanging my head. "I kind of left the door unlocked."

"So, they must have picked the lock?"

"No. I said I left the door open."

"I gotta tell you, it's a good thing you didn't just leave the door open, cause you can't make an insurance claim if that was the case. Just to verify, you said they probably picked the lock, right?"

"Absolutely. They must have picked the lock."

The officer nodded.

"Thanks for that," I said, feeling my face get hot. "Where do we go from here?"

"Well, I go back to the station, file my report and then we go after these bastards." He made gestures with his hands in an attempt to make a stronger point.

"You don't have to give me false hope."

"Oh, thank God!" His shoulders and face relaxed at the same time. "I can't tell you how hard it is to try and tell people we're going to catch the people that commit these petty crimes. Don't get me wrong. We'll probably catch these guys, but we won't be able to connect them with this robbery."

"Thanks for being honest."

"In the future, remember to lock your door and try not to drink so much." He walked out of my apartment with his head held high.

Who the fuck was this guy to tell me not to drink so much? Sure he did me a big favor, but so what? I felt like going to the liquor store and buying enough booze to stay drunk for a week, just to give him a big 'fuck you.'

The thought was derailed by an ache in my jaw. I thought about how much of an asshole I had been to Becky. I wondered what she thought of me that morning. Did she know I was too drunk to know better, or was she registering for membership in the 'I Hate Wade Club'?

I wanted to call in sick again. I didn't want to face Becky, or Mike for that matter. I sulked around my apartment for a while weighing my options. Consecutive sick days required a doctor's note. I could have bullshit a doctor into giving me a note, but I just didn't feel like making the effort. Plus, my movies and video games were stolen.

The entire time I got ready for work and the entire drive to the store I felt like I was on my way to something important. Like a job interview or my own death sentence. I felt like I had a drawer full of knives in my stomach and they were all pointing out. I wasn't sure if it was the hangover or nerves.

Walking through the store it seemed like every pair of eyes was on me. Instead of my cheeks getting warm and red, I felt slimy. Each person that added their glare to the crowd's made my skin greasier.

I wondered if they were looking at me because I had been missing for a few days or because I was the guy who had fired several people. Or maybe they heard that I had become some kind of alcoholic and they were watching for my next drunken episode. I felt hated and somewhat feared. Then I saw Megan.

She looked at me the exact same way she had looked at me the week before and the same way she had looked at me the day we met. Without saying a word, she invited me to come and talk to her. She wasn't judging me and she was willing to listen.

I didn't go to her though. I couldn't. It seemed easier to just let everyone hate me. So I just walked past her along with everyone else.

I felt a hand clap me hard on the shoulder. I turned to find myself face to face with Jameson who had a huge smile on his face.

"Welcome back, Wade. I can't tell you how glad I am to have you back."

There was a long list of people that I didn't want to see at that moment, and Jameson was at the top of it. I could only bring myself to nod in response since I was pretty sure if I opened my mouth I would start yelling obscenities at him.

"I have a few things to take care of, but we should talk later. Again, really glad to have you back, champ."

I nodded again as he walked away.

I walked back to my department. My entire team watched me from afar. I assumed they were pissed at me because of Dev. I couldn't blame them.

"Yeah. I'm looking for a computer," said a man from behind me.

I turned and found a pompous looking prick that didn't even look up from his cell phone to talk to me.

"Over here," he said walking away.

I sighed. "Sure."

He stopped in front of a tower and finished typing a message on his phone before finally looking at me.

"OK. So, this is the one." He motioned to the machine we were standing in front of.

"Great. Want me to bring it to the front of the store for you?"

"If I buy it, sure."

"You said this was the one you wanted."

"It is. But I need you to tell me what the price is."

I pointed at the large price tag stuck to the computer.

"All our prices are on display for your convenience." I could already hear the bitterness seeping into my tone.

"I know what the price tag says. What I need to know is how much I'm going to pay for this computer."

"You mean you want to know what it's going to be after taxes?" I knew he didn't mean that. He wanted a discount.

"Maybe I'm not talking to the right guy."

"You are," I said. Usually I would have dicked with him for a while longer, but I didn't feel like it. "I can knock off fifty bucks." A token gesture.

He grimaced. "I'm afraid that's just not going to cut it."

"Sorry. We don't make a lot of money on computers. I can't do any better."

"But you make some money on them, right?" he asked.

"Sure."

"How much are you making on this computer?"

"Right now? Nothing."

"Right. If we can talk seriously for a minute, if I were to buy it and pay what was on the price tag, how much would you make?"

"Well, on a serious note, we'd make about $200. Probably a bit less."

"Was that so hard?" he asked.

"Nope."

"I feel like you've got a sale on your hands if you can knock off that $200."

"I'll bet you do."

"Excuse me?"

"What do you do for a living?" I asked leaning on the computer we were haggling over.

"I thought we were talking about the computer."

"Forget the computer. What do you do?"

The prick put his fists on his hips, trying to look authoritative.

"Not that it's any of your business, but I'm an investment specialist. What's it to you?"

"I have an investment question for you."

"This should be interesting." We were battling to see who the bigger prick was. It was a tie so far.

"Why do you want the economy in the shitter?"

"I don't want the economy in the shitter."

"You must. Tonight you walked into this store and demanded that I sell you a computer with zero profit. You probably do that a lot. Let's say all businesses started doing that. You'd probably be pretty proud of yourself, cause you'd be saving a lot of money. But then all businesses go bankrupt since they're not making profit. All those jobs are lost. People aren't buying as much anymore, and even if they are, there aren't any businesses left to sell anything. Since nothing is being bought or sold the stock market basically doesn't exist. Now you're out of a job and robbing some little old lady for a loaf of bread. And it all started because you wanted a cheap computer. Seems a bit selfish, doesn't it?"

He looked at me for a minute with a shit eating grin on his face. It was the kind of smile that pricks wore when they were angry. What kind of idiot smiles when he's angry?

"You know something?" said the prick. "You're a real asshole."

I slowly climbed on top of the waist high shelves that displayed all the desktop computers and raised my arms.

"People!" All the customers and employees nearby looked in my direction. "You need to understand something once and for all. We. Don't. Like. You. It takes every last bit of my energy not to yell at you every day. You come in here saying stupid shit like, 'the customer is always right', and 'what can you do for me?' We don't want to do shit for you. In our eyes, you're all pompous mother fuckers that think you're entitled to shit you don't deserve.

"No, we won't give you a discount. The cheapest shit in the store is cheap because it's shit. If we sell out of something that was an advertised sale, that means you lose out and you should have gotten here sooner. You're terrible human beings yet you somehow find ways to blame us for it. I don't even know how that's possible, but you did it.

"I have some advice for you, so listen up. When you come in here, treat people with respect. Listen to our advice. Pay the prices you see printed on the tags. Say, thank you, and get the fuck out! If you choose not to take my recommendation then you can all fuck off and I hope to see you in hell."

Jameson ran up to me with his mouth hanging open.

"Manager's room. Now."

I hopped down from the shelf and stormed away from my audience. Angry shouts erupted from the crowd, some of them even tried to follow me for a physical altercation.

I heard Jameson trying to defuse the situation as I walked away, "Folks, what can I say? We all get stressed from time to time. I can assure you he didn't mean any of that."

Once in the manager's room I sat with my arms crossed and waited. Jameson burst in a few moments later, his face a shade of red I had never seen before.

"Give me one fucking reason why I shouldn't fire your ass right now."

I looked at him and grinned. "You know what? I can't think of a single one."

"Lewis told me you were having problems, but I didn't want to believe it. I lied to myself saying you were just sick. What's going on with you?"

"I don't know."

"Fuck, Wade. You're the best out there. My go-to guy. Besides Lewis, there's no one I depend on more than you."

"I guess I'm really letting you down, then."

"Lewis told me you were upset about Dev, but come on, man."

"Come on, what?"

"Did you really trust him?"

"Yeah. One hundred percent." I came to life, unfolding my arms, standing from my chair and letting my voice rise.

"Wade, you can never trust those people one hundred percent."

"Those people? You obnoxious fucking prick."

"Watch it, buddy. You're close to unemployed. Don't push me."

"Fuck you."

"You know what?" Jameson continued. "I know you better than this. You're still sick. I remember one time when the flu snuck up on me. I didn't even realize I had it, but for a week I was bitchy and just not myself."

"Sounds like a menstrual cycle."

"Ignoring that, you're clearly still sick. Therefore, you'll go home right now and come back tomorrow when you're feeling better. OK?"

I sat staring at Jameson with a hundred things on my mind that I wanted to shout at him. Things all the way from how inept he was to how short he was. I had to say something. He wasn't going to let me go until I said something.

"Whatever."

He grinned, happy in the belief that he had resolved in issue.

Before leaving the store I spent $800 on my credit card and left with a new XBOX and a whole library of games.

CHAPTER 28

My night was spent playing the new video games. That continued into the early morning, and late morning, and early afternoon. My mind had been so occupied with killing zombies that I had forgotten to sleep. My stomach growled, reminding me that I had also forgotten to eat. Not only was I avoiding sleep and food, I was scheduled to work in an hour.

I called in sick. Video games were way more fun than customers. Sleep could wait a little longer, but I did need to take care of my hunger before anything else.

I didn't feel like cooking anything.

Fifteen minutes later I was standing in Taco Bell looking over their menu. Two high school girls were in line in front of me spewing words at each other.

"Oh, my god, so like, Tim, in my English class..." Her voice rose every few words, making it sound like she was asking a litany of questions. "He was totally bugging me today. He kept like, putting stuff on my shoulder, 'cause he sits behind me, and I was like 'stop it', but he just kept doing it all class." That was all from the first girl and it only took her a few seconds to say it.

"Oh, my god! That sounds like Ryan in my math class. He sits behind me too, and the whole class, he like, kicked the back of my feet, cause I like to keep my feet tucked underneath my chair, and he like kicked my feet for like a whole class."

I wasn't trying to listen to their conversation, but I couldn't block it out. It was so annoying and yet too close to me to ignore. If I closed my eyes I couldn't tell which one was talking.

"I told Tim if he didn't stop it I was going to like, tell Mrs. Norris and he like, laughed at me. He's so stupid."

"Ryan kept kicking me, then he'd say 'sorry' and like laugh after."

"He told me to go ahead and tell Mrs. Norris cause he didn't care or whatever."

"I said I knew he wasn't sorry and he was just being a jerk."

"Then he started poking me in the back with his finger."

"So he started kicking harder and kept saying 'sorry' and laughing."

"And it started to hurt 'cause he was poking me like so hard."

"I know. The kicks were starting to hurt, too."

I was amazed. They were having two completely different conversations with each other. I never wished to be deaf before that day. The stupidity washed over me and I felt like weeping for the next generations of our planet.

One of them noticed my blank stare.

"What the fuck are you looking at, creep?"

"I'm sorry," I said. "It took me a minute to realize that was a real question."

"What are you talking about?" said the other girl.

"Nothing."

"Oh my God. Loser," said the first girl.

I had tried to avoid a confrontation. They just couldn't let that happen. I leaned in close to the two girls.

"And you two little bitches are the stupidest sounding people I've heard all week, and I work in retail. There are far better things to talk about than a couple of retarded boys that won't stop bothering you during math class. Here's a tip: start sucking their dicks. They'll stop. I promise you, they will stop. But in the end, if you two are a representation of the girls at your school then I feel bad for all the guys. 'Cause during a time when they should be chasing tail and having reckless sex, they have to listen to you talk. Now order your food and fuck off."

"Whatever, loser." They spoke in unison, like they shared one brain. That meant they each only had half a brain, which made a lot of sense.

I ate in the dining room. I felt compelled to spend thirty consecutive minutes outside of my apartment. My own dwellings were increasing my depression.

When I got back to my apartment I watched one of the crappy movies that hadn't been stolen. I was nodding off to sleep on the couch when my intercom buzzed. I woke up and lay there, wondering if I had dreamed the buzzing sound or if it had been real. My eyes slide shut when the buzzing came again.

"Hello?" I said into the two-way system.

"Hey," was all that came back.

"Who is it?"

There was a long pause. "It's Mike."

Now it was my turn to pause. "Hey. What's up?" A few days ago I would have shouted for joy. That was no longer an option after the amount of times I had reached out to him only to be ignored.

"We should talk."

I hit the button to unlock the door and sat on my couch again. Minutes later there was a quiet knock on the door and Mike cautiously stepped into my apartment.

"Hey, Mike." I stood up from the couch to face him. "I didn't think you'd ever step foot in this apartment again."

"I felt some moral obligation to make sure you weren't lying a pool of your own vomit."

"You've been talking to Becky."

"Yeah."

"Does she hate me?"

"No, she doesn't hate you. She doesn't really like you very much, though."

I rubbed my jaw. The pain had dulled a little.

"Mike, you gotta know that I didn't blow you off on purpose to hang out with Jameson. I would never do that."

"I know that now. Just took me a bit to realize."

I grabbed two bottles of beer from the fridge and passed one to Mike. He took it with a smile.

"Are you sure you should be drinking?"

"We've missed out on a lot of beer together. No point in wasting time. You're just lucky that I actually have two beers left in this place."

We each took a long drink of beer.

"I wish I could say I only came over to make amends, but I didn't. You gotta go back to work, man. You gotta be the old you again."

"Why? What's going on?"

"Jameson's walking around the store telling people that he's going to fire your ass."

"Is that how you figured out he wasn't my new best friend?"

"That had a lot to do with it. Yeah."

"Asshole."

"Yeah, yeah. But that's why you gotta come back."

"Whatever, man. I don't think I care. Let him fire me. It might be the best thing to happen to me. To you, too."

Mike snickered.

"I'm serious, Mike. Look at us. Two guys at our prime and we're working in retail. We both have so much more potential than a dead-end job like this."

"And do what? Investment banking? It's not that bad. The pay is good and I don't want to think about looking for another job in this economy."

"Fuck the economy, and fuck the store, too."

"I don't think I've ever seen you this," he paused, searching for the right word. "Frustrated."

"I am frustrated! I feel frustrated and I feel stuck. I used to love this job."

"What happened?"

"Time, I guess. I loved it for a while, then I liked it. Indifference, dislike, and now I think I hate it. I've seen what the next level looks like, and I hate it even more." I took another drink of beer. "They made me fire people. They made me fire friends, acquaintances and Christine. Actually, firing Christine was kind of fun."

Mike nodded as I spoke, truly understanding my point of view. "If you came back, nothing says you have to go to the next level."

"Not right away," I agreed. "But there's pressure coming from all levels of management for me to move to the next level. If I turn them down they'll find reasons to drive me right out of the store. So, I say let them fire me now. Hell! I've given them enough cause. In fact," I grabbed a random piece of paper and a pen and wrote 'I quit' in large letters. I signed at the bottom before handing it to Mike. "Give that to Jameson for me."

Mike slowly turned the paper over in his hands, staring at it with a sadness in his eyes.

"Whenever Jameson started acting like a real prick you were always the guy who brought him back down. Without you around, his ego has been out of control."

"It's only been a few days."

Mike shrugged. "I know, but he's been walking around intimidating people for fun."

Was that where I fit in? Was it possible that my real position in that store wasn't one that the company created, but one that the people, my co-workers, had created? Was I some kind of champion of the people? I felt a little good about myself for the first time in days. The feeling didn't last.

"Ridiculous." I was speaking to myself, but Mike nodded, seeming to think the comment was directed at Jameson's behavior.

"There's something else," Mike said. "Frank's been calling for you."

"Shit!" I had completely forgotten about my best customer. Abandoned him.

I quickly drank the rest of my beer and grabbed my car keys.

"Thanks for coming, Mike." He stuck out his hand offering a shake, but I slapped it aside and hugged him before running out the door.

*   *   *

I walked into Frank's house without knocking. He was, as always, in his favorite chair watching a movie. I quietly walked up behind him.

"Been a while," said Frank, without even looking back.

"How do you do that?"

"I may just be an old car guy, but I know a thing or two. Sit."
I took my usual seat on the couch.

"You haven't been at work lately," Frank said. It wasn't a question. He already knew. He was just stating a fact.

"Yeah, I've been feeling under the weather lately."

"Is that what you call it?" Frank turned his eyes away from the TV to look at me. "I talked to your friend Mike for a while."

"And what did he tell you?"

Frank turned his gaze back to the television. "He told me that you were sitting at home drinking yourself stupid every night, like a damned fool."

I didn't even think Mike knew that much. "It wasn't every night."

"Still pretty stupid, if you ask me. What did you find at the end of an empty bottle?"

"Another bottle," I said and laughed. My laugh faded quickly when Frank didn't even crack a smile.

"You hate your life that much?"

"I did. It seemed like everyone in my life hated me. Mike's talking to me again, and that helps. I think I hit some kind of breaking point. Something made me stop caring. So I work at a crappy retail store. So I might get fired from that crappy retail store. It all seems so trivial now. Whatever happens, happens."

Frank quickly stood from his chair walked over to the DVD player. He stopped the current movie. He did a quick search through his DVDs until he found what he was looking for. Instead of playing the movie from the beginning, he went to the scene selection menu and selected one somewhere in the middle of the movie.

"Why are you..." I started to ask.

"Shh!" Frank nodded at the TV screen.

I looked at the screen and saw Brad Pitt holding a gun to the back of a young Asian man's head. Pitt was asking the young man questions about his future, his life. The young man answered through tears. At the end of their interaction, Pitt told the young man to make his life better or Pitt would end it. The young man ran and Frank hit stop on the DVD player and looked at me.

I looked at Frank and thought about what he had just shown me. I would end up thinking about it for the rest night.

"Now get on out of here. Figure things out."

I smiled at Frank's bluntness and walked over to the door. I turned back to see Frank putting the first movie back into his DVD player. He stopped for a moment and put a hand on the back of his neck. It was a stance that I could only describe as stressed or concerned.

"Thanks," I said.

As I left his house my brain kept picking at the meaning of the scene Frank showed me. For an old car guy, my dad sure knew a thing or two.

CHAPTER 29

Walking back into the store the next night for my closing shift, I felt the same wave of nausea from the previous time, emotional déjà vu. I also felt the eyes of every employee in the store. This time I met each and every gaze with a smile. It was a smile that said I had made some mistakes, but I was back.

As I smiled at my co-workers the blank looks on their faces grew into return smiles with a hint of hope.

Megan was nearby and had completely stopped stocking a shelf to smile at me. I wanted to talk to her, but I had things to take care of first.

Mike was sitting behind the repair desk and nodded when he saw me. I returned the nod as I headed into my computer department and gathered my team. They looked at me warily.

"I know none of you like me right now for what happened to Dev. I don't blame you one bit. I don't like what happened to him either. I don't know exactly what I'm going to do about it, but I'm going to find a way to make it right. That's a promise."

A few of the guys smiled a nodded. A few others let their facial expressions tell me that they didn't believe me. I had nothing else to say. I expected a few of the guys to ask a question or two, but no one spoke. They all slowly dispersed and went in search of customers.

I turned and looked at the store. It kind of felt good to be back. No one was more surpassed than me.

"Excuse me," said a rather large gentleman.

"Yes, sir. What can do for you?"

"I need help picking out a laptop. Do you know the laptops?"

"Absolutely," I said with a smile. "Follow me."

We walked over to the row of portable computers.

"Let's start from the beginning," I said. "What do you want a laptop for?"

"I want to go on the Internet. I might play a computer game every now and then. It needs to play movies. That's about it, I guess."

"A guy who knows what he's after. I like that."

I showed him several computers and explained the differences. He decided on one of the high end computers.

"My boss wouldn't like me saying this but, you don't need a computer this expensive. There are cheaper ones that will do everything you're looking for."

"I'm sure there are," the man replied. "But, I don't want to have to upgrade in a year or two, you know?"

"Fair enough. Let's find a register and I'll ring you up."

The man handed me a credit card for payment. Over the years I had gotten into a habit of checking the name before anything else. The name on the man's card said Laurie. I had never met a man named Laurie, and it wasn't uncommon for a man to come in with his wife's credit card.

"Is this your card?" I asked.

"Yeah."

"Great. I'll just need to see some photo ID and we'll have you on your way." This was not a common practice but when there was some doubt about the person presenting the card it was best to pretend it was standard.

"Sure thing," the customer said, handing me a driver's license.

I examined it thoroughly without staring at it in an obvious way. The picture matched the person standing in front of me, and the name matched the credit card I had in my hand.

My heart skipped a beat when I saw the gender classification on the card displayed an F. Realization became a brick that the hit me in the face. I wasn't assisting a gentleman with a computer purchase, I was assisting a manly looking woman. A woman who I had been calling 'sir' the entire time.

I lost control of myself and burst out laughing. Laurie looked at me with a grin on her face. She didn't look pissed or confused as I struggled to compose myself and started breathing regularly again.

"I'm really sorry," I said, still trying to get myself under control.

"Don't worry about it. It happens all the time," she explained. "I know I look like a man. I'm a truck driver. All my co-workers are guys. They rub off on me. I stopped caring about what people thought a long time ago. Let them think I'm a man. Doesn't bother me."

"That doesn't make it okay for me to laugh."

"Wade, sometimes in life, you gotta laugh."

"I think I really needed that laugh."

"There you go. You helped me with a computer, and I helped you have a laugh. I guess that makes us about even."

I smiled. "I still have to charge you."

Laurie snapped her fingers. "Damn. Worth a try, right?"

We finished the transaction and I walked Laurie to the door. I thanked her again and despite her claims, apologized twice more.

Mike walked up to me immediately after, looking around cautiously.

"Meet me in the warehouse in two minutes," he said.

"Why? What's going on?"

"Two minutes."

Mike walked away still looking in all directions.

I went to the home theatre department to talk to Sawyer, but he was off somewhere else. Becky and Rory weren't in their departments either.

When I walked back into the warehouse they were all there standing in a semi circle talking quietly. They stopped when they saw me.

"Is this some kind of intervention?" I asked.

Becky spoke up first. "Mike thought it would be a good idea for us to fill you in on what's been going on while you were gone."

"Yeah. Mike told me Jameson was walking around claiming he was going to fire me. I'm not too worried about it."

"That's not all, man," said Sawyer.

"I told him Jameson was throwing his weight around," Mike explained. "I didn't go into detail."

"He's been throwing insults at us, and at some of our employees. Calling people useless and incompetent," said Becky.

"No one's tried to stand up to him?" I asked.

"We tried," said Becky.

"We all tried. Once," Mike explained. "And we were all threatened with termination."

I looked to Sawyer and he nodded.

"Even some of the part timers tried to stand up for themselves," said Sawyer. "He threatened to fire them too."

"Does he give any reason?"

"No," replied Sawyer. "He walks right up to people and tells them if they don't smarten up he's going to fire them. Dude's out of control."

"He's been hovering over people and if they do one thing wrong he sends them home without pay," Mike explained. "Even if it leaves us short staffed."

I looked at Rory. He was the only one who hadn't said anything.

"What do you have to say?" I asked him.

"I don't like to say bad things about the boss, but he's been pretty inconscrewus."

He meant incongruous.

"OK. I agree with you guys that it's bullshit, but why tell me?" I asked.

"It's like I told you," Mike said. "You've always been the guy that keeps him in check."

That feeling of being a real leader began to rise in me again. I fought it off. I wasn't worried about being fired for missing time, but I wasn't about to start a fight.

"What about Lewis? What's he doing in all of this?"

"I think Jameson might have threatened him, too. He's been keeping out of it completely."

"So this is where you all are?" Jameson bellowed. He had snuck into the warehouse, listening for an unknown amount of time. "My whole supervisor team all in one place."

"We just wanted to make sure Wade was all right," Becky suggested.

Jameson walked up next to me, studying me from head to toe.

"He looks fine to me. Are you fine, Wade?"

"I sure am. How are you?"

"Well, Becky. Now that you know Wade is fine, maybe you should head back to your department."

"Absolutely. Is it getting busy out there?" Becky asked.

"That doesn't matter. You'll get out there unless you want to be promoted to a customer."

That leadership feeling rose up inside me. The feeling grew stronger as I watched Becky slowly walk past Jameson with her head down. As she looked back over her shoulder at me with a look of defeat the feeling exploded.

"She just asked a simple question," I said.

Becky stopped at the warehouse door, but didn't turn around. Jameson looked at me. I could tell by the look on his face that he was feeling dominant.

"She was questioning my authority, as if to say she shouldn't be out there unless it was busy."

"No. She already said she'd go out there. She asked if it was busy as an afterthought. She wanted to know what she was in for when she got out there."

"She doesn't need to know what she's in for. She needs to go out there."

"The management training we attended said to always know as much as you can about what you're heading into." That wasn't exactly true, but it sounded close enough that Jameson would never question it.

"Fair enough. Attention all supervisors. It's not really

busy out there, however, I would like you all to report to your departments like good little soldiers."

Everyone's eyes dropped to the floor and they started moving toward the door.

"Don't do that." Everyone stopped moving as the words left my mouth.

"Excuse me?" said Jameson.

"Don't patronize us like that. I heard you've been doing that a lot lately. I heard you've been sending people home, intentionally leaving the store short staffed and threatening to fire people without probable cause."

I was pushing the boundaries of what I could and couldn't get away with, but that didn't matter anymore. I was going to fight as hard as I could, and if that meant Jameson firing me, that was fine.

Jameson looked at me, the dominance fading from his face. He looked around at the rest of the supervisors who were staring and waiting for his response.

"Wade, I think maybe we should take this conversation offline."

Offline was corporate bullshit for a private conversation. But what it really meant was that Jameson was losing this battle and he didn't want witnesses for the rest of it.

"No, Jameson. Let's not take this offline. Let's keep this online."

Jameson looked around at everyone again. His face was turning red.

"You can't threaten people the way you've been doing," I said.

Jameson's stare was turning angry. "If any employee is not meeting standards it is my duty as the store manager to provide a warning."

"It's also your duty as the store management to fill out a full report on that warning and get the signature of the employee being warned. That way these things can be tracked, to protect the store, and to protect the employee."

A field of smiles bloomed around me. Becky and Rory tried to hide theirs, but failed miserably. Mike and Sawyer had the biggest smiles of all and didn't bother to try to hide them at all.

"I just haven't gotten around to the paperwork portion, yet." Jameson was reaching for any excuse he could find.

"It's too late now. The paperwork is supposed to be filled out at the time of the warning. Otherwise, a warning is not supposed to be given. It's the kind of paperwork that can't be manufactured at a later time."

Jameson had nothing left to say. He put on a fake smile. "Looks like I sent the right guy to management training, huh? Thanks for setting me straight on this aspect of our procedures. I'm still a little wet behind the ears, so I'm not quite up on everything. So, thanks again." He was still smiling.

No one returned his smile.

"We're all going to go back to work now," I said. "But I want you to know that if I hear any more about you threatening people, belittling people or just generally bullying people around I won't be having a conversation with you. I'll be having a conversation with Brent Baker. And I'm pretty sure he likes me more than he likes you."

Jameson forced a smile onto his face again and looked at each of us in turn. He opened his mouth to retort, but turned and left the warehouse without another word.

We all shared a moment of victory, shaking hands and hugging each other before heading back out to the sales floor. I hung back for a moment reflecting on my confrontation with Jameson. I shouldn't have said half of the things I said. If Jameson was a little smarter, he could have fired me that moment. The relieved looks on my co-workers' faces were worth the risk.

Between good customers and great co-workers I was starting to remember why I liked this job.

On my way out of the warehouse I noticed Megan tucked away in the opposite corner of the warehouse with a basket full of products. When she saw me she smiled and dropped her eyes to the floor.

"Were you sitting in here listening to that whole thing?" I asked.

"I was getting some stock. I wasn't listening on purpose, but I ended up overhearing a little."

"How much is a little?"

"All of it."

I took a few steps closer to her.

"You know, I heard something about this corner of the warehouse," she said.

"What's that?"

When I was close enough she wrapped her arms around my neck, pulled my body against hers and kissed me. Her grip was violently passionate, but her kiss was soft. I felt her pelvis grind against mine and she moaned softly.

Half of my brain couldn't stop thinking about her body, the way her hair smelled, and how soft her skin was. I should have listened to that half of brain.

The other half thought about how I shouldn't be taking advantage of a younger co-worker. I considered Megan to be too smart with too much potential for something like this. That was the half of my brain that I hated.

I struggled with the decision while enjoying Megan's lips for a few seconds more, then pulled away.

"What's wrong?" she asked, breathing heavily.

"This. What I'm doing."

"I want to. I started it."

"It doesn't make it right for me. In any other circumstance..." I thought better about finishing that sentence.

"Look," I continued. "There are so many reasons why I want to stay here with you right now. But, I have to go."

I backed, hating myself for doing it. I walked out of the warehouse, across the sales floor, out the front doors of the store. I allowed myself to breathe and fell against the front of the store. A few days ago, I would have blown off work and taken Megan to my apartment for a buffet of all you can have sex. In some ways I felt like I was back to my old self. Other ways I was a completely different person. Either way, I couldn't stop thinking about secret #4.

Secret of Retail #4: Never get involved with someone from work.

Things almost always got messy. If the relationship went bad there was an awkwardness that fell over everything. Eventually one person would feel forced out of his or her own job. To be honest, I could probably handle that. But it wasn't me I was worried about. It was her.

Megan was too nice of a girl to end up like that. To end up being hurt by an asshole like me. Maybe I could have changed. Maybe I already had changed. But I doubted it.

"I don't know what you did to Jameson." Lewis strolled out of the store and leaned against the wall beside me. "But he took off a few minutes ago and he was acting real strange. Timid."

"I was told he needed be knocked down a few. So I did it."

"You're a better man than I."

"Don't be so sure of that, Lew."

"No. I'm serious. I tried to stand up to him, but he just ran me over with threats."

"Well, he's back in line now. So, business as usual, I guess."

"I don't think so." Lewis stared out at the sky, lethargy deep in his eyes.

"What do you mean?"

"I don't think I'm going to stay."

"Why not?" I asked.

"It's not the same job anymore. Everything that made this job fun seems to have disappeared. I'm only here for the paycheck."

"Isn't that why we're all here?"

"To an extent. I think you're supposed to believe in what you do. I don't believe in what I do."

"You think anyone here believes in what they do? Come on, Lew."

"Seriously. I used to think that people needed a store like this. Where else are they going to get electronics and advice of people who knew about this stuff? People don't need a store like us. They can get electronics anywhere if they really want them. We're contributing to more problems with society than solutions. The average person has a ridiculous amount of debt and our solution is to offer a store credit card.

"When I became a supervisor, I was providing a service to those that might become supervisors one day by passing on what I knew. Same thing when I became a manager. I may have helped out one or two people, but after watching so many of them leave the store and go do better things with their lives than I'd ever do... The only thing I passed was the buck."

We sat staring into the sky for a few minutes. I knew how he was feeling. I hadn't believed in my job for quite a while. Still felt that way. How could I try to argue that he was wrong when I believed the same things he did? After a few moments, we walked back into the store without another word between us.

I looked around for Megan, worried that she was feeling

upset and rejected. She wasn't on the sales floor. When I went back to the warehouse where I had left her. She had already replaced me with another guy. They were making out like the world was about to end. Obviously, even if she was upset, Megan was going to be fine. In fact, she looked like she was fine already.

Megan and the guy switched positions so her back was to me and I saw the guy was Trent. He saw me standing there and gave me a thumb's up without interrupting his lips. I smiled and returned his thumb's up. I always knew Trent would do well here.

CHAPTER 30

When I got to work the next afternoon, Jameson was walking around smiling, chatting with all the employees, telling them how great they were and slapping them on the back.

"He's been like this since the store opened," Mike said as he walked up beside me.

"He's been at this for three hours?"

"Yeah. He must be trying to make amends. Prick."

"He needs to make amends with Lewis."

"Why?"

"He wants to quit."

"You're shitting me."

"No. He told me last night."

"Really?"

"Yeah."

"That's not all bad. You're a shoe in to take his place."

"I'm not sure I want his place."

"Hey, man. You already do the job. You might as well take the pay."

I watched Jameson as he ended a conversation with another employee. He looked genuinely happy. He practically ran over when he saw I had entered the store.

"Wade!" he called as he ran.

"I'm outta here," Mike said and snuck away.

"Wade, I'm glad you're here. It's good to see you."

"You certainly seem chipper. You getting some kind of bonus or something?"

Jameson laughed and waved a hand at me. "No. I'm just glad to see you. And I want you to know, that I appreciate you setting me straight last night. Really, I do. I didn't realize how out of control I was."

"I guess we all lose ourselves once in a while."

I turned to walk away, but Jameson stepped in front of me still wearing a big friendly smile. "I do have some very exciting news for you, though."

"Oh, yeah?" I was already getting tired of friendly Jameson. I almost preferred asshole Jameson. At least I knew what to expect from asshole Jameson. "What news is that?"

"Do you remember Brent mentioning we were getting a big celebrity visit from Brianna Hill?"

"Yeah."

"Well, that visit is tomorrow."

"That is exciting." I turned to walk away again, but once again Jameson took a step in front of me.

"We're required to have a staff member sit with her at the table while she signs autographs to assist her." His smile grew even larger. "I've arranged for that person to be you!"

He bit his tongue and clapped me on the shoulder.

"You're going to spend the whole day with one of the hottest stars on the planet, you lucky dog!"

Finally, Jameson walked away. I was a little stunned. Maybe friendly Jameson wasn't going to be as bad as I thought.

I started toward the back again when I saw Rory on the edge of my department waving me down.

"Hey, Dub, there's some girl asking for you."

My heart started beating faster as I considered the possibilities. Tess, Elizabeth maybe even Bridget.

It turned out to be two girls. One looked pissed off and the other looked pissed drunk.

"There he is!" said the drunk one. "Hi, again." She waved, trying to make it look sexy. It was barely coordinated.

"Hello," I said.

"This is the guy who always helps me when I'm in here. He helped me just last week. Right?"

Secret of Retail #8: When you work full time in retail just about everyone in the city looks somewhat familiar.

"Let's focus on today," I said, steering the conversation away from awkwardness. "What can I do for you?"

She started to laugh and then looked at me very seriously and said, "Someone to take me home, pick up a bottle of wine on the way and fuck my brains out."

"Sara!" said the drunk girl's friend.

Sara laughed even harder now. "Calm down, Melissa. We joke like this all the time."

I looked at Sara's friend and subtly shook my head.

"I'm sorry," said Melissa. "She said that you're the only person in the store that could help us. To be honest, I think she has a crush on you."

"Melissa!"

"I'm just saying. You totally do. You've talked about him a dozen times already."

"Shut-up, bitch!"

"Don't yell at me," Melissa said.

"Okay," I broke in. "Let's all calm down and get what you need."

Sara went from looking pissed off to drunkenly aroused. She opened her mouth, probably to say something about needing to get fucked again, but Melissa spoke up first.

"We need some kind of cable. We were at my house about to watch some movies when we found my cat had chewed this." She pulled a mangled cable out of her purse.

"No problem." I took them to the home theatre department and showed them the replacement cable.

"Thank you," said Melissa. "Let's go Sara."

"Wait, wait. Give him your address." Sara was digging in her purse.

"What? No!"

"Maybe he'll want to watch a movie with us tonight."

"Sara, that's not a good idea."

Sara opened her mouth to protest when I grabbed a blank scrap of paper and pretended to read it.

"Got it right here," I told Sara. "Just in case."

She smiled and winked before turning to walk to the cash registers.

"Thanks for that," said Melissa.

"No problem. Listen, maybe I should get your address. Maybe once Sara has gone home I can come over and make sure you got that cable hooked up properly."

Melissa laughed. "I don't think so, big boy, but thanks for the cable."

I watched her walk away with a grin on my face.

"See?" said Sawyer walking up behind me. "You went too direct. What did I tell you about that shit?"

"Never go direct. Always guide her into asking you out," I repeated like a drone.

"My personal statistics have shown a 95% success when using this method. 30% with the direct method."

"I wonder if that 95% would still be so high if you were eight inches shorter and white."

"There you go with that racist shit again."

"Hold on a second," I said holding up a hand. I was watching a young guy walk around the computer software department. He was looking around, but not for someone to help him. He was looking to see if anyone was watching him.

"I'll be outside," I said to Sawyer.

"Don't think this is over," Sawyer said to my back.

I walked out the front doors of the store and leaned against the wall to the right of the exit.

A few minutes later the young kid walked out of the store, head down, moving fast.

"Two choices," I called.

The kid jumped at the sound of my voice and spun around to face me.

"What?"

"You have two choices."

"What the fuck are you talking about?" he said as he turned to leave.

"I'm talking about all the merchandise from my store you have stuffed in your coat."

That got his attention. He stopped walking away and turned back to me.

"I didn't steal nothing," he said, not looking me in the eye.

"That's a double negative, kid, which means you just admitted to stealing."

"I didn't steal anything."

"So, you're not a complete moron. That's good."

"I'm outta here." He turned to walk away again.

"Choice number one," I said loudly, and he stopped walking but didn't turn around. "You can continue to claim you didn't steal, I get a couple of my friends from inside, not that I'd need them, to help me bring you back inside and this turns into a criminal matter."

I stopped talking. I wasn't going to give him choice number two. He was going to ask for choice number two.

The kid turned around slowly to face me once again.

"What's choice number two?" he asked.

"Choice number two is you hand over everything that you stole right now, and then you disappear."

He only paused for a few seconds before he unzipped his jacket and started handing me software. I expected it to be video games. Instead the software he handed me was all 3D rendering and animation software.

"Why did you want this kind of stuff?" I asked.

"I'm going to school next year."

"To be what?"

"A game developer."

"Get accepted anywhere yet?"

"Yeah. A couple places."

"You must be smarter than you look."

"Shit. It ain't that hard."

"Do you realize a criminal record would fuck all that up for you? No school, no job."

"School's expensive enough. This software's fucking crazy expensive, too!"

Despite the kid's behavior, I felt bad for him. I felt like tucking the software back into his jacket and sending him on his way.

"If you're half as smart as you're starting to seem, there are bursaries you can apply for. Write an essay, get some cash. I'd look into it if I were you."

"Yeah, okay." He sulked a little as he turned to walk away.

"If you get really desperate," I called after him. "Our competitors down the street aren't half as watchful as I am."

He looked over his shoulder and grinned at me.

"Not that I condone that kind of thing."

CHAPTER 31

The next morning, I sat in the break room for a few moments before the store opened. Brianna Hill's people had sent over a rider for us to fulfil.

The door opened hard and fast enough to hit the wall before bouncing back. I had just enough time to see Rory on the other side before the door slammed shut. The door opened again, slower this time, and Rory walked in with pink cheeks.

"You're a real bastard, you know that?" he said.

"Why?"

"You slack off from work for a whole fucking week, sitting at home saying 'poor me, poor me,' until Mike snaps your ass out of it. Then you're back to work for two days and you get to sit with Brianna Till."

I rolled my eyes. "It's Brianna Hill."

"What?"

"Hill."

"Whatever, man. All I know is she's damn hot and you get to spend the day with her and get paid for it."

"You're practically married. What do you want from me?"

Rory thought about it for a minute, staring off into space. "To switch bodies for a day."

"Come on, Rory. Do you think someone like that is going to take any kind of interest in someone like me or you?"

"If I had known I just had to yell at Jameson to get that spot I would have done it weeks ago."

"Dude, you're making way too big a deal out of this. You know what I'm going to be doing? Making sure she has working pens. Handing her bottles of water. Making sure people don't spend too much time confessing their love to her. Walking her to the break room when she needs a break."

"The break room? She's going to be in here?"

"Yeah. Jameson made it available for her."

"What. Does that mean—"

"That it's not available to you? Yes."

"What the fuck?! Where am I going to eat lunch?"

"You never eat your lunch in here. You hate eating your lunch in here."

"But I like having the option!"

Rory was about to continue protesting when a large man wearing a black suit opened the door and scanned the break room.

"Is one of you Wade?" he asked.

"I am," I said.

"I need you to remain here," he said to me, and then turned to Rory. "And I need you to vacate the room, please."

Rory looked ready to fight. He looked from the guard to me and back to the guard. "This is my break room, you know?"

"Not today," said the security guard.

Rory left in a huff muttering something about his lunch being ruined.

"Miss Hill will be here in 3 minutes."

"Okay."

I didn't know what else to say. Being in a room with a complete stranger and complete silence was awkward in just about any situation. But being in a silent room with a stranger who looked like he could break me over his knee was a whole new level of awkward.

"Are you a fan of Brianna's music?" I asked.

"I make sure that Miss Hill is safe. My enjoyment of her music is inconsequential to that."

"Yeah, I'm not a fan either," I replied.

After another two and a half minutes of trying to make small talk with a man made of concrete, two more large men entered the room ushering little Brianna Hill between them.

She stepped out from the two man protective cocoon like someone struggling to get out of a car with deployed airbags.

She sighed and brushed at her clothes.

I expected something else. She was much shorter than her videos made her look. She was attractive, but she didn't look like a sex goddess the way her posters looked. I guess life looks different through a lens covered in Vaseline and Photoshop software.

"You don't have to walk so close to me. This shirt wrinkles very easily," she said.

"Miss Hill," said the original guard. "This is Wade. He's going to assist you today."

She looked me over with disgust on her face.

"Let's get a couple things straight," she said.

"Sure," I said with a smile.

"You're here to assist me. I don't want people lingering in

front of me for more than 15 seconds. No one touches me. If they want to shake my hand, they can't, and you have to tell them they can't. We can't stop people from taking pictures of me, but no one gets their picture taken with me. I don't like it. If you see anyone who looks even the least bit suspicious make sure you tell James right away."

"James?" I asked.

"Me," said the original guard.

"You got it," I said.

"When does the store open?" she asked. If Rory could be here now he probably wouldn't think I was so lucky.

"Half hour."

"OK. I'll start signing in 90 minutes. Until then, disappear."

Without another word I left the break room, I didn't get two steps away before James laid a big meaty paw on my shoulder.

"Wade."

"Yes?"

"Miss Hill would like a non-fat Chi Latte, extra foam and cinnamon."

"Uh, sure."

I drove to the nearest Starbucks and cursed Jameson's name the whole way there. What had seemed like a privilege was going to be a huge pain in my ass. I should have known that nothing good could come from Jameson.

I knocked on the door on the break room and handed James an eleven dollar coffee.

"Miss Hill would like an everything bagel, lightly toasted, with low fat cream cheese on one half."

I heard Brianna say something from inside the break room, but couldn't make it out.

"And Miss Hill would like all the poppy seeds removed from the bagel."

"So, it's not really an everything bagel, is it?"

James looked at me for a few seconds before he closed the door in my face. I set out on another errand for a spoiled bitch, grumbling even more than the first time.

When I returned with the bagel, the store was already open and there was a small line-up in front of the table Jameson had set-up for Brianna.

I knocked on the door and handed James the bagel.

"Miss Hill doesn't want you to have to leave at lunch time to get her food."

"Good," I said a little too quickly.

"So she wants you to go get it now and we'll keep it in the fridge here in your break room."

"Great," I said, not caring how obvious my sarcasm was.

James was unaffected anyway. "Miss Hill would like a Caesar salad, but with a light ranch dressing instead of Caesar. She'll need half of the croutons in the salad and half on the side. She likes some to be crunchier than others. The salad has to have tomatoes mixed in, with cucumbers on the side."

"Is that all?"

"And a bottle of coke. But half coke, half diet coke."

"That means I'll have two bottles of half coke and half diet coke."

"She doesn't want two bottles. She only wants one."

"What do I do with the other bottle?" I asked.

"I don't care."

"Don't you think this is getting a little—"

James closed the door in my face once again. For the third time in less than an hour, I attempted to please the unappeasable. I went to a grocery store and picked out withered lettuce, tomatoes that weren't quite ripe yet and cucumbers that were far over ripe. I found a package of croutons that had been opened and grabbed a bottle of regular ranch, but only because there was no such thing as double fat.

Once I had all the ingredients I tossed the bitch's salad myself, in the passenger seat of my car with my unwashed hands and put it into a disposable Tupperware bowl that I had laying around in my back seat.

When James opened the break room door I smiled and handed him the salad.

"It's the best I could find," I said.

"Miss Hill would like—"

"Let me guess! Miss Hill would like a milkshake made with real strawberries, half soy milk, half skim milk, a half scoop of frozen yogurt and no more, no less than two straws. Am I close?"

James eyes widened the slightest bit.

"Miss Hill would like to have a word with you."

"Oh."

I walked into the break room to find Brianna sitting in a stack of three chairs with her feet up on a table.

"Hi, there," she said. It wasn't exactly friendly, but it was a big improvement from our first encounter.

"Hi," I said.

James stood with his back to the door and the other two guards stood with their backs to one of the walls.

"I wanted to tell you that I'm kind of impressed."

"Why?"

"You handled all of my orders in good time. I've had some assistants who took an hour and a half just to get me coffee."

"Well, it was no big deal."

"I'm almost tempted to offer you a job. Go on tour with me. Get me whatever I want."

I wondered if James had a gun and if he'd shoot me in the head if I asked nicely.

"I'd make a lousy personal assistant. You'd probably end up firing me for telling you to go fuck yourself."

I wished I hadn't said the words before I was even done saying them.

Brianna stared at me for three painful seconds before she burst out laughing. Relief washed over me.

"You've got balls."

"Yeah, I guess."

"I'm used to being around people that just pander to me. 'Oh, Brianna, I love your music!' 'Oh, Miss Hill, I'm such a big fan.' I know where my fan base lies, and it's not with guys your age, is it?"

"It's not with me."

"See? I like the honesty."

She looked at me for a moment like a child admired a new toy.

"You ready to do this, Wade?"

"Whenever you are."

We all exited the break room together. James instructed me to go first, probably in case there was a sniper. Behind me were the two nameless bodyguards, then Brianna, with James on the very end.

The line-up of fans erupted when they caught a glimpse of Brianna shuffling between the bodyguards. Once they performed a quick scan of the line they stepped away from her and she held her arms out toward the fans, blowing kisses and smiling.

I sat down while she finished acting like she loved her fans. Jameson was suddenly standing directly in front of the table with a big goofy grin on his face. He clapped me on the shoulder real quick, but kept his eyes on Brianna.

"Hi, Miss Hill. I'm Kevin, the store manager here and I have to say, I am such a big fan of yours."

"Thank you so much."

I couldn't stop myself from speaking up.

"Hey, Jameson, what's your favorite song?"

He didn't look at me, but I recognized the smile he puts on when he's been caught in a lie and doesn't have a back-up lie ready.

"I don't know," he finally said. "I guess I just like them all."

Brianna tried to hide a giggle behind her hand.

Jameson took a few steps away from the table, waving awkwardly.

"I guess... I'll just... let you get to it."

I waved the first person in line forward, and the autographs officially began.

Brianna smiled at each fan as if she were meeting her first and biggest fan. Despite her earlier instructions, she eagerly shook hands with anyone who extended their own.

I was even more surprised by how she treated me. She thanked me with words and a smile for each bottle of water and pen that I handed her. I slipped a note to Rory asking him to get a good Caesar salad for Brianna's lunch. He was more than willing to go.

"So, how long have you been working here?" she asked.

I looked around confused. It sounded like she was talking to me while still signing photographs of herself and smiling to her fans.

"Are you talking to me?"

"Yeah. These autograph signings make for a long day. I need someone to talk to."

"Oh. Okay. I've been here," I paused to think about my time served as I handed her another 8x10. "Almost five years now." I scrunched my face up in disgust. "Oh my God! Years! Five of them!"

Brianna laughed.

"What do you want to do?" she asked.

"I asked myself that question for a long time, and always had trouble finding any kind of answer, until a few years ago."

"What did you come up with?"

"To stop asking myself that question."

She laughed again.

"What made you want to get into singing?" I asked.

"That's kind of a dumb question, isn't it?"

"No. Why?"

"Doesn't everyone want to be famous?"

"No. I don't think everyone wants to be famous."

Brianna stopped mid-signature and looked at the man standing in front of her. He was middle-aged and either getting a signature for his daughter or a new center piece for a creepy shrine.

"Do you want to be famous?" she asked the man.

The man looked at her and shrugged. She gave him the picture without finishing the autograph.

"Well," she continued. "I always wanted to be famous, and I always loved to sing. Put those two things together and here I am."

"So you wanted this from the beginning?"

"From as far back as I can remember."

"I haven't wanted anything for that long."

We continued chatting idly while she signed autographs until it was time for Brianna to take a break for lunch.

Brianna's bodyguards led her back to the break room while I stood in front of the remainder of her fans.

"Okay, folks. Miss Hill is going to take just a little time out to grab a bite to eat. She'll resume signing autographs shortly."

I was unanimously booed by the crowd and someone threw a sharpie at me.

"Hey!"

I was about to head back toward the break room when I saw Jameson waving me down from the customer service desk.

"Wade! Over here!"

"Yeah, I see you, you goofy jackass," I muttered under my breath as I walked over.

"How are things going?" he asked.

"Things started out a little rocky, but it's going pretty well now."

"She's hot, eh?"

"Yeah, I guess. Is that what you called me over here for?"

"Did she mention me at all?" he asked.

"Yeah. She asked who the little creepy dude was."

"Seriously?"

"No, Jameson. I was kidding."

"Oh. Good one. Listen, Brianna's leaving before the store closes for the night, so I'm going to leave you the keys to close up the store and take off. Okay?"

"Really? You're leaving?"

"Well, I figure you've got Brianna under control and since she leaves before we close there won't be anything to keep you from handling closing duties either."

"There's always supposed to be a manager on duty, which there won't be, because I'll be sitting beside Brianna until she's done. Who's going to handle customer issues?"

"Rory's here."

"Rory?"

"Come on. Let me get out of here."

"Hey, man. It's your store. If you don't mind it being run like this for the night—"

"Great!" he said with a huge smile, clapping me on the shoulder and handing me his keys.

"Great," I repeated, much less enthusiastically.

I went and found Rory to tell him he was in charge until I was done with Brianna.

"Are you serious?" he asked.

"I wish I wasn't."

"So I get to tell people what to do?"

"Sort of. You have to be fair about it."

"But they have to do what I tell them to, right?"

I hung my head in frustration.

"I wish Sawyer was here." I raised my head to look at Rory again. "Yes, people have to do what you tell them to, but you can't be a dick. If it's not in their job description you can't tell them to do it."

Disappointment bloomed in his face.

"This is your chance," I told him. "Your chance to show everyone you're management material. Don't fuck it up."

Once again I headed toward the break room.

"Wade," said Rory.

I stopped and turned to face him. "Yeah?"

"I won't abuse my dynomysticism."

I had no fucking clue what he meant.

By the time I got back to the break room Brianna was ready to return to the table and sign more autographs.

I led her back to the table to a much milder round of applause from the remaining fans. Those that were left didn't take long to get through. Brianna's smile wasn't quite as enthusiastic as it had been earlier in the day.

"Do you think I'm losing popularity?" she asked after the last person in line got their autograph.

"What do you mean?"

"Do you think my album is played out?"

"Your songs never appealed to me in the first place."

"You know what I mean," she said hitting me playfully.

"I don't think so. We still sell a lot of copies. Why?"

She stared at the empty space where her fans had lined up.

"This wasn't a very good turn out," she admitted.

"Seemed pretty good to me."

"And how many Brianna Hill meet and greets have you been to?"

I smiled.

"More people will come. Look at your watch. It's getting close to dinner time."

"Nice try."

She stared at a pen she was rolling between her fingertips and wore a sulky look on her face.

I was surprised to find out that even superstars felt self-conscious. We sat in silence for a while. I watched a customer walk in through the front doors and said, "Home theatre."

"What?" asked Brianna looking at me.

"Nothing. Just this game I play sometimes."

"What game?"

"One day, I discovered that I could watch a customer walk into the store and know what department they were going to."

We watched the man walk through the store and head down the aisle of televisions.

Brianna laughed. "How do you do it?"

"I don't know. I'm sure on a subconscious level it has something to do with the customer's age, the clothes he's wearing, the way he walks, maybe even posture."

"That's amazing!"

"Not really."

"What about these people?" she asked pointing at a young couple coming through the doors.

"Tablets."

We watched them head directly to a display brandishing a large apple logo.

"Two in a row!"

"I can do this all night."

"Let me try, let me try."

She looked at another young guy walking through the front doors.

"iPod?" she guessed.

"Nope. Movies."

He walked past the first two aisles of movies.

"Ha!" Brianna gloated.

Then he turned down the third aisle.

"Don't mess with the champ. By the way, laptops." The next guy walked past us at our table and all the way to the computer section.

Brianna eyed three girls walking into the store.

"These ladies must be here for some CDs," she guessed.

"No," I said. "They're here for you."

The girls walked up to the table, barely containing their excitement. I held out a brand new pen for Brianna. She smiled at me and gave my hand a quick squeeze. I was amazed. Brianna Hill had a human side and I had found it.

CHAPTER 32

After chatting a while longer and signing autographs for a few fans as they sporadically appeared, Brianna decided to end the signing a little early.

James told us the limousine was at the rear of the building, outside of our warehouse, to avoid any 'incidents.'

I walked Brianna and the bodyguards through the warehouse. The two nameless guards quickly went outside. James stood and waited.

"Give us a minute, James," Brianna said.

James looked torn between following orders and keeping watch over Brianna.

"Yes, Miss Hill. I'll be right outside."

Once we were alone Brianna turned and faced me, but stared at my feet while pretending to dig at something on the floor with her toe.

"Thanks for looking after me today. You made a pretty good assistant."

"It wasn't so bad."

She took a step closer and, with some effort, looked me in the eyes.

"You know, I wasn't joking when I said I could use a man like you on the road."

It was a tempting offer. Celebrity parties, world-wide tours, and the money was probably ridiculous. But being an assistant meant being the responsible person every day at any hour. That didn't sound like me.

"I don't think it's the life for me," I said.

"And this is?" she asked.

Ouch.

"It might be."

She took another step closer. Our bodies were inches apart.

"Then how about taking care of me tonight?" she asked in whisper.

She stood on her toes and pressed her lips to mine. Her songs claimed she was a great kisser. She was OK, but I expected a little more from an international sex symbol.

For a second my mind wandered and I considered the warehouse cameras. We weren't standing in the dead zone. In fact, we were standing in the direct view of one of the main camera. I didn't care. Even if Jameson reviewed the footage, he would just tell me he was proud of me.

"Come with me," she whispered in my ear. "Just for tonight. Come with me."

"I've gotta close the store." The words came out slowly as I tripped over each one.

"Let someone else do it." She chewed on my ear lobe.

I wanted to go. If Brianna fucked like she kissed she'd be

average in bed, and that was a hell of a lot better than sitting at home trying to decide if I should masturbate to classycougars. com or hotwetteens.com. At the very least it would be a great story to tell. Not that they'd believe me.

We kissed a little more while I tried to convince myself that Rory was capable of closing the store if I left.

A loud crash sounded from deeper in the warehouse.

"What the fuck?" I asked.

I walked the width of the warehouse, peering down the rows of shelves and came across a horrible scene. A large screen television had fallen from the top shelf and landed right on top of Greg.

Greg.

I stood for another few seconds in shock before I was able to force my body into motion. I ran over as fast as my legs would take me, but they were numb and I felt like I was wading through jello.

Greg was lying motionless. Dead? No, he couldn't be. Could he?

I slid to my knees beside him. I checked for a pulse. There was no pulse. No. There was a pulse. I think. It seemed weak. I didn't know what a weak pulse felt like.

I yelled at Brianna, "Call 911!"

I didn't know if she was still there, but I thought I heard the distinct beep of a cell phone being dialed.

I didn't know what to do, but something tickled at my memory. Something told me not to move Greg if there was a chance of spinal injury. That much came from movies and TV shows. I looked Greg over to see if there was a sign of where the TV had struck him. There was no blood that I could see. No bruising. No red marks.

I lowered my ear to his nose and mouth and listened for

breathing. I didn't hear any. I couldn't hear anything. Everything was muffled. I thought I heard Brianna talking.

"Tell the paramedics to come to the back of the store. It'll be faster," I said. Even my own voice sounded distant.

I ran back to the bay door, fumbled the key into the padlock and threw the large door open. Brianna's bodyguards turned to look at me, hands moving to hips.

James seemed to recognize panic on my face.

"Where's Brianna?"

"She's fine. Someone's hurt. Paramedics are on the way." The power of logic was slowly coming back to me. "Get that limo out of the way."

James motioned to the other two guards and then followed me back into warehouse. I ran back to Greg with James a step behind me.

Greg was still unconscious. I don't know why I had expected otherwise. It had only been a minute.

I picked up the warehouse phone stabbed the buttons to make a page over the intercom.

"Rory to the warehouse?"

I hoped my voice sounded calm and level, but I wasn't confident in that.

When I turned back to Greg, James was lying on the floor, his head bobbing back and forth, studying from different angles.

"Don't touch him!" I yelled.

He continued to look as he explained in a calm voice. "I'm looking to see if there's still contact between him and the television. If there isn't, we can move the TV out of the way."

He looked closer and closer yet.

"He's under it, but it's not touching him."

I scrambled to the other side of the large box. James and I lifted the TV and set it aside.

Once the TV was gone it looked like Greg was sleeping on the floor. He looked pale. That could have been my imagination, but it worried me anyway.

Rory came strolling into the warehouse and smiled when he saw Brianna standing there.

"What's up, dogs?" he asked.

No one answered, we all just stared at Greg.

"Why's Greg lying on the floor?" asked Rory.

"He's hurt," I said. "A TV fell on him. An ambulance is on the way."

Rory looked at Greg and the back to me.

"Is the TV broken?" he asked.

I gaped at Rory.

"Who the fuck cares if the TV is broken?"

Rory looked down at the floor, color filling his cheeks.

The four of us stood there, studying Greg's face and hoping to see some sign of movement. The flicker of an eyelid, a cough, a sign of pain, anything.

Sirens sounded in the distance and I felt the smallest flicker of hope. I ran to the bay doors and waved my arms as the ambulance drove into view. The driver parked close to the bay door.

The paramedics got out on each side of the ambulance and pulled open the back doors. With well-seasoned grace, they pulled a gurney from the back and deposited a small duffel bag and a spine board on top of the gurney.

With little effort, they lifted the gurney and its contents into the warehouse and climbed up after it.

"This way," I said, and hurried back to Greg.

As we walked, I explained what had happened, how we found him, and what we had done so far.

The paramedics walked calmly behind me, saying nothing.

When we reached Greg they knelt beside him and went to work. One of them opened his eyelids and shined a penlight into Greg's eyes. The other pulled a neck brace out of the duffel bag and handed it to the first one.

The other one looked up at us. "What's his name?"

"Greg," I volunteered.

The paramedic looked back to Greg and called his name several times.

They murmured things to one another as they worked, but spoke too low for me to pick out much. I thought I had heard the word responsive and hoped they hadn't said 'non' before it.

After the neck brace was in place they gently rolled Greg on his side and slid the spine board underneath him. Several straps were snapped into place before they lifted the spine board, and Greg, up and secured it to the gurney.

Everything moved a lot slower than it did in movies and on TV. Actors, who weren't really paramedics but played them on TV, always seemed to be running. These paramedics moved at calm and steady pace. They gave the impression that there wasn't any kind of emergency.

Yet after only a few minutes the paramedics were carefully wheeling the gurney into the back of the ambulance.

Rory, Brianna and I all stood outside watching, still in shock. James stood with us but wore his usual calm mask. He must have seen all kinds of crazy things in his line of work and this wasn't much to make his head turn.

Rory walked up beside me.

"I didn't care about the TV. I just didn't know what to say," he said. Shame was pouring out of him aurally and visually.

"Here," I said, thrusting the store keys into Rory's hand. "You're in charge."

"Where are you going?"

"I have to go with him. I have to. I'll be back when I can."

"But, what do I do? I don't think I can..."

I put a hand on each shoulder and looked directly into Rory's eyes.

"If you put aside all the uncertainty and façade and just do what you know is right you'll have no problems. You can do this."

Rory nodded back, looking unsure but willing.

I turned just as the paramedics finished their preparations and I put one foot on the rear bumper of the ambulance. The paramedic in the back with Greg held out his arm.

"Unless you're family, we can't take you with us. Sorry."

"I'll meet you there," I said.

The other paramedic closed the doors, then hopped into the driver's seat and fired up the engine and the sirens.

I walked over to Brianna and took her hand.

"I'd like to take care of you tonight, but I can't. I've got to take care of Greg."

"Are you sure about this?" she asked. "The offer I'm making is once-in-a-lifetime."

Brianna Hill the diva was back. She didn't seem like she would be as much fun.

I ran around the side of the store to the front parking lot and got into my car. The drive gave me time to think about all the potential mistakes I might have made.

Leaving Rory in charge of the store. Would he go on a rampage bossing people around? Would he do everything properly?

Passing up a night with Brianna Hill. Now what story was I going to tell people to try and impress them? What would Sawyer say?

If I hadn't been kissing Brianna maybe I could have preventing Greg from getting hurt.

Greg was in good hands now. I wondered if I was needed at the hospital.

You're going, I told myself. I needed to go to the hospital. If not for Greg, then for myself. I was in charge, and he got hurt. I had to make sure he was going to be all right. He had to be all right.

When I got to the hospital I rushed in and found a nurse sitting behind a desk.

"I'm looking for my friend, Greg."

"What's his last name?" she asked.

I stared at her, dumbfounded. I didn't know. I hadn't even taken the time to get to know the kid's last name.

"What did he come in for?" the nurse asked.

I explained the situation and she checked a clipboard and then checked her computer terminal.

"He's here, but I have no information."

I put a hand on the back of my neck and looked at the ceiling

"If you sit in that waiting room right there," she said pointed to a small room of chairs right across from her desk. "I'll let you know as soon as anything happens."

"Thank you."

The waiting room was like a prison. Small area, drab walls, and no possible way to get comfortable. It was probably worse than a cell.

I flipped through a few out-dated magazines. I thought about making a few phone calls to let Mike and Jameson know what was going on, but my cell phone was dead. I flipped through channels on the TV that was suspended in the corner of the room, but nothing could keep my mind occupied.

My mind wandered through all the possible outcomes of the night. Human nature caused me to consider the worst possibilities.

How could I tell Jameson that an employee had died on my watch? Fuck Jameson. How would I tell Greg's parents that I had let him die?

I started to wonder if I could end up in jail for some kind of negligence. There would be video footage of me making out while a television was falling on one of my employees.

After an hour of torturing myself the nurse stood in the doorway with a sympathetic smile on her face.

"Hi, Wade. How are you?"

It felt a little weird to hear her say my name. I didn't remember giving her my name.

"Any news?" I asked.

"Not yet. Do you need anything?"

"No."

She disappeared again and I decided to take a walk around the hospital.

The hallways were dim from poor lighting, the only adornments on the wall were warnings for ailments, and I cringed to think of the grime covering the floors. No wonder hospitals were so depressing. All the bad news people have received in hospitals is enough to create a negative stigma, but walking through the hallways made me feel like I'd never see the sun again.

That hospital smell was getting to me. That smell that seemed like it was beyond clean, but at the same time seemed to be masking some other smell the hospital was trying to hide.

I decided to retreat back to the waiting room where it was a little brighter and smelled a little better.

I tried various sitting positions in the chairs. Sitting up straight, slouching, sitting on the edge, bent forward. I even tried pulled a second chair in front of mine so I could put my feet up.

"I know. They're not very comfortable." The nurse was in the doorway again.

I stood quickly, glad to have a reason to get out of those chairs. "Any word?"

"Yes. Greg suffered head and spinal trauma. He's lucky, though. He's not seriously hurt. He may require a little physio and massage therapy over the next little while, but other than that, he'll be fine. We're keeping him a few nights for observation. Standard procedure with head trauma."

Relief washed over me.

"I am so glad to hear that."

"Right now he's not supposed to have any visitors other than family, but if you wait here for a few minutes I can see about getting you in."

I looked at her, confused. "Not that I don't appreciate the help, but why are you going out of your way for me?"

"You went out of your way for me. You sold me a computer a few weeks back, and it was the best customer service I've ever received."

"You're breaking hospital rules based on that?" I asked.

"It's a bigger deal that you think. At another store I was told something was out of stock. The guy went over to the next aisle and started talking to his co-worker. He laughed and said, 'I don't feel like working, so I just told some lady we were out of stock.'"

There were a lot of things I would do to avoid work, but that was too low, even for me.

"That, and even though you're not family, I can tell you really care about your friend. The poor guy could use a friendly face. His parents are out of town and can't get back until tomorrow."

I continued to sit and wait as the nurse disappeared again. Knowing Greg was okay, the chairs seemed more comfortable. I started to fall asleep, slouched in a chair, when the nurse came back into the room.

"You can go see him now, but it has to be quick. I had to do some convincing with the doctor."

We started walking down the hall together.

"How'd you convince him?"

"You're going to have to pretend to be something you're not."

"Sneaky. So, I'm his brother or something?"

"No. Our files are pretty up to date, so the doctor knows he doesn't have a brother."

"Who then?"

She smiled and winked at me.

"I told him you were Greg's lover."

* * *

Greg smiled as I entered the room and gingerly pushed himself into a sitting position.

"Wade. What's up, man?"

"Oh, nothing," I said with a smirk. "Just hanging around the hospital. I was just over in the maternity ward. You know, easy chicks."

Greg laughed a little, but stopped with a wince of pain.

"Sorry," I said.

The room was pretty standard. Despite the dingy look from the overhead fluorescent lights, the smell of sterility was everywhere. It hosted two beds, Greg's and one filled with an old lady who was either sleeping or dead.

"Is it true that a TV fell on me?"

"Yeah. A sixty incher."

"Damn. No wonder I hurt everywhere."

"You don't remember it happening?"

"I remember putting Big Bertha away, and I hit one of the shelves pretty hard with her, but nothing fell. After that, I remember putting some routers away on the bottom shelves, then I woke up here in a shit load of pain and doctors and nurses all around me."

"At least you didn't have to finish your shift, right?"

Greg had another short laugh cut off by another wince.

"Sorry," I said again looking at the floor. "Do you need anything? Can I get you anything? A book or a magazine?"

"Nah. I've got the TV here. That's all I need."

Greg laughed a little again, with a slightly smaller wince following.

"What?" I asked.

"I talked to my dad just before you came in. He's pissed. He says he's going to sue the shit out of the store. I may not have to work for my college tuition after all."

"What are you going to college for?"

Greg let out a heavy sigh. "I have no idea."

"I know the feeling."

An awkward silence fell over us. I started thinking of our futures. Greg was young, everything was ahead of him. Was I really that much older? Was my future already in the past? Then I remembered something I intended to do much earlier.

"When you're trying to text at work, text with one hand while holding a product in the other. If someone walks in, cover your text hand with the product. It'll look like you need two hands to carry something pretty light, but who cares? And if you want to be a real pro, start texting with your phone still in your pocket. It takes a while to get familiar enough with your phone to send messages without mistakes, but once you're there it's worth it."

Greg smiled again.

"Are you a text messaging pro?"

"Are you kidding me? I've sent three messages since I walked in the room."

Greg was smirking ear to ear.

"You know, Greg, for a guy who just got crushed by a TV, you're in a pretty good mood."

"How can I not be? They told me that I could have ended up paralyzed or dead. Instead, I'm just in a little pain and might need regular massage. Doesn't sound that bad to me."

"They're not talking about the kind with the happy ending."

"You don't know that. I've got pretty good health insurance."

"Will you two keep it down?" said the old lady in the next bed.

"Come on," I said. "The man just avoided death. Give him a couple of minutes."

The old lady sat up in her bed and gave me an evil look.

"Well, some of us are still trying to keep death away, and to do that we need rest, and it's really hard to rest when there are people in the room talking about this and that and all I want..."

I cut her off by pulling Greg's privacy curtain around us.

"Faggots!" she shouted through the curtain.

Greg and I both laughed. The old lady's call brought a nurse into the room who promptly told me visiting hours were over.

"All right. Make sure this man gets a sponge bath from your hottest nurse. It's on me."

I shook Greg's hand and gave the old lady my cheesiest smile and wave as I walked by. She gave me the finger in return.

CHAPTER 33

On the drive back to the store all I could think of was how great Greg's attitude was and if I'd be able to keep that kind of outlook if a TV fell on me. I'd probably be bitter. Pissed off at the world. Focusing on the negative and not giving a thought to the positives.

It was almost closing time when I walked into store. The fatigue of a long, emotional day seeped into my body and made the walk from my car to the front doors seem long. Rory met me at the front doors.

He handed me back the store keys with a solemn look on his face.

"I did things just like you would have. How's Greg?"

"He's sore, but he's going to be all right. I'd better go call Jameson. Let him know what happened."

"He's here."

"He is?"

"Yeah. Him and Brent and both here."

"Brent? Brent Baker?"

"Yeah. I called Jameson to let him know what was going on, and he called Brent. I guess Brent was at a store an hour away, so he booted it over here."

Pressure built up in my head, making my brain throb. I could feel my night getting even longer. I walked over to the manager's room and found Mike standing just outside the door in plain clothes.

"What are you doing here?" I asked.

"You got me, man. Jameson called half hour ago and told me to get my ass in here. He said there was a big emergency."

"There was. Greg got hurt in the warehouse. He's in the hospital."

"Is he going to be okay?"

The door to the manager's room was ripped open before I could reply. A red-faced Jameson stood there staring out at us.

"You two. Get in here."

Brent sat in the manager's room typing on his laptop and messaging with his blackberry at the same time.

"Sit," Jameson commanded.

Mike and I sat beside each other on one side of the table while Jameson took a seat next to Brent on the other side of the table.

"I assume you were at the hospital with Greg," Jameson said. "What the hell made you think it was okay to leave the store with Rory in charge?"

"You left—" I started to say.

Brent held up a hand and all talking stopped.

"How is Greg doing?" Brent asked.

"Pretty good, considering."

"Considering what?" Jameson said.

"Considering a TV fell on him."

Mike gaped, eyes wide. "A TV fell on him?"

Jameson's face turned brighter red and Brent held up both hands making a calming gesture.

"I'm glad to hear he's doing well," Brent went on. "That being said, we have some damage control to do."

"Damage control?" I asked.

"His dad is pissed," Jameson said.

"Yes," Brent said. "Greg's father is quite upset, understandably. He's said that he intends to file a suit against the company, and to be honest, he's going to win. Since the fault is on our side, we'll settle with him before it ever gets to court."

"It sounds like you've got everything figured out," I said.

Mike nodded. "Yeah. What damage control is there to do?"

Brent looked down at the table.

"This part is never easy," he said. I knew what he was going to say next. "This kind of thing requires repercussions to be dealt."

They needed a martyr.

"Let's drop the corporate mask," I said. "You need to fire someone."

"Fair enough," Brent agreed. "No sugar coating. Someone has to go."

An uneasy silence fell over the room. Brent obviously didn't have to worry about his job and Jameson didn't look worried. That meant my job or Mike's.

"Now," Brent continued. "Wade was in charge of the store when it happened. So, we have to consider that." He stopped and cleared his throat.

"Jameson put me in charge so he could leave early. Consider that."

Brent ignored me and looked at Mike.

"I'm told that it was your responsibility to secure the televisions on the top shelf. So, there's that to consider as well."

"Bullshit," Mike said. "I was securing those TVs when Jameson pulled me out of the warehouse because he didn't want to talk to customers. He told me he would finish strapping the TVs down himself. He should be the one to go."

Brent looked at Jameson with an eyebrow raised.

"You said I was safe," Jameson said, his voice turning whiney.

"Guys," said Brent. "The company puts a lot of time and training into store managers." Clearly not enough.

"Why are you telling us all of this?" Mike asked.

"Isn't it obvious, Mike?" I asked. "They're going to make us decide. You and me." I met Brent's eyes, and he looked away, pretending to check something on his phone. Jameson did the same when I tried to meet his. "Fire me."

"No," Mike said. "I'll go. This fucking guy hates me anyway." Mike put a finger in Jameson's face.

"I was responsible for everyone in the store. It should fall on me." Poor choice of words.

Mike stood up and jabbed his finger at Jameson again.

"If it wasn't for this motherfucker right here, it never would have happened. Why are you such a prick all the time? Why are you completely unwilling to do anything you're supposed to do as a co-worker, as a manager or even as a human being? You walk around the store day after day like you own every single brick. But you still avoid any and all responsibility. You're not just a terrible boss, you're a terrible person. Does your wife hate you? I'll bet she does. Even if she doesn't say it, I'll be she can't wait for you to leave the house each day. She probably dreams of stabbing your eyes out with a fork and letting you walk into traffic. I know I do. You're the biggest asshole I know, and I can't wait until the day all this falls on your head. There! Now I'll bet you can't wait to fire me."

If only Mike had done that earlier. It would have been a fight but he would have had Jameson's respect afterwards.

No one said a word as he headed for the door. Walking past me he put a hand on my shoulder and gave it a squeeze.

I wanted to say something to stop Mike from leaving. Was it still within my power to stop this? Could I change anything? Mike's rant made it seem like things were final. But if I spoke up before he left, maybe I could convince everyone to change their minds.

Among all the noise in my brain a quiet voice asked me if this was going to be one of those moments in my life that I would look back on and regret.

I reached a hand out to stop Mike, but he was already out of reach and the door closed behind him.

"I guess that's settled," said Jameson.

"No, it's not," I said and turned to Brent, pleading with him. "I can't let him do it."

Brent looked at me. He almost seemed to have a look of pain on his face.

"You have to admit. This does seem like the better choice," he said.

"I don't care. If you respect me half as much as you say you do..." I trailed off, not knowing how to finish.

Brent studied me for a minute.

"I'll leave the final choice with you," Brent said. "But only if you take some time to think about it."

Jameson exploded out of his chair. "There's no point. There's no way Mike is keeping his job now."

"If that's what Wade decides, then yes he will. Don't forget that there was no manager present at the store when it happened."

Jameson looked away in disgust and defeat.

"Think about this very carefully, Wade," Brent said to me. He looked at me intently as he spoke. "We're going to need another manager at this store and that job is yours. You stay, you get a promotion, along with a pay raise. You leave and you have to start over with another company working your way up from the bottom. Think about it. I'll talk to you in a couple of days."

I stood, opened the door and looked back at Brent.

"Do what's best for you," he said.

I left the manager's room and walked through the store. It was minutes until close.

I walked aimlessly, the only thing saving me from bumping into shelves and stacks of product was my subconscious memorization of the store's layout.

When, I stopped walking I was standing in front of the bank of digital cameras. I looked at them without really looking at anything.

Mike.

Could I really let him lose his job while I took a promotion? It occurred to me that Mike hated the job and being fired might be the best thing for him. If he was happy, did that make it okay to take a promotion?

"You sure have a lot of cameras here," said someone standing beside me.

I hadn't noticed anyone approach. I slowly turned my head and saw it was the lonely man. The customer everyone avoided. The customer that wasted everyone's time and never bought anything. The customer that seemed to always be around.

"Do you need help?" I asked.

He laughed.

"That's a relative question, don't you think?"

I didn't answer.

"I guess we all need a little help now and then. That's what I always tell my son. When he needs help he's too bullheaded to admit it. I try to help him out, but he won't accept it."

"Maybe he feels like he needs to take responsibility for his own life."

"You're probably right. Everyone needs help, though. My parents helped me when I was growing up. You've got to take it when it's available. Cause it won't always be there."

"Good point."

"Sometimes I think he doesn't want my help out of spite. We don't get along all that well."

"How come?"

"I don't know. My wife, his mother, passed away when he was young."

"Sorry to hear that."

A smile touched his lips.

"Thanks. His childhood growing up was tough on both of us. I had to work all the time. He spent more time with babysitters that he did with me. During his teenage years we had a lot of shouting matches. It was rough, but we made it through." He sighed. "Even now that he's moved out on his own we're not real close. We talk. Sometimes we meet for lunch or dinner. He always insists on paying." He smiled again.

"That's nice of him."

"It is nice of him, but he can't afford it. He's working, but I don't think it's going to be his career. I don't think he knows what he wants to be. I don't think he even knows what he's good at. He doesn't really know who he is."

We shared a moment of silence.

"He's trying to be you," I said.

"What do you mean?"

"From the time he was conscious of you and what you did

for him, all he knew about you was that you worked your ass off every day and did everything on your own. You provided everything, no matter how tired or broke you were. You may not have always been there for him but you were always doing something for him."

"You think so?" he asked.

"He may not realize it, but yeah, I think so. And it's because he's so much like you that you end up butting heads so much. People who are alike usually do. You take stances in all the same areas, have similar resolves and principals. When he was growing up you didn't need anyone's help, and now that he's at a similar age he doesn't want to take any."

"But, I got a lot of help. I used to borrow money from my brother. A good friend of mine used to fix my car just about every week to keep the junk pile working since I couldn't afford a new one. One of his babysitters used to work for free once in a while when I couldn't afford to pay her. I had a lot of help from a lot of people."

I looked at the lonely man in silence for a few seconds.

"Maybe you should tell your son that."

The lonely man stared at me for a second. Then he turned his head and let out a long sigh, then laughed.

"I should come and talk to you once a week instead of my therapist."

CHAPTER 34

Weeks after Greg's accident, I was stood in front of the row of laptops. I went to a random laptop and typed a little before moving on to another laptop and typing a little more.

I continued bouncing from laptop to laptop when I heard a familiar voice from behind me.

"Can I get some help here?"

I spun around and found myself face to face with Tess.

"Hi!" I said with a large smile.

"Hi." She looked around the store, somewhat confused. "You're not working here are you? I thought you worked down the street."

"I used to work down the street," I said. "I quit."

"And now you're working here?"

I laughed. "No, no, no. I think I'm done with retail for a while. I'm looking for a wedding gift for Mr. and Mrs. Rory and Taffy Simpson."

"So, I can't call on you for technical support anymore? What are you going to do?"

"I'm going to be back in school in the fall."

"Oh, yeah? I just graduated. What are you going to take?"

"Psychology. For now. We'll see if it sticks. I have a habit of quitting."

"What's with all the strange messages on the laptops?" she asked looking at the screens.

I smiled, forgetting that I had done it. While bouncing from laptop to laptop I pulled up a blank word document and typed messages like, 'The next customer I see is getting a punch in the face!' and, 'Free physical abuse with any purchase!'

I liked that some customer might read the messages and be afraid to approach any of the employees. Some manager would find the messages and have a serious look at his staff.

"I guess you could call it an early psych experiment," I said.

Tess smiled politely.

"It was good seeing you," she said. It was the kind of thing people always said to one another without meaning it, but something told me she actually meant it.

"You too. Take care of yourself."

She smiled and began wandering back through the store.

"Did you come to get me fired from here, too?" said Mike, walking up behind me.

"Yeah, right."

The day after Greg's accident Jameson had Mike fired without talking to Brent about it. Jameson thought it would force me to stay. Instead, I quit as soon as I found out.

Sawyer told me Jameson was put under investigation the next day.

"Check it out. Here comes my latest hire," Mike said.

Dev came walking over to me with a big smile on his face.

"Hey, bossma...Wade. Mike told me everything that happened between you and Jameson. I'm sorry about what I said to you. If I knew..."

"Dev, you had every right to say what you said and more. I'm just glad to see you're not adding to the welfare line."

"You think just because I'm brown I'm going to end up in the welfare line. Racist!" Dev grinned, shook my hand and walked over to a few wandering customers.

"How do you like the new uniform?" I asked Mike.

"It's different, but somehow the same."

"How's management here?"

"Pretty good. Turns out they do make managers with brains, so that works well."

We both laughed.

"I have to get back to work, but I'll buy you a drink at the wedding tonight."

"All right. There's just one thing I've got to pick up before I go."

I walked around the store until I found what I was looking for.

"Hey, Tess?" I said.

"Yes?"

I felt like I was walking into failure, but I didn't really care. More than once I had talked with Tess, baiting her to get a date, but nothing seemed to work. So far, I had followed all of Sawyer's rules to getting that first date, including 'Don't ask directly.'

"Would you like to have dinner with me sometime?" What would Sawyer think of me now?

"No," she said. A small smile grew on her face. "But I may let you buy me a coffee sometime."

*   *   *

I didn't mention the very first secret of retail. It's the least known but probably the most important.

Secret of Retail #1: Get out before it's too late.

Working in retail too long turns a good person into a bitter shell. Staying too long drained my faith in people as a race. For every good person I met, I met ten assholes. For every person that was glad to have my help, there were five that wanted to complain. I forgot every good deed that this race of so called human beings ever committed and my mind was filled with every terrible thing a man ever did to another man. Every accomplishment man ever achieved faded away and all I was able to think was:

The world is full of stupid people.

Dear Reader

Thank you for reading Secrets of Retail. I hope you liked it. If you did, or even if you didn't, I want to hear from you.

- Leave me a review at amazon.com, iTunes, or wherever you bought this book from.

- Get on social media
  Facebook: facebook.com/jwmartinonline
  Twitter: @JDubMartin

- or e-mail me: joe@jwmartin.com

I don't have a staff or an assistant. I personally read every review, tweet, facebook comment, and email that comes my way. Writers love nothing more than hearing feedback from readers, so let me hear you. You'll most likely hear something back.

J.W. Martin spends his nights and weekends writing in Ontario, Canada. He has a very understanding wife and two hilarious sons, without whom he would get much more writing done... and would be completely miserable.

www.ingramcontent.com/pod-product-compliance
Lightning Source LLC
Chambersburg PA
CBHW030314200626
46816CB00006BA/1772